The River Caught Sunlight
by Katie Andraski

ISBN 978-1-940192-26-0

Published by
◄ köehlerbooks™

210 60th Street
Virginia Beach, VA 23451
212-574-7939
www.koehlerbooks.com

THE RIVER CAUGHT SUNLIGHT

KATIE ANDRASKI

VIRGINIA BEACH

CAPE CHARLES

This is for Bruce, who supported me through much of the writing of this and for the Normans Kill people, especially Bob, Jean and Clayton, fierce, great souls themselves.

.

CHAPTER ONE

January, 1983. Coeymans, New York

Janice Westfahl saw, rather than heard, a stitching of pops. Small puffs of smoke billowed as a rock wall crumpled, then shimmered to the ground. A few seconds later she heard thunder that might have frightened her had it not been a clear summer day.

The word *pulverized* played out right before Janice's eyes. A sheer side of a mountain dropped to the ground, blown to smithereens. *And we all fall down. Wasn't that the child's game?* Her classmates' dresses billowed as they dropped to a crouch. Janice leaned into Caleb, his arm around her, hugging her close. Her body rippled with the joy of being so close to this man who worked the ground. When they'd met she'd fallen in love with his big machines slowly, ever so slowly, trundling over The Farm, turning over the dirt, beating the grasses, cutting them. Then she'd fallen for the companionable hours they'd spent riding in his tractors. And now he hauled rock in a quarry.

The whole time he'd been watching her reaction, his pale blue eyes studying her, but she couldn't meet his eyes. She looked at the blue scar left by the explosion with no pity for the mountain that was being felled for material to repair the New

York State Thruway.

"Up close those pebbles are car sized boulders," he said.

"I'm glad I saw it," Janice said. "You're something to work there." She'd not meant to fall in love three years back. But his big machines—his tractor, his combine, the gizmos he used to break the earth—seduced her, though he'd been clear he was not the marrying kind.

"It makes ends meet."

"Aren't you afraid?"

"Not particularly. They clear the site when they set the charges. The dynamite is worthless without blasting caps."

"I couldn't stand the noise."

"They give us ear protection."

"The phone is the loudest equipment that I'll use," Janice said quietly. In two days she would be leaving for her job at Godspeed Books, a publishing company outside of Chicago. Her job would be to garner national media attention to her authors and their books.

"Let's get married." Caleb's voice sounded raspy as wind blowing through dried grass over the top of stale, crusty snow. He tipped her chin up, so she had to meet his eyes. They reminded her of puddles reflecting the sky. He didn't let her see into them.

"Sure." Janice squinted. Her heart was beating fast. The man she'd loved because the light fell on him, because he was beautiful and took her up in his tractor, was actually asking to marry her. Sure, she'd rather learn how to drive the big machines than wheel and deal outside of Chicago. Sure.

Caleb drew her to him, his lips electric, his beard scratchy. He smelled like baking corn, and she felt surrounded by his passion, her own passion bubbling like a spring.

"Don't leave," he whispered, his eyes still shut. Something vulnerable about his face she'd never seen before.

"Aw Caleb," Janice sighed. "Why now, why when I made a promise to take this job a thousand miles away?"

"My friends told me I was a fool to let you get away." He

wiped her hair off her face, even though her hair was short and didn't need brushing aside.

"I thought you weren't the marrying kind. You've been clear about that." He'd stood her up when they'd made a date the first summer. She blamed herself for coming on too strong and promised they could be friends. Just friends had been fine as long as she could ride behind him on the tractor during the summers when she was home.

He looked out the window. The dust was settling. "People change."

"Caleb I love you. I've always loved you."

"You too," he said.

"Let's set a date. Maybe a year from now, so I could get some experience in my job and look for something back here. What about Christmas? Then you won't have to worry about remembering our anniversary." Janice tumbled over herself.

"Whatever makes you happy," Caleb said, a little resigned.

After he shifted into gear and was driving down the highway, he laid her hand on his thigh and rubbed his thumb over the top. Her hand felt so soft between the hardness of his leg and hand. She thought how those legs braced him as he picked up bales of hay, the strings boring into his palms, even through his leather gloves. He'd toss the fifty pound bales to the top of the stack like they were nothing and set them on edge so air could circulate, letting the heat that built up ease out of the green hay.

"I'll pick you up tomorrow at one. We can go to a motel," he said just before she got out of the car. He tried to make it sound like the joke it had always been. Janice looked at the red siding on her parents' house and the white shutters. The Little Barn towered alongside them.

"I'd like that." Janice wasn't sure she was ready to make love because she believed what the Bible said about waiting until marriage, but it would be nice to be alone with him without either one of their mothers in the next room. Besides he'd teased her about going to a motel for the last three years. She'd said *yes, no, maybe* and they'd laughed it off. He'd always said he didn't want to blow her mind because he knew how innocent she was. But this was different.

Caleb held her against him, too strong for her to pull away. He kissed her hard on the lips and released her. She was about to say she loved him again, when he put his finger on her lips, the dirt worked into the lines. "Tomorrow then."

Janice nodded, his finger rubbing across her lips, she was so full of pleasure and dared not say anything. She walked unsteadily to the house. At the door, she waved as he pulled away.

"Caleb, asked me to marry him and I said yes," she announced to her mother when she came inside, her voice full of smiles.

"I thought you were going to Chicago." Her mother sounded distracted like she hadn't heard Janice, like she didn't believe Caleb was serious, like his proposal wasn't worth her spending emotion.

"Of course I am."

"Get your clothes out, so I can iron them." Her mother was pressing a pair of Janice's pants. She added that she had a house to show in a few hours. She didn't have much time.

"We're getting married next Christmas."

"We'll see." Her mother didn't look up, but lifted the pants and set them down so she could iron the other side.

"It'll happen," Janice said, her heart lifting up. Two good things brought her hope—her job in Chicago, and Caleb declaring his love. Well, not exactly his love. But he'd asked for her hand, he'd held it gently, he'd kissed her. She pulled her clothes out of the laundry hamper and brought them to her mother.

"Did he give you a ring?" her mother asked. Steam hissed out of the iron. She pushed the point into the seam between the shoulder and the arm.

"Maybe tomorrow."

"Don't you need to pack?"

"I have time."

"You've got your whole life ahead of you." Her mother sighed.

Janice looked forward to her new job but dreaded living

in a row house in the city and not being able to walk outside at night. She would not be able to see the stars or cry out loud or laugh without anyone watching from their windows. She did not know if she'd be good at this job, only that God called her to do it. She felt like she was dying before she died by giving up a life she knew and loved, because something inside, she thought it was God, drove her ambition to leave home and start a career in publishing.

"Janice, Janice, Janice. It's only barely just begun." Her mother set the iron up on its heel and drew her into her arms. Where before it seemed a stretch to wrap her arms around her mother, like hugging the big willow down by the Normans Kill, now her mother felt as thin as the mountain ash in the front yard. She was cold as bark.

Janice swallowed hard and stepped back. Before, she had been ashamed of how heavy her mother had been. Now she missed her thick, round mother.

"I'm twenty-seven. I'd hoped to be married by now. I didn't want to marry late like you and Dad."

Her mother smiled. "I promise you, that you'll marry when the right man and the right time comes."

"Caleb has come. I'm ready to settle down."

"We'll see."

"You don't sound like you believe it."

"See what this year brings."

Janice wished her mother could be happy for her, but she wasn't. She never was. When she would feel joyful, her mother had been sure to say, "This too will pass," which made sense when there was trouble, but why did she have to remind her the good times would be gone all too soon? Janice took her whites and permanent press clothes into her bedroom and began folding them into her suitcase. She looked at her collection of Breyer horses prancing and grazing and just standing on her shelves. As a child she would stare at them and imagine they were real and what each would be like. By her junior year of high school she played out those fantasies in writing.

Janice waited by the window for an hour and a half before she figured Caleb wasn't going to show. To think she'd seriously thought about giving up her dream for a man who couldn't even keep a date. To think she'd said yes, and that she'd been awake nearly the whole night imagining the solitaire diamond he was going to pick out, just like the one her father gave her mother last Christmas. She had seen herself standing, white satin cascading around her, as Caleb stood at the front of the church, dressed in a white wool suit, his hands folded at the buckle. And she would feel the electricity in his lips through her body. Somehow she would have convinced him to wait until their wedding night, at least to go all the way. But no, it had been a big, fat, cruel, joke. She should have known he'd been playing with her when he'd asked, just like the joke about going to a motel room.

But no, she'd been suckered and now her soul was tearing in two like the veil in the temple torn in two on Good Friday. She found it hard to breathe. She bumped into things. Her eyes felt swollen even though she hadn't cried. It felt like raw, unmitigated fear, to be left standing by the window like this. She hated that her mother had been right.

Walk. Walk it out, she thought. *Walk The Farm one last time.* Her mother entered the kitchen just as Janice pulled open the door to leave. Tears were rising and she sighed to catch her breath. Her mother did not need to see her cry, no not with how thin she'd become, or the fine lines in her face—lines in mud that dried too fast—that aged her a decade past her sixty years.

"He doesn't want to see you. Let him go." Her mother sounded harsh but her face looked sad.

Janice hadn't even thought to go to Caleb. Later, maybe later, she would drive over there, and find out why he did not show, especially today, when she was leaving tomorrow. But now she wanted The Farm to listen while she wailed how hard it was to leave with his invitation to marry hanging between them, even though she needed to leave. She'd been called to leave. It was time to leave. Not even Caleb offered adventure like the one waiting outside of Chicago.

"You said you'd see a doctor after Christmas."

"Don't change the subject." Her mother leaned against the doorjamb, her face was all deep lines and creases. *Rivulets*, Janice thought of rivulets of water that had long since left after leaving their trails.

"I'm not. I'm worried about you is all."

"Nothing hurts." Barbara's mouth turned down like she was going to cry. "Except my heart aches for you. You're special to suffer so much."

"Why couldn't he at least say goodbye?"

"I don't know." She paused then folded Janice in her arms. "God has important work for you to do."

Janice put her hands to her face and sobbed, ashamed to seem so pathetic to her mother. Her mother rubbed her back. "There," she paused to catch her breath, "there is a good man waiting for you. God has something special. You must believe it."

Janice stood there, smelling her mother's mix of cigarette smoke and Youth Dew perfume and something older, earthy like the deep, cold bottom of the pond. She felt hot in her coat and boots, hot in her shame. She did not want her mother to say, "I told you."

"You'll feel better after your walk." Her mother handed her a dishtowel to wipe her face and blow her nose. "I am so proud of you. To think my daughter is going to be promoting the likes of Jeremiah Sackfield. You have a special call."

Her mother's eyes had standing water in them. But they looked relieved and calm.

"Go. Go for your walk. I'm making creamed chicken and biscuits for supper."

"But why did he stand me up?" Janice repeated. She felt like Caleb had taken her love and friendship and torn them in two. "He asked me to marry him. I didn't ask. He asked. It was his idea. I was happy watching the mountain blow up. Being his friend was enough. I was leaving. Why did he have to hurt me like that?"

"He will be failed from what he should have been. You mark my words."

"Don't say that just because you're angry."

"It's what I see," her mother said. "Now, go."

The cold air smacked her face as Janice walked up the road toward the pines, hoping against hope that Caleb might still come, that he got his times wrong, saying three instead of one. She looked for the dust that would rise as his truck touched their mile-long dirt road, but there was none.

The two border collies trotted alongside her, their tails curled over their backs. They read the smells and lifted their legs, marking their territory. Janice walked straight instead of turning when the road turned towards Genovese's fields and eventually the main road. Even though it was January, there was no snow, and the ground was so hard she felt every bank and dip under her boots. The day was turning amber as the sun eased toward the Helderbergs, an escarpment of old limestone that stood on the western horizon. This would be last time she would see these sights for at least a year.

Tomorrow she would board a flight to O'Hare, where she'd drive to her new apartment, an upstairs flat in Elmhurst. The next day she would start her job. Janice couldn't think of a job that fit her talents as perfectly as doing publicity for a Christian book company. She'd use her teaching talents to educate the media on their books. She'd use her poetry to write snappy phrases that would catch journalists' attention. As a Christian, she'd use what she knew of her faith to connect with other Christians in the media. She came by selling honestly, with her mother a successful realtor and her dad an ad agent for the *Times Union* newspaper.

* * * *

She walked toward the trail that took her through the tamarack trees down a valley to a nameless stream that emptied into the Normans Kill, the river that formed the north and eastern boundaries of The Farm. She was grateful it hadn't snowed so she could walk with no more hindrance than weeds and sumac. Years ago they'd cut Christmas trees from this slope, but they'd matured so they towered over Janice as she followed the horse trail she'd cut when she and her brother, Lucian, rode their horses through similar valleys that angled all the way to Slingerlands, a village several miles away.

The trees brushed across her face. Her boots twisted on the uneven ground. The dogs snapped at her heels. Her lungs burned in the cold air. The ground dropped down gradually. Her body heated up. Her knees ached. She imagined riding her horse at breakneck speed. Like Paul Revere, she had to deliver a message or the world as she knew it would not exist. She ran, yelling, almost for joy. King and Arthur barked, picking up on her urgency. She reached the bottom, her boots stumbling as the land evened out. The dried goldenrod slapped her thighs. She saw a flash of white out of the corner of her eye and looked up at a deer bounding through the mature hardwoods on the opposite side of the valley. She'd never seen a deer this close before. King and Arthur charged after it, breaking through the brush and clearing the unnamed stream in one leap.

"King. Arthur. Come," Janice yelled. Dogs chasing deer could be shot. They were her mother's. Would they hear her voice? She jumped across the streambed, and stumbled to her knees. She called them again. King, the red dog, whirled around, looking at her, his ears pricked. She sat on the ground weeping, the stiff weeds pricking her bottom.

She did not want to leave this ground. She did not want to leave Caleb. "Mommy," she cried. She knew her mother would not see the year out. Once a person lost weight from cancer, they were a goner. She knew that's what it was, but her mother refused to see a doctor until she left. She heard high pitched barking and the dogs barreling toward her, faster than when they ran for the deer. She rolled over on her back and looked up at the pale, tangerine sky.

Night was coming. She could fall asleep right in this spot and not have to get on that plane tomorrow and fly to an apartment and prove herself at Godspeed. Even though she loved this farm, she also needed to leave. It was she, not her brother, Lucian, who'd attended Wheaton College, a long day's drive, and continued on to graduate school, in Fayetteville, Arkansas, a hard two days of driving and difficult connections by air. King dove his nose into her face, licking her cheeks. Arthur, black with a white bib, pawed her belly. Suddenly she was laughing and petting them and rolled up on her butt. Their tongues warmed her cheeks.

Even now, in the dead of winter the sinkhole was not frozen, the mud soft and pliable. Maybe this was the salt lick that showed up on the old maps.

As Janice stood she thought about the deer that had bounded through the woods, her legs unlocked and free, her tail waving like a white lily in a strong wind. There were places a person could walk that were solid, sound, gave purchase as you ran, and others that sucked you down, that held you until you died. The trick was figuring that out before you stepped down and leaned your weight on ground that might not support you.

The sky deepened into blue as the sun dropped below the horizon. Janice had one more thing to do before she turned for home.

She fingered the White Linen perfume bottle. The glass felt like it could break open if her gloved hands squeezed hard enough. She'd thrown it in her pocket to spritz herself when she and Caleb were in the hotel room she'd hoped would become more than a joke between them. She pushed through the dried goldenrod and followed the stream to the Normans Kill. The evening star hung above the pasture on the opposite bank. She had to hurry. There would be no stopping to pray or sit and read her Bible beside the river as she had done so many times. She listened to the water sliding under the ice. The dogs trotted to the other side, jumping up the opposite bank. They disappeared over the lip, into the wide, flat pasture. "Arthur. King. Come!" She figured they were sniffing old cow pies and lifting their legs.

Janice squatted and pulled off her gloves. The air bit her fingers. She unscrewed the cap and poured out the perfume. It smelled more poignant and clean in the cold air.

Up at the house the tin horn sounded a deep, sonorous note that only she and Lucian knew how to blow. It echoed through the valley, their family's signal to come home. That horn was likely one of those the anti-renters blew to warn each other the sheriff was coming to collect rent they could not pay. Her mother bought it at an auction in Berne, a town deep in the Helderbergs.

How could Janice leave a place so full of stories? Henry Hudson had anchored the Half Moon at the mouth to begin trade with the native tribes for the Dutch West India Company. Other stories drifted down, seeming to cling to the valley: Dutchmen slaughtering Mohawks, who slaughtered them; French Huguenots raiding a neighbor's pigsty, biting every last pig to death; Marie Antoinette's ladies-in-waiting settling in the valley, fleeing the beheadings of the French Revolution. Even Janice's parents were proud they drove off Mayor Corning who planned to buy their valley within three hundred feet of their back door, not pay squat and make a park. Her parents celebrated when the judge ruled Consolidated Gas needed to move their pipe.

And the odd thing was the river was named after the cruel man. Not Godyn's Kill after one of Kilean Van Rensselaer's lieutenants. Nor Mill Kill after Bradt's work, but after him, the Norman. The Normans Kill. Norman's river. Norman's Kill. A river dammed. Trees cut and milled. Game shot and eaten.

Janice saw him teasing his children and wife, making promises he never kept because the extra money went back into the mill and the ambition of him, the exhaustion of the work, driving him to use his fists on his own people to become a family story dropping through three hundred years as surely as the Normans Kill waters drop eight hundred feet from headwaters to mouth. Where it began and where it ended were spectacular cliffs. Back at French's Mills the river had dropped through cliffs and over long plates of stone, a railroad and car bridge crossing not far above. By the time it reached the Hudson, it had cut through hundreds of feet of stone, the New York State Thruway and 787 spanning rainbow arches, way high over the rapids. Then it leveled out to sashay through the huge oil drums of the Port of Albany.

Janice dipped the bottle into water that burned her hand like she'd buried it between two burning logs. The glass started to slip. She squeezed harder, holding the mouth a little above the surface, so air would escape, letting the bottle fill to the brim. She sat back and capped it, slipping it into her pocket. She unzipped her coat and shoved her bare hands into her armpits to warm them. King and Arthur trotted across the river, their tails curled up behind them. Then they jumped the open water.

The sound of the horn again. The stars were poking out of the sky. Between her and home were the woods, and there was no moon. She'd never walked in the woods at night without moonlight. A branch cracked behind her. Her heart pounded as she hauled herself up the bank the ridge behind her that was so narrow she could straddle it like a horse. She held her hands out to catch branches, so they wouldn't whip her in the face.

The dogs' white bibs flashed alongside her. The ridge widened and flattened, and she walked through the dried mandrake patch. She ducked and pushed branches out of her way until she stepped into the wheat field that Caleb had planted in winter because her mother refused to let him plant corn. She hadn't wanted him to block her view. She called it ugly. So he'd agreed. Caleb was a good man, and she admired how he worked the ground, the power from the dirt and sun and rain welling into plants, making them grow, making them into food. She sighed.

A flashlight appeared at the gap between the white pines bordering the road. Janice shouted and ran towards it. The dogs sprinted back to her. "Where've you been?" Lucian panted, his eyes wide and furious. When they got that way Janice was reminded of an angry cat, with its electric tail and puffed up fur. "We've been frantic with worry." The dogs made figure eights around them.

"Saying goodbye to The Farm." Janice pulled off her glove

and felt for the bottle of Normans Kill water in her pocket. She twisted the cap even tighter.

"Caleb's up at the house. He's not going to stick around," Lucian said. "He offered to look, but he doesn't know these woods." Caleb stayed up top where the fields were. He had no reason to know the woods, except to push them off the tillable soil. They bordered The Farm on three sides, holding up the long, steep banks of the Normans Kill keeping them from slipping on the blue clay subsoil.

"Mother said she saw you cut across the headlands. We were afraid you'd sprained an ankle or something."

"Time got away from me." Her heart beat faster. Maybe Caleb meant it when he'd asked her to marry him. Maybe he'd been dealing with an emergency. Maybe he'd brought her a ring. Janice wished she'd left the perfume in the bottle.

Janice and her brother walked silently back through the gap in the trees and found the road. The dogs trotted ahead of them, the white tips of their tails bobbing. Lucian only stood as high as her shoulder, a man more square than tall. Janice often thought of him in mythical terms, like a troll guarding the bridge. Her father used to tell him he had to learn to use his fists, because, "You have to fight when you're short like we are."

Janice and Lucian were very different and had never been close as children. His intelligence was in his hands. He knew how to take apart radios and put them back together. Her brother could play guitar, do Judo and use computers like nobody's business. He'd shown her a cloud chamber where an accelerator could send high speed particles into a mist.

She loved books and prayer and walking in the woods. They both liked the adventure of riding their horses through the valleys between here and town, and it was on those rides that they bonded most and talked about their lives and dreams.

They came in sight of the farmhouse and every last window on the first floor was lit, which was unusual because their father believed in shutting lights off in unused rooms. The new roofs on the barns glinted in the starlight.

Almost as if he was reading her thoughts, Lucian said, "I need to put a roof on the house this spring. I've patched it about as much as I can."

The roof had leaked in her room yielding a stain had spread across the ceiling. It almost frightened her when she looked at it before turning out the light. Whole patches of plaster had fallen upstairs. Janice shuddered at the work it would take to repair it. Did anyone even know how to repair plaster these days? "You put a lot of work into keeping this place up," Janice acknowledged. Her shoulders felt heavy as though that plaster had crumbled around her.

"It'll be worth it someday."

"Isn't it worth it now?"

Lucian looked at her as though the answer to that question was obvious. But his face softened. "Janice I wish you were staying," he said, taking her arm and stopping her. "We could make an apartment for you upstairs. You could still have your horses. Maybe something would come of you and Caleb."

"Maybe." Janice looked at the new Dodge Ram parked alongside the smaller of their two barns. "How about you? Why don't you move out and get an apartment?"

"I can't leave Mom and Dad. They're getting so they can't take care of the place on their own."

"It's not like you're going to Chicago."

"How about it? Won't you stay?"

"I don't think I can." Janice looked at the house that was built like a church or a barn, with its long nave and two aisles on the sides, the windows where the pews or stalls would be. "I promised Godspeed that I would pitch their books. No job around here could offer something that is so perfect for who I am."

"Just don't let them work you too hard." Lucian started walking again, the gravel crunching under his feet. "Or they'll expect that out of you." He paused like he was afraid to say what he had to say next. "Take your Sundays as a day to yourself."

"Speaking of which, I was proud to hear you're an elder.

That's something."

"Well, thank you, Sis. Some parts I like and others I don't."

They were walking down by the pond now, the ice, a solid gray surface, the scratches from their impromptu hockey games etched across it. Just at that moment the ice cracked, a loud sonorous boom, not unlike a bullfrog's call. The dogs shied and started barking as though a gun had fired over their heads.

"I'd imagine," Janice said.

"You know. Politics. People complaining about Pastor. People complaining about the people complaining about Pastor. But I like seeing that the lawn is mowed, the phones work, the driveway is plowed, that sort of thing. I like feeling like I'm finally serving the Lord and His church."

"You've served Him your whole life."

"It hasn't always seemed like it."

"My job feels like a call too," Janice said. "I can't not do it."

"I understand," Lucian said, "but I'll miss you. We'll all miss you. Before I forget," he paused and reached into his pocket, "here's something I thought you'd like." He handed her a small white box. "I won't be able to see you off at the airport."

She took off her gloves and stuffed them under her armpit. The air numbed her hands immediately. Lucian switched on the light.

"It's beautiful," Janice whispered. Underneath the layer of cotton was a gold unicorn head, the one leg curled, the other striking out. The horn spiraled. A thin chain was attached.

"Do you like it?" Lucian asked, the shadow from his light making him look hungry and sincere and intense as a saint.

"I'll treasure him," Janice said, "but my hands are too numb to put him on now."

"Here, I'll help you." Lucian set the flashlight and box down and pulled off his gloves. He lifted the delicate chain and stepped behind her, looping it in front of her and closing the latch. She tucked it underneath her jacket.

"Oh Lucian, thank you." Janice turned around to hug him, but he leaned down to pick up his gloves and light.

"You never did find the unicorn did you?"

"I doubt I ever will," Janice sighed. As a girl she'd called walking The Farm "going to look for a unicorn." There was enough mystery, maybe she'd find one. When they walked up to the house, Caleb was sitting next to the cherry table, his back to the window. He wore his green Pioneer gimme jacket and held his IH cap in his hands. He opened his arms, but Janice stood back, even though more than anything, she wanted to step into those arms. The dogs followed Lucian into the living room and flopped down between the couch and the coffee table. She looked into his blue eyes that held no apology for the pain he'd caused this afternoon, only an explanation. It was easier to look at his flattened hat hair, lovely gold hair, than it was to look at his eyes or his arms, the round balls of muscle she knew were under his jacket.

"Your mother's not happy with me," he said.

"Neither am I."

"You look cold."

"It's a brisk night."

"Why would my sweet Janice go for a walk in this weather?"

"Why would my sweet Caleb stand up his sweet Janice?"

"The quarry called. They have two thousand ton they want moved."

"You couldn't call?"

"They don't have phones."

"Why didn't you call before you left?"

"I forgot."

"He says he forgot," Janice said to the air. "How could you forget?" She stared at him. She hoped she could look as ferocious as her brother.

"I have a thousand acres around the county to run, this job at the quarry, taxes to figure, groceries to buy. There's a lot on my mind." He dropped his cap on the table.

"You hurt my feelings."

"I came to say goodbye."

"You asked me to marry you."

"It was a joke."

"A joke."

"No more serious than going to a motel."

"But I said I would marry you." Janice had been taken for a fool.

"Janice, come here." He pulled her into his arms, so there was no question whether or not she would hug him. She buried her face under his coat where she smelled his sweat and motor oil and hot, hot corn like it smelled when it tumbled in the dryer. He held her close and hard. "I'm going to miss my sweet Janice."

"You don't have to."

"I have to let you go." She felt his chin bob on her head. Janice did not return his hug, but his arms, his chest felt so safe. "Our mothers would shoot me."

Janice ducked away from his arms, his chest. She hated how her mother had been right.

"I have something for you." He fished into his pocket and pulled out a small picture of him leaning against the back of his White tractor. His legs were crossed at the ankles with one Red Wing boot cocked to the side. His arms were crossed so that his fingers were wrapped around that lovely bulge of muscle. He looked defiant like he was about ready to stick out his tongue at the camera. Double tires off to either side of him with treads that left V prints in the road that reminded Janice of geese wedged across the sky. "I thought you'd like something to remember me by."

"I remember that day," Janice said. "You couldn't get the male hitch to match up to the female."

"Isn't that how it goes?" With that Caleb leaned down and kissed her on the lips, barely touching them. "You take care now," he said, picked up his hat and was almost out the door when Janice said, "Wait!" sharply, like she was halting a horse.

There was impatience in his eyes. "Wait," she said again. "I have something for you."

She walked back into the house, into her room, where she'd set a sheaf of poems she'd written about him. She slipped them in a white envelope she used for sending out work and pushed the metal clips on the back so they were flat.

Caleb looked uncomfortable waiting by the door, holding his hat.

"Here, I made these for you," Janice said, holding them out to him. Inside were several poems she had written about him. They were about his tractor; the soil; how the summer light fell on him; sounds of the farm; planting corn....

"You should have these."

He hesitated, before he accepted them.

She stepped up and kissed him and hugged him. "Goodbye." She didn't know if she was saying goodbye to him or the poems—they were her only copy—or her life on The Farm.

Janice stepped to the window and watched him pull his cap on, smoothing it down the back. He did not look back as he opened his truck. He tossed the poems on the seat next to him. He flipped on his lights even before he started the engine. Not fast, not slow, was how he drove away. She watched until the cloud of dust settled and his lights disappeared from the last rise in the road before it turned toward Font Grove Road, the main road. A mile out to the main road, that's what they always said. A mile between them and their nearest neighbor. And tomorrow she'd be able to look through her window into her neighbor's bedroom. Janice sighed. She would be doing God's work, the work she was made to do.

CHAPTER TWO

August 1983, Tybee Island, Georgia

Who said ocean air was refreshing? To Janice Westfahl it smelled like rotted weeds. She wanted the smell of fresh cut hay, square and stacked loosely enough for air currents to find their way, cooling it, so the barns wouldn't burn. She'd felt it, that heat when she stuck her hand between bales, a simmering, fragrant heat.

For two weeks, she'd heard Jeremiah Sackfield's spiel about how the United States was going to hell in a hand basket if Christians didn't get active in government, media, university teaching, and law. The country needed a Christian revolution, Jeremiah proclaimed. For Janice, Sackfield was a showman, an opportunist, and she was his enabler. She helped promote his book, *An American Treatise*, onto the Christian bestseller list. Thank God the tour was done, except for this last meeting with laundry magnate, Matthew Sparks, who promised to buy some books.

They were sitting at the Crab Shak, a seafood joint, outside of Savannah, Georgia. Carapaces of lobster and crab claws piled up around them. The owners weren't kidding, the place was a shack, with peanut shells on the floor and screens for windows, so the ocean could waft its salt breezes through the place.

Jeremiah shook a crab claw. "The violence of the Sixties blew the evils of segregation to smithereens and pulled us out of Vietnam, another evil. Wait until these people read *An American Treatise*. We might see some action. In the very least a tax revolt that might shut down the government."

He was dark, intense, even though he was blonde and blue-eyed. *Boyish, until you listened awhile,* Janice thought. She was bored, turning her eyes out toward the water. She thought of Caleb; right about now, he would be driving his tractor across alfalfa, the pump of his baler kicking the hay into tight, square bales. Janice slid her hand into her briefcase, and tipped the bottle of Normans Kill water over her finger and touched the water to her neck like perfume. It smelled rusty like rain as it taps the ground.

"Do you know what these are?" Matthew Sparks leaned towards Jeremiah holding innocuous looking twists of wire and paper. His eyes, his hair, his slightly sunburned skin, seemed more off-color than she first thought. Janice hadn't gotten a bead on him because his face kept slipping from one emotion to another even though his voice remained jovial and relaxed.

"Blasting caps," Janice blurted, recognizing the dangerous sticks powerful enough to blow off their faces.

Jeremiah held a crab claw in one hand, a fork to peel the meat out in another. His eyes flicked back and forth signaling his panic. He couldn't say, "It was a joke."

"Very good." Matthew turned to Janice. "You're a little dangerous."

"You bet."

She had learned from Caleb that you stick the cap in the first stick of dynamite, drop it down into a hole, below the water table. Then you drop the next stick. And one on top of that. The wire wrapped around it carried the spark.

"Where'd you find her?" Matthew turned to Jeremiah, his face full of approval. "I came with the publisher," Janice huffed. *Remember to breathe. Remember to pray. Deliver us from evil.*

"She's the best of the best," Jeremiah said, peeling the meat out of the crab.

"Do you have a license to carry those?" Janice asked.

"That I do." Matthew shook his palm as though he wanted to hand the blasting caps to Jeremiah. "Add a little fertilizer, some dynamite, and a spark. You've got some power."

"Maybe you could help us." Matthew's hand. The roll of wire over a paper stick. Still over their meal. Held like a peace offering.

Lightning flashed out at sea. Caleb had said that as long as you keep them away from a spark or lightning or dynamite, they can't hurt you. We keep the dynamite and caps a mile apart.

"Why ever would you bring those here?" Janice's voice thumped with the beats of her heart.

"To make a point." Matthew's voice sounded as definite as the grey line of ocean. "We could move this to the next level."

"That's only the last resort," Jeremiah said, carefully setting down his crab claw, holding his hand up. "We have a long way to go before then. A long way." His voice had never sounded so calm.

"You sure?"

"Absolutely." Jeremiah's eyes held Matthew's until he squirmed like a toddler made to sit too long. But still he held the cap, his hand glistening. It had to ache by now.

"We slaughter a million babies a year."

"I know," Jeremiah said, waving to a waitress and pointing to his empty Bud Light bottle.

"Sometimes a revolution sets a few fires."

"I know."

"Segregation ended. We pulled out of Vietnam. Sure a few buildings burned, but things changed fast." Matthew's voice was high and angry. "We could do the same."

Thunder rolled a little closer.

"Will you put those things away before you blow off his face and you've got nothing. No cause. No Second American Revolution. Nothing," Janice demanded.

"They're perfectly safe."

"No sir, they are not."

Slowly Matthew pulled his hand back. He set the cap in a wooden box and closed the lid, setting it to the side.

"Now if you'll excuse me," Janice said. The cracked pink crab legs, black clamshells, and destroyed lobster claws were piled on a platter. Her stomach gurgled. She didn't know if she would make it to the bathroom, and if her bowels were this rattled, she didn't know how she would manage her flight to Chicago.

"Can I order you another Diet Coke?" Jeremiah called after her.

"Please," she said, hoping it might settle her stomach.

Janice leaned against the phone booth like she used to lean against the ironwood trees on The Farm waiting to dial until she was sure she wouldn't have to run back to the ladies room. What a messy time low tide was, showing black seaweed on the beach, stagnant pools, and junk. Her eyes followed a rope that rolled in the sea swells. She wondered if the dry sink toppled upside down had been someone's priceless antique. Flotsam and jetsam. In the distance, the ocean looked blurry. A tanker sat this side of the horizon, making her slow way up the inland waterway.

Janice wiped her nose trying to stop the stink of salt air. Her mother's hello sounded like a sad whisper until she heard Janice's voice. Then her voice sounded strong, almost fierce.

"They're talking crazy. Bombs, the whole bit," Janice said, her panic bouncing off the glass door. Goose bumps rose on her arms and legs in the cool ocean breeze.

"The Lord won't let anything happen that's not meant to."

"I don't belong here." Janice stuck her fingernail under a sliver and lifted it away from the paneling, leaving a long, pale scar.

"The Lord brought you there for a purpose," her mother said so earnestly, Janice imagined her mother buckling her Bible in two.

"I want to come home." Janice leaned against the back of the booth.

"You need to finish what you started," her mother insisted. "You need a year's experience before another employer would look at you."

"They want to start a revolution. They want to take over the country."

"Then you'd be making history." Janice had a hard time keeping track of the sadness, fury, pride, and calm that echoed in her mother's voice.

"What are you saying?" Janice pushed her fingers in the crack in the door, the door flying open, pinching them.

"Sometimes you have to stay put."

"In a revolution?" Janice sucked her fingers to draw the pain.

"Remember me telling you the Lord was preparing you for a special calling? Maybe this is it. Maybe you can slow things down, make them listen."

"I could change my ticket, come home tonight."

"Don't you dare."

"But you need me."

"We're doing fine here." That calm again, that sounded like it was almost true.

"That's not true." Janice's heart banged against her throat. Her mother had been diagnosed with metastatic lung cancer right after Janice had arrived at her job. The nine months the doctor had given her were just about up.

"Finish what you started," her mother repeated, but her voice cracked over the word, "started." They closed the call by saying they loved each other.

Janice leaned against the back of the booth. All she had wanted was her mother to say, "Of course you can come home. We'd love to have you. I need you to help me." Any one of those would have been like a cool hand to her terror. She swallowed back her loneliness and stared at the tanker moving out of sight. The last time she'd been home they'd argued something awful. Sure they'd talked since then, but she wanted to know she and her mother were all right, right there, right in person. But she'd have to wait a few more days.

When Janice had returned to the table, a hundred thousand dollar check made out to Godspeed Books sat where her plate had been. She tried not to look at it. She took a sip of her Diet Coke. The wooden box was no longer on the table.

"If changes aren't made soon, we'll see a collapse like the Roman Empire or we'll see a revival that will send everyone back to church," Jeremiah said in his preacher's voice. "God's judgment is pending. I predict people will be euthanized because they aren't convenient—the right race, the right religion, too old, too sick, too disabled, too young."

"What makes you think Christians can make a better society?" Janice glanced over at Jeremiah who looked startled, quickly recovered, and glanced down at his watch. "We're not better people." She'd wanted to say this for two weeks.

"Christ called us to redeem the world. That includes every society on the face of the blessed earth." Matthew leaned his voice hard on the "deem."

"I don't think it's our job."

"Then whose job is it?"

"Christ's. Didn't he say, 'It is finished'? The world has been redeemed."

"But we have to finish the job."

"We've got a plane to catch." Jeremiah cut her off, glancing at the check lying by Janice's plate. "Janice, you won quite a coup, didn't you?"

Janice was dazed by the amount of the check lying on the table for Jermiah's book.

"Day after tomorrow, we'll be on the *Today* show," Jeremiah said proudly, patting Janice's hand.

"There you are, doing exactly what we're talking about. Using the world's tools to promote the Kingdom. You're not so far off as you think," Matthew said. "I was a little worried that our point woman wasn't on point."

"Oh I am," Janice quipped.

"Tell your boss, your gracious hospitality arranging this meeting made all the difference. I'm using Jeremiah's book in a promotion. I'm giving your book to members of action groups I'm organizing here in the southeast." He reached for the bill. "It's been a pleasure."

They all stood. Janice's skirt stuck to the bench. She reached around and pulled it away from her damp thighs and bottom.

"We'll keep in touch," Jeremiah said, taking Matthew's hand. He limped toward the door, his head coming up to Janice's shoulders.

"You keep doing good work for The Cause," Matthew said to Janice, his eyes bright and glazed like he had a fever.

"You're the best of the best my dear." Jeremiah poked her arm. She covered his hand with hers and took the back seat. Matthew would drive them to the Savannah International Airport where they would board a flight to New York for a few interviews before the *Today* show.

Getting booked on the network had been an amazing break for Janice, as the first publicist for Godspeed Books, especially since she'd been in the job less than a year. But she couldn't take her brother's advice. She worked many Sundays to keep ahead of the clerical work, seeing that review copies were sent out, press releases were written, and addresses were entered into her rolodex and mailing list.

* * * *

Like her brother, Jeremiah was shorter than she was, but he was packed full of intensity. He was the flagship author of Godspeed Books, which, before Jeremiah, had poor sales. His bestselling book about how evangelicals used their faith to justify being mediocre sold a couple hundred thousand copies. So his next two books, *An American Treatise* and *A Christian Bestseller: Why Not?* were sure to sell even more.

Unlike her brother, Jeremiah limped because of a childhood bout with polio. That seemed like such an old-fashioned disease and it added to a wounded healer aspect that Christians seemed to love. She offered to carry his bag. She could not have him overcome with fatigue for his interview with Jim Sanders tomorrow, and the *Today* show the following day. Besides, his bag would balance her load. He shook her off saying he was fine.

As the plane leaned back and kicked off the tarmac, the lights of Savannah dropping away, the ocean a pale blue in the late afternoon sunlight, Janice asked Jeremiah how he met his wife.

"I fell in love with her at first sight." Jeremiah's smile flashed wide and open. "She looked like a Celtic queen even though she was only eighteen. And placid—there was something very grounded and calm about Elizabeth."

"I thought you'd have a ten-point check list." Janice turned her back on the smear of city lights, to watch Jeremiah. He looked completely happy when he talked about his wife.

"She thought I was kidding when I told her I was going to marry her," Jeremiah said. "I'd walked up to some girls, sitting on a blanket eating cheese, bread and wine, generally enjoying the day. A fine, bright day it was too. I'd struck up a conversation and told Elizabeth that we'd marry."

"Wish someone would tell me they're going to marry me." Caleb had asked, but he didn't mean it.

"Would you like a drink?" The flight attendant asked.

"A Whiskey Sour. The lady would like a Tab." He nudged Janice. She reached into her purse and pulled out a few dollars. The flight attendant stuffed it in a plastic cup.

Jeremiah took a sip. "But you couldn't travel and do your job the way you do if you were married. Someday you'll look back on these days, wishing you had them back."

Look back on these days? Wish she had them back? She didn't think so.

"People who serve God, like you're serving Him with your wonderful publicity talents, and attention to detail, should not be married."

Janice ripped open her almonds so hard, half spilled out on her tray.

"Careful."

"You say so."

"Where would I be if you weren't there to show me where I needed to go?"

Was it the booze mixed with exhaustion making him so open? Janice wasn't sure, but she didn't like anyone being that dependent on her, let alone him.

"So then what happened? With your wife?"

"Other men were jealous. She's a beautiful woman. Very striking. I love her for loving me, just as I am." Jeremiah poked himself in the chest.

"You're very lucky." Janice drank her Tab. Bottom's up. Maybe it would help her stay awake until they checked into their hotel.

"All this revolution talk is...." He used an expletive. "What's real to me is what happens between the four walls of my house. That's reality—my wife and children. I don't care about the revolution. So my dear Janice, I want you to do a bang up job with my books, so I can finish fixing up my house, so we can use the commode without looking at lath and plaster and horsehair."

Was Jeremiah staging a revolution so he could fix his bathroom? Was he, ambivalent about the whole cause? He was easier to take, the whole thing was easier to promote, if he was simply greedy, and not a fanatic who thought violence was the only way to save the country. *But what if he sparked a real revolution? Then what?*

"Matthew wasn't fooling with those explosives," Janice said.

"Oh he's harmless. He's just trying to make himself important. Don't let him trouble you."

"Those caps are dangerous."

"You handled him very well. Thank you."

By the time Jeremiah leaned back and mercifully shut his eyes, Janice was praying, *"If this is Christianity, I don't want it. But Lord I want you."* She felt so lost. An old song she remembered her father singing rolled through her head. *"The Lord knows the way through the wilderness. All I have to do is follow."*

She shoved her knees against the seat in front of her and dropped her shoulder against the window. *Lord be gentle,* she prayed. *Lord have mercy. How can I keep doing this job? How can I not?*

She set the bottle of Normans Kill water on the tray table in front of her. A thin line of sediment had settled to the bottom. She wanted the ground with an ache more intense than sex. She wanted to lie down, feeling the earth's energy flooding her. Janice uncapped the bottle, lifting it to her nose. She took a whiff, the sediment swirling, the water turning cloudy. The smell reminded her of the mile-long road where she walked out her prayers every night ever since she was a girl. She'd prayed aloud, inviting Jesus into her heart when she was five. The preachers talked about how God was lonely, how he didn't have many true friends on this earth, and Janice wanted to be one of them. As with any friendship, she'd worked on it, taking time every day to read what God had to say to her, and to talk back to him. Sometimes she listened. She knew enough about God to know his love was fierce, that he didn't take kindly to hypocrites. Whitewashed graves he called them. Pretty on the outside. Rank on the inside.

Janice capped the bottle and slipped it back into her briefcase before Jeremiah woke. She wanted the Normans Kill, where she could step from the bank to a rock, and plunk herself down, with acres and fields between her and anyone who could hear her scream how terrified she felt because the nine months Doc had given her mother to live were just about up. No one deserved to hear her, except God, who said Himself, she could come to Him for anything she wanted, even the depths of her pain and fear. She wanted to tell God all her desires: *Heal my mother. Completely and utterly heal her. Send me a man of God, so I don't have to be so alone, and so I can make love.*

As the jet banked for its final approach to New York, Janice gazed down at the blackness of the ocean and sky scraping lights of buildings even she could recognize—the Empire State Building, the Chrysler Building and the Twin Towers of the World Trade Center. She wished she could call her dad to come get her.

CHAPTER THREE

August 1983, New York City

Janice stood in the marble foyer of Weekly News waiting as the one armed guard called Jim Sanders' office. She'd met Sanders a few months ago when she'd traveled to New York to pitch Godspeed's books as a brand new publicist. Even the book review editor at *Time*, Stefan Kanfer, and Robert Silvers at *The New York Review of Books* had granted her appointments because they were curious about this little publisher interested in publishing Christian literary fiction as well as the radical Jeremiah Sackfield's books.

Godspeed Books was on a mission to redeem American culture by salting it with books informed by a Christian worldview. Janice had bought into the Christian fiction part, but felt hypocritical and complicit pitching Jeremiah's story. The one armed guard cradled the phone between his ear and his shoulder, nodded, and wrote out a pass for the fifteenth floor.

As she stepped onto the elevator, the red and white visitor's pass clutched in her hand, her briefcase burned through her other hand and her feet ached from two-inch heels. How she hated dress shoes; how she missed her farm work boots.

"Are you all right?" A man asked, his voice like water that

backs up just a bit before it falls over a cliff. His hair was pulled back in a ponytail.

She nodded, "I'm tough."

"You don't look it," he said.

Janice dropped her eyes, saw drops hitting the mud spackled floor. She saw his Nikes shift from one side to the other. *Up Where We Belong* by Joe Cocker and Jennifer Warnes played softly as the elevator streamed upwards. *How ironic,* she thought.

"My mother is dying, and I was hired to promote...never mind," she quipped to the stranger. She raised her eyes and saw the man looking at her kindly. She took deep breaths to calm herself. Maybe he wouldn't notice her tears if she acted like she wasn't crying. "But my job has gone south, way south and way right. I'm up to my eyeballs in the Up Right, Down Right, Just Plain Right types. I'm a poet."

"A poet?"

Janice nodded watching the lights move through each number. Only one was lit, the ninth floor. He was going where she was going.

"You know that poets die trying to save their countries."

"But sometimes they get away," Janice smiled.

"They pay a price." His eyes ached with so much sadness, Janice had to look away and think about the sun dropping behind the Helderbergs or she would lose it entirely.

"We all pay a price."

"That we do."

The elevator stopped. The man opened his palm toward the door. Janice hefted her briefcase and stepped out. She turned towards Jim's office. "Who are you seeing?"

"Jim Sanders."

"I'll take you there. I'm his assistant, Allan White. Your name?"

"Janice Westfahl."

"Here you can have my coffee. Looks like you could use some." Janice took the Styrofoam cup, feeling the warmth as she wrapped her hands around it.

"Jim, Janice Westfahl is here to see you."

Jim was pecking on a manual typewriter, his hands stabbing at keys. A computer terminal was behind him, it's green cursor blinking. There was a telescope angled at the building across the street, but the lense was tipped up to the ceiling. And stacks of books as high as Janice's hips covered every inch of the floor except for a pathway to the desk. He looked like an eagle, his eyes fierce, studying them both, his mouth crooked enough to draw attention to his lips, to a face that was just off the movie version of male beauty, which made it even more interesting. He wore jeans, loose around his butt, a white shirt open at the collar and a tweed jacket with elbow patches. Janice thought in poetry when she got around him because he made her heart sigh.

"Let me finish," he said.

"Here have a seat," Allan said, setting Jim's coffee on a clear space by his desk. He turned and picked up the stack of books and newspapers and set them out in the hall.

"Thank you," Janice said.

"I'll be down the hall." Allan nodded and then ducked away.

Janice took a sip of the coffee, very sweet with cream. She could feel the buzz hit her and nearly make her head swim. Slapping rain, the fat drops that fall when a storm is about to hit, that's what his typing sounded like. Janice looked at the *Weekly News* cover of Cheryl Tiegs posted on the wall. There was also one of Billy Graham and three faded pictures of the Pope. She noticed her pitch letter, sitting upright against his dictionary and thesaurus. She'd stuffed it with a packet of clippings, letters and a bound galley of *A Christian Bestseller: Why Not?* Part of convincing Jim to write her story was how easy she made it for him to write. She'd noticed how reviews and news stories often used her press releases in the body of their text, without giving her credit. Despite what her teachers said, plagiarism was the order of business in the real world.

"All right, what can I do for you?" Jim turned and looked at her, with those fierce as a golden eagle's eyes. They braced her.

"They're serious about starting a revolution. They want to usher in the Kingdom of God by force."

"The Kingdom's already here. Jesus wasn't kidding when he said it was like a grain of mustard, and would grow to become the biggest tree. What do you think has happened over the last two thousand years?"

"But they want to save America by overturning it. I sat next to a guy with blasting caps," Janice didn't like the fear and anger in her voice, but she couldn't help it. "He said he was a demolitions expert. He could bomb the Supreme Court if he wanted."

"Don't worry about the Downright types."

"This guy is filthy rich. He wrote out a check for a hundred grand without batting an eyelash. He's going to give Jeremiah's *An American Treatise* to small groups, so they can be revolutionaries." Janice felt how hard the seat was where she was sitting. Her hips ached. At twenty-seven she was too young to have arthritis wasn't she?

"At least he's promoting literacy."

"Funny. Ha. Ha."

"I believe in the apathy of Americans," Jim continued.

"But you didn't see how they came up to talk to Jeremiah about how they were dedicated to picketing abortion clinics."

"They have a right to protest."

"You didn't see the look in their eyes."

"People are too comfortable to make those kinds of changes. Sure Jeremiah can beat his fists against the silent majority, but it won't do much."

"I can't do it anymore. I can't promote a man who looks like Hitler every time he talks, and people buy into what he's saying."

"Janice, you're paid to promote what crosses your desk." Jim patted a copy of *An American Treatise*.

"I could go home, take care of my dying mother, and not be at war with myself."

"Look, you're like a lawyer defending a criminal. For our system to work, guilty men need lawyers. And good men represent them and try to get them off. You're doing the same thing by publicizing them, even though you don't agree."

"I feel like I'm losing my soul."

"You shouldn't. These groups are powerful when they are secret. You're breaking that power by publicizing them."

"You think I should stay?"

"You have an amazing window on these people. It's great material for your poetry. You're going to have some wonderful stories to tell one day."

"And Jesus warned it's not a good thing to gain the world while losing your soul."

"He also said you have to die before you die. Maybe it's your job to blow their cover."

"I don't know," Janice said.

"Call me if you need me. I won't betray your trust." Jim stood up.

"I will," Janice said, standing up, gripping her briefcase and holding out her other hand. He pulled her in and kissed her on the cheek. She felt the coolness of his lips all the way down the elevator, all the way until she smelled the diesel exhaust from buses, the smell of Caleb's tractor working a field.

Then she walked fast to Federal Express where she dropped Matthew's check in an envelope and mailed it to her boss, Pete DeVries. She followed up with a phone call to let him know it was coming. "You take a week after this is over. Go be with your family," he offered. Janice thanked him and hurried out the door to the Barbizon Plaza so she could take Jeremiah back to *Weekly News*.

* * * *

"Jim is closer to where I am as a Christian than the Upright types," Janice said with a sigh as she and Jeremiah waded against the current of people—women dressed in business suits with running shoes on their feet, men in wool suits, all their eyes focused on some point in the distance, nobody catching her eye.

"If you think that, you're the worst kind of hypocrite promoting these books. You should look for another job."

"I don't know what to say." Janice glanced at a tangerine pants suit hanging off a mannequin. Jeremiah stepped out ahead of her. Maybe she would look for another job.

"Jim Sanders of *Weekly News* is about as far away from my own views of God and faith that a person could get. Why according to his own writing, Jim doesn't even believe in a personal devil, or the inerrancy of scripture, or the virgin birth."

Janice looked up at the store's name. The Madison Avenue Boutique. She'd have to come back this evening. Jeremiah walked back and turned to the window, his hands behind his back. "Very nice. Now let's go. We'll be late."

"Jim straightened out my confusion." Janice said pulling her briefcase up in front of her, wrapping both arms around it, covering her heart and her belly.

"Confused. Oh that is something different." Jeremiah's eyes and face and voice became very gentle. He put his hand on her arm, but gently. He'd never touched her gently before. "Janice, searching is good. I was afraid you were set in some liberal unbelieving faith."

"No, of course not."

The orange pants suit stood quietly behind the glass, the same color hunters wear, so they can be seen in the woods. That's why Janice liked it. She wanted to be seen in the woods, the same dark wood, where Dante found himself before he walked through hell.

"Liberal Roman Catholics believe differently than you do."

She noticed the pants suit had matching pumps. She'd never bought shoes that matched an outfit before.

Jeremiah continued by saying how good it would be for her to nail down her worldview.

"You're saying I should slide my beliefs into nice little slots?"

"Something like that." He clapped her on the back and then explained it had taken years of reading and writing to sort it all out.

"What counts are ideas," he said.

"No, what counts is our bodies. Jesus came in a body," she retorted. "People filter everything through their experiences and feelings because we were created to live in a world we can touch and smell, taste and see," Janice said.

"No, Janice, no. Feelings don't matter. Look, if I depended on my feelings and experience I'd be just like that piece of paper flipping every which way, not firmly planted on the sidewalk, the concrete meeting my sore feet."

"Your sore feet. Bodies. Jesus died and rose and will come again for bodies, not ideas," Janice whispered.

"Janice, take the time and pin down what you believe."

"We're all heretics," she said. She didn't have to believe everything just right to know God.

"Heretics burn," he said.

"We'll see." They stepped into the shadow of the buildings.

"You'd be better off if you sorted it out."

"I prefer my God wild. The Bible says, he makes the wise man a fool, the fool wise; he uplifts the lowly and beats down the proud. Not knowing comforts me." And why wouldn't she find comfort in a God who was utterly in control, who knew how to work it all together for good, though it was hard to see the good just now—the thing she'd dreaded the most her whole life was upon her—her own mother's dying of lung cancer. How would she ever manage without her?

"That scares me," Jeremiah said. "I don't know how you stand not knowing what you believe. Besides, God is a God of order, not chaos." He stopped and pointed up. "Look at the straight lines of the buildings and tell me God isn't a God of order."

Janice tilted her head back and gazed at the square girders and the men walking around on top of them, flashes of light where they were welding them together. Order. Right angles. Fire joining steel to steel.

When the *Weekly News* elevator opened, the receptionist showed them to a waiting area. She handed them each a copy of *Weekly News*. Janice pulled out *Teaching a Stone to Talk* by Annie Dillard and read about the shadow of the moon racing across the earth. She finished that essay and looked at her watch. A half hour had passed, but that wasn't unusual since Jim usually made her wait. She opened the book. Jeremiah jumped up and stalked around the lobby, his arms behind his back.

"What's he doing?" Jeremiah whispered.

"How should I know?"

Jeremiah walked over to the elevator and looked at it. "No thirteenth floor. I'm continually amazed at the superstitions of contemporary man. Listen, let me do the talking."

"Fine," Janice said. She didn't look up from her book. "If you do as well as you did with the *Chicago Tribune*, and show some vulnerability, you'll do all right. What have I been telling you? Jim's a good guy."

"Jim Sanders." He said his name so brusquely, Janice jumped to her feet, thumb in her book.

"A fan?" he nodded at the book, his voice warm and friendly.

"She talks about being dressed right for the job," Janice said referring to Dillard's essay about the Arctic expedition that took silverware to the North Pole.

"Come on back." He stepped aside, letting Janice lead the way. She knew his door by the faded *Peanuts* cartoons. She had just been here less than two hours ago but she was nervous and a little guilty. Would Jim blow her cover? What would happen if Jeremiah found out she wasn't utterly loyal?

Jeremiah sat in the assistant's chair to her left, Jim in his own chair to the right, and Janice in the middle, right in place to catch the sparks flying, pricking her as they disappeared like Fourth of July sparklers.

Janice read the titles of books stacked knee high in the office, the titles shoved onto shelves, while he talked with Jeremiah. She noticed how *Holy Terror*, a book about how the Upright types were a frightening lot, had been moved from the stacks to Jim's desk.

She was surprised at what a good rapport they had, that Jeremiah was almost respectful, humble, not imperious like he'd been with Dennis Manley, vice president of the Upright, Down-right, Just Plain Right Americans for Social Justice.

"Sometimes we can't know God. He springs out of a cloud of unknowing. Knowing Him is actually not knowing him, a blur," Jim said, his ankle resting on his knee, his leg forming a box, his hand holding his argyle sock.

"I disagree. God does not leave us without knowledge. He revealed himself through Jesus Christ, and in the written pages of the Bible." Jeremiah shifted back in his chair, his feet barely touching the ground. "Christians must be involved in all of life, especially governing bodies of all levels."

"He is nearest when he is far, farthest when he is near." Jim turned his mouth to Jeremiah, but those kind eyes turned to Janice. She felt them touching her face, glanced up and looked away, feeling uneasy. It was like he'd thought about her plight and had things to say just to her. Would Jeremiah pick up on how this wasn't a real interview?

"I don't understand," Jeremiah said abruptly. "I'm not here to talk to you about off-the-wall mysticism."

"He draws near to the broken hearted. Saves those who are crushed in spirit," Jim said, flipping through a manuscript on his desk. He showed the title to Jeremiah and Janice. *A Cry of Absence.* "My friend wrote this after his wife died. It's about how some people have a winter sort of spirituality, and that's just as real and faithful as those who always feel God's presence."

"Of course," Jeremiah said impatiently. "What else do you want to ask me?"

"No more pietistic saying prayers by the bed, separating your faith from your everyday life?" Jim set the book down and reached for a legal pad and pencil sitting on a pile of books.

"Right. We believe in becoming involved in all of life, art, the media, and politics. This culture won't make it unless Christians infiltrate every aspect of it, unless they salt the meat so to speak."

"My family used to have a smokehouse to preserve hams and beef. So you're like smoke curing the meats?" Jim looked up at him, pausing in his writing, not hiding the irony in his face.

"That's right. *An American Treatise* urges Christians to disobey the laws of the land if the laws of the land continue to support injustices like abortion on demand," Jeremiah said.

"You'd condone the means justifying the ends?" Jim said quietly as he scribbled on the pad, the pencil scratching thick gray lines across the paper.

"A million babies a year is this nation's Holocaust. Who stands up for them if we don't? A baby in the womb is utterly defenseless. Anyone else, even a small child, has the opportunity to run from their murderer. An unborn baby has no such chance."

"So you condone violence?"

"Only as a last resort."

Jim put his reading glasses on and read, "But it says here, "We don't have much time to work through political, legal and judicial channels. Every day thousands of babies are being slaughtered. Their lives are on our heads. Desperate times lead to desperate measures. As in a just war, violence is sometimes called for. How many lives would be saved if the local abortion mill were destroyed?" Jim looked up, his eyes fierce, daring Jeremiah to respond to his own words.

"I wrote that, yes," Jeremiah said.

"You're breaking the law."

"Martin Luther King talked about just and unjust laws. If a law goes against God's law, we can break it. It's pretty clear murdering babies goes against God's law."

"But you're not a desperate mother."

"Look, I made my wife pregnant when I was seventeen."

"Often it's the ministers who are the first to bring their daughters in for abortions."

"My parents' religious reputation was at stake, but they simply said, 'We'll help you.' And they did."

"You gave the baby up for adoption?"

"I married the mother. We're still married. Where would I be without my son Allan?"

"I have to respect that," Jim muttered, his head down scribbling notes.

"I've counseled men and women who'd aborted their babies. It pisses me off how they'd been sold a bill of goods, how their grief was real and deep and hard to bear, made harder because they were told their baby was just a clot of tissue."

"Do you want him to quote the pissed off part?" Janice asked quietly.

"No of course not. Say angry. That's off the record," Jeremiah let loose his foot, to swing just above the floor.

"It's a pluralistic society," Jim said quietly, looking up while his pencil scratched across the page.

"That shouldn't justify murder," Jeremiah said. "How will God judge this country with a million a year dead? Pragmatically, look at the people who won't be coming into the work force, who won't be contributing to society. Social Security won't be able to support our generation because there won't be enough children to pay into it. What if another Martin Luther King had been aborted?"

But what about the women butchered in back alley abortions? Janice thought but didn't dare say. *And who will help the women who get pregnant and the father won't support them? Who will help the family that can't afford one more child? Is adoption a solution?* Janice had heard that often children who were adopted were abused, that giving a child up for adoption was excruciating. *But wouldn't knowing your child was alive out there somewhere, be better than knowing you'd killed your child inside your womb?*

"We agree there." Jim shoved *An American Treatise* along with galleys of *A Christian Bestseller* into his briefcase, one of those old fashioned fat bags that clipped together on top like a doctor's bag. "I've got all I need. I'll call you if I need anything else," he said to Janice, standing up, signaling the interview was over.

"Sounds good." Janice tried to hide her shock that he so readily agreed with Jeremiah, without arguing the complexities. She looped the strap of her briefcase over her shoulder.

Jeremiah was the last to stand, pushing himself up by the chair rails. He shook out his leg making it look like he was shaking his pants out of the creases in his legs. He thrust his hand out to Jim and shook it one, two, three times. "Thank you very much."

"No problem," Jim said looking over at Janice as he led them out of his office to the elevator. Those eyes caught hers again, with that kindness that made her blink and look away.

After Janice pushed the elevator button, Jim leaned down and kissed her cheek saying, "Remember what I told you. You're doing important work." She felt his lips warm against her skin, then the cool air of the hallway. She felt like a young girl who wouldn't wash her face for days, and she wanted to hold his hand long enough to steady her up to the next ridge, which is how she felt, like she was climbing this long mountain, and she was shot from weariness and there was more to come, but her legs wanted to buckle, slide like the pebbles away from the desolation that waited up top.

"See, he agrees with me." Jeremiah clapped Janice on the back as she watched Jim walk toward Grand Central, his graying hair cut raggedly along his upturned collar.

"That went very well," Jeremiah said as they started along Madison Avenue toward Central Park and the Barbizon Plaza, even with his limp, Janice had to trot a few steps to catch up.

* * * *

Just before Janice woke to take Jeremiah to the *Today* show she dreamed she was walking along the mile long road, kicking an occasional stone, singing, when she saw a city alighting on the headland by The Farm. It was something to see, like driving into Chicago on a misty night and the skyscrapers loomed overhead, and she had to fight the temptation to take her eyes off the Eisenhower and the brake lights in front of her, to look up, up, up at the long furrows of lights disappearing in the low lying clouds which made them even more infinite and huge than they were, and her eyes ached trying to see the end of it.

She saw cars stopping at red lights and going at green lights and felt how they moved forward, then stopped, then moved forward again. Apartments and warehouses and churches shot up around her as the city settled down on the headlands. So many wooden water tanks stood on the roofs, Janice wanted to count them, and there was promise of a very exquisite, expensive meal, something ethnic, something she'd waited to eat her whole life.

Janice's walk became a jog, then an all out run like when she was terrified of an animal's scream in the next valley over, but this wasn't terror but longing. She felt her breath shortening; she felt the sweat pouring down her back, and her thighs rubbing one against the other. She would not be dressed neatly when she sat down to eat, but she didn't care, as long as she was invited to sit down at the table.

She was grateful when the arm for a train crossing dropped down and stopped her, the lights winking on and off, that arm pulling down the phone line. Janice could hear it snake in the wind, that arm with the blinking lights, a low bass sound, like the wind in the pines, and Janice was surprised a wire could make such a living sound. The balls of her feet burned from running. She sucked in the smell of diesel exhaust. Her mother waited at the crossing, only young like she looked in Lucian's baby pictures when she held him, her eyes full of happiness and hope. Janice and her mother watched the engine's headlamp bear down. Then it glided by, a Santa Fe locomotive with its red nose and gray body, surprisingly quiet.

"For as long as I can remember I've loved trains." Janice smiled at the power of the big machines, lifting her up, lifting her heart up.

"Your grandfather photographed them," Barbara said smiling.

They watched cars big as two story houses slow down. Oval windows filled the upper story of the train with people looking down on them, their faces happy.

"The station is down there." Janice pointed to the brick building that was standing where the Little Barn should be. But the darkened house and the maple tree and Janice's mountain ash were still there.

"I've always wanted to take the train to the West Coast," Barbara said, as the train rolled to a stop, sleeper cars opposite them. A door opened and a porter set down a stair stool.

"Then you should," Janice said.

It would have been a good dream if they'd hugged when they parted. But the phone rang, the front desk calling to wake her. All Janice felt was her womb loosening like getting her period or the beginnings of labor.

* * * *

Janice was grateful for the tangerine pants suit she'd bought to celebrate the end of the tour. This outfit helped her feel as alive and attractive as a quiet fire on a cold night, right on down to the matching heels. She felt chilled at 4:00 a.m. but pleased when Jeremiah remarked about her new outfit, "It suits you."

"You didn't know you had a devil with you, did you?" Jeremiah asked as they pushed through the Barbizon Plaza's revolving door, the bottom of it whooshing with Janice doing most of the pushing.

"You don't honestly think you're the devil do you?" Janice asked as they broke into the gray morning light.

"I was a wild man when I was in high school. I'd be gone for days at a time, and my parents wouldn't worry about me. That was the 1960s, man."

"You'd run away?"

"I would take off my clothes and put on a sheepskin, then take chickens out to the woods and stalk them with a sharpened stick. The blood was fun." Jeremiah rubbed his hands together and grinned. The patches on his tweed jacket looked like bruises in the half light.

"Fun?" Janice asked.

"I was expressing my predatory instincts." Jeremiah sounded proper like it was reasonable to enjoy making a living, breathing creature be dead the next minute. "We are at the top of the food chain you know. Killing lesser animals is natural."

"Sounds more like cruelty to me," She murmured. And then, "Oh Lord have mercy."

"What was that?" Jeremiah stopped, looking like she'd tossed cold water on his face.

"Nothing." Janice stepped over the crack between two panes of cement.

"I thought for a minute you were going to speak in tongues. You sounded like someone revving up for it." Jeremiah turned from her and continued limping down the sidewalk.

"I don't speak in tongues," Janice said. "Never have. Never will. God can pass me by as far as that gift goes."

"That stuff is simply too odd. I ever tell you I walked in on a circle of girls praying at Joyful Rest, each one of them speaking in a different language, a candle in the middle of the circle?"

"No, what happened?"

"I threw my hands over my ears and backed out slowly, until I could turn tail and run to my mother, crying uncontrollably. I was about seven. Since then I get the willies when someone starts to mutter prayers under their breath. So Janice, do me a favor, don't take it up."

"I won't. Promise," she said feeling Jeremiah's power as they walked along the Avenue of the Americas to Rockefeller Center. All that intensity, his eyes flashing a black light she could feel on her face. Her teeth ached. She had to trot to keep up.

Was he was telling her straight? Was he a devil? Or a prankster? Janice stepped in front of him and bowed, spreading her arms wide. She could feel a breeze and imagined her arms were wings, the wind strong enough to push her into the air. She straightened up."

"What are you doing?" Jeremiah said exasperated.

"Praying," Janice said. "Praying for you because you'll need all the prayers you can get during this interview."

"I'm going to start out by saying, 'Hey Ellen Adams, you bitch.'"

"Jeremiah, don't wreck what you've worked for. People look up to you. You don't scare me," she blurted the words, not sure how she was supposed to respond, but knowing part of her job was convincing him to behave, so Godspeed could sell his books.

"I'll be good." Jeremiah folded his hands in front of him and smiled. The shine off his hair practically sent a column of light into the pre-dawn darkness.

"Show compassion. Throw them off guard," Janice said. "Now that's a thought. A conservative who actually cares about the liberal sitting across from them."

"I don't want to talk about it anymore. I've been up all night thinking."

Janice switched her briefcase from one hand to the next, looping the shoulder strap, to the other side, but still it pinched. The books she carried to give to the producers in hopes they might run a story, had grown heavier by the step.

Her purse slipped off the other shoulder and flopped by her calves. There was a fat water blister on the balls of her feet.

As they came up to Rockefeller Center, Janice felt a weight laid on her as if Jeremiah had gone limp, utterly depending on her to take him to the door with NBC written on the marquee. Through the year Janice had become good at reading the large directory board. She'd smile at the security guard, telling him her name and the person she was scheduled to see.

Despite her misgiving about Jeremiah, there was no denying that Jeremiah's book should be acknowledged as a *New York Times* Best Seller instead of being cast off as a A Christian Bestseller. The mainstream media discriminated against conservative Christian books. Liberal elitists were even banning them from libraries and schools. *Not fair, not right,* Janice thought. *That's censorship. An American Treatise* was selling twenty-five thousand copies a month. The kicker was *Christian Bestseller: Why Not?* wouldn't be released for another couple of months. But the *Today* show had wanted Jeremiah right now for a series they were doing on censorship, a perfect venue for Jeremiah to out the liberal book media.

* * * *

The guard directed them to the Green Room that wasn't green but beige with a coffee maker and a plate of donuts. There were two televisions in two corners and one couch and several easy chairs. The place seemed more like a closet for waiting guests than the elegant room Janice had imagined for guests of the *Today* show.

A woman dressed to the nines gave Jeremiah a release form and cards for his name and address to let people know how he could be contacted in case they had any questions. "The writer for the segment will be here shortly if you want any tapes of the show."

Ellen Adams of the American Library Association and Bruce Walker, the owner of a Krochs and Brentanos showed up about the same time. They sat down and immediately began talking, hands folded out like they were praying. Ellen's bright red fingernails gave Janice the chills. Her matching lipstick made her face look even sharper. This was not a woman to cross. The bookstore owner, Bruce Walker, wore a tweed jacket and khaki Dockers. He was swarthy like a pirate, without the beard, but his lips were pinched in like he was taking a long swig on a beer bottle.

Janice hoped Jeremiah wouldn't flip like he had walking here because if he did, Pete, her boss, would blame her for not keeping him under control. The industry would shun Jeremiah like they had authors who'd written about talking to angels they called spirit guides. Returns would flood in from bookstores and Pete would lay her off.

Jeremiah introduced himself, unafraid to shake Ellen's hand with the sharp red fingernails, his eyes flashing, his mouth smiling, his words just this side of stuttering.

The producer, Tiffany Reynolds, with her pug nose and

freckles, looked like she'd stepped off a horse. She wore pleated pants and a blouse, the same classic styles that Janice wore. She shook Jeremiah's hand and pulled him to the side talking with him. "Of all the people we've interviewed on the subject of book banning, you're the most interesting."

"Conservative Christian books are being excluded from the mainstream press and kept out of mainstream bookstores. Those are the books being banned," Jeremiah said. "It's not right that Christian books have sold more than acknowledged bestsellers, but are never included on *The New York Times Best Seller* list."

"You be sure to say that on air," she said, brushing her hair out of her eyes.

"Doesn't it make you nervous that fewer are deciding which books are being published? Which books are being sold? What does that say about freedom of the press or even freedom of speech? Doesn't it trouble you that the books upholding decency and Christian values are the ones being ostracized?"

"You make very interesting points," Tiffany said, holding her clipboard close to her chest, her arms crossed in front of it.

Then Tiffany turned to Ellen Adams and Bruce Walker, her air friendly and welcoming, but Janice noticed she did not take her hands off her clipboard to shake their hands. As she herded them to the studio door, she turned to Janice. "I'd take you to the Control Room, but you'd better stay here if you want to see the show."

"I'd love to see the Control Room," Janice said. The room was pitch black with TV screens in a row above them and colored lights on the control panels. Most of the screens showed different angles on the show. Tiffany wore an earpiece with an attached microphone. The darkness, with the splotches of light from the monitors, made it hard for Janice to focus.

The hair on the back of Janice's neck stood up, and her stomach tightened when she heard Ellen Adams say, "How can you expect us to put your books in the library when they aren't even in *Books in Print*?"

"I checked last week to see if they were there, and they

weren't."

What did she mean they weren't there? Months ago, Janice had filled out the ABI forms for *Books in Print*, a huge, fat book that listed the books and their ISBN numbers. Janice liked to think of them like a baby's howl when they first entered the world, those numbers, evidence the book was alive and could find her audience. She had stuffed them in their envelopes and sent them. She sent galleys to *Booklist*, *Publishers Weekly* and *Library Journal* for pre-publication reviews. One of the reasons evangelical books weren't included in these publications was because the evangelical houses didn't send books there. She'd worked hard breaking new ground by simply doing the clerical work required and meeting their three-month pre-publication deadline.

"My publicist is very efficient. If they're not there, it's because both *An American Treatise* and my forthcoming, *A Christian Bestseller: Why Not?* are being ignored because of the Christian genre."

"I doubt that," said Ellen Adams.

"We put a one hundred thousand dollar ad campaign together for *An American Treatise*, so it's incomprehensible that the book could simply be ignored...And in case you *haven't* heard *An American Treatise* is about how Christians should use civil protest, even uncivil protest against anti-Christian American policies like abortion on demand." Jeremiah turned the camera and said, "You can find it at B. Dalton and Walden."

"So you can line your pockets and make lots of money?" Ellen Adams asked softly.

"To quote St. Paul, 'A workman is worthy of his hire.'" Jeremiah leaned back and slid back in the seat as if her comments weren't worth acknowledging.

"You people like to hide behind the Bible," Bruce Walker said, his pursed lips moving like he was sucking on a beer bottle.

"It is the bestselling book of all time. You people hide behind the dollars and cents of that," Jeremiah said tapping the sole of his shoe. "Yet a school teacher can't set a Bible on her desk without being fired. Town squares can't have a manger scene."

"What does that have to do with books?"

"Everything. Why is it the decent part of society gets censored while the pornographer promotes his smut with court sanctioned protection?"

"Once you cut the pornographer's rights where does it stop? *Lady Chatterly's Lover*? Do we ban that? Or *A Wrinkle in Time* because it has witches? You Upright types can't have it both ways."

"Of course we can. *A Christian Bestseller: Why Not?* talks about how the media and academic elite are biased against anything with an evangelical perspective." He turned to the camera and smiled, "It will be available in Walden Books or B. Dalton in a month."

The show cut to a commercial. Janice swallowed hard because Ellen Adams had put her red fingernail right on it. Jeremiah had plans for his royalties. But wait a minute, didn't every author want to line their pockets and make money?

"You've got a live one there." Tiffany touched Janice's arm and led her out of the Control Room back to the Green Room. Her kindness sliced through her defenses right to her grief. Janice swallowed air, trying to concentrate on what her fingers were feeling—the bite of the handles on her heavy briefcase.

"He's a handful."

Janice looked on the carpet blinking hard.

As Jeremiah opened the door his eyes darted back and forth like he was looking for a hiding place. He smiled when he saw Janice and clapped her on the shoulder. "How did I do?"

"Fine." Janice switched hands on her briefcase. She noticed Ellen Adams and Bruce the Bookstore Pirate coming through the door followed by Tiffany.

"Jane Pauley asked me the first question and let me do the talking. She leaned over during break and told me it was good television," Jeremiah said proudly.

"You did a good job," Tiffany said shaking Jeremiah's hand, holding it like she was holding a lightning bug cupped in her fingers.

"Thank you for showing me the questions. You gave me an edge." Jeremiah winked.

"We try to be fair," she whispered, the whole tone of her voice changed, lower somehow, maybe angry.

"Give me a couple books." Jeremiah nudged Janice, who reached into her briefcase handing him several copies of *An American Treatise*.

He handed Bruce the Bookstore Pirate and Ellen Adams copies like they were his biggest fans. She handed him an essay on intellectual freedom written on yellow parchment paper.

"His book is in *Books in Print*." Janice was startled by how her voice sounded like a growl. "You can scratch my face with those red fingernails, but you will not tell a national audience I am not doing my job." A shot of adrenalin surged through her because she hadn't meant to speak her mind. It wasn't Jeremiah sabotaging her job she had to worry about. Oh no, it wasn't him.

"How's that?" Ellen asked mildly as if she hadn't heard Janice.

"I sent the forms myself." Janice's heart was thumping so loudly, it was all she could hear.

"I got on the database and did a title search." Ellen folded her hands, those red fingernails in front of her belt.

"*An American Treatise* is in there," Janice said. "It was reviewed by *Publishers Weekly*, your own *Booklist*, and *Kirkus Reviews*."

"So his book *isn't* being ignored," Bruce said. "Your author, what's his name? He admitted that the major chains were carrying it."

Janice tried to look neutral because Bruce inserted himself into Janice's trouble with promoting *A Christian Bestseller: Why Not?* She didn't think the media ignored Jeremiah because of censorship. The way she saw it, no one had bothered to promote Christian books to the mainstream media. Janice was breaking new ground, making new friends. She resented how Jeremiah's message undermined her work and her integrity, as she built those relationships, not only for him, but also for God-speed Books.

"I have no desire to scratch your eyes out, or his, or anyone else's," Ellen said quietly. "By the looks of them, your nails could use a manicure."

Jeremiah threw Janice a dark, startled look and jumped in. "Godspeed Books has some lovely children's books."

"Here are a few." Janice reached in her briefcase and pulled out the brightly colored picture books, glad to lighten it.

"Thank you." Ellen Adams' eyes glazed over as Bruce Walker turned toward the door. She walked after him quickly, her fingernails flashing at her sides.

When Janice and Jeremiah stepped out on the street, Jeremiah asked, with fear in his voice, "Janice what was that about back there?"

"I hated her lies and those crimson nails," Janice whispered.

"It's my job to be out of control. Your job to put the brakes on. Got it?"

"Got it." She swallowed hard.

"She should register them as weapons." Jeremiah's eyes flashed. He chuckled, continuing, "You heard me come to your defense. She played right into our point."

"I don't know what happened," Janice said, but she knew. She was tired of being nice to everyone though her job demanded it. She was worried about her mother. The nine months her doctor had given her were almost up. The cancer was going to win.

"I'm rubbing off on you, that's what. I'll have to behave myself, or I'll send my publicist off her rocker. Takes all the fun out."

"I'm sorry," Janice said, refusing to meet his eyes, a little startled by her own outburst. A Central Park carriage horse stood with his head down, dozing, his lower lip hanging down. "You're showing amazing courage with your mother so ill and all. Janice, I want you to think of me as your friend. I won't say anything to your boss," Jeremiah said.

Friend? How could she think of Jeremiah as a friend when his talk of revolution and turning America into a Christian country had driven her to betray him? It didn't matter that he pulled back and said it was a crock. A revolution was a revolution. From what she knew of Christians' behavior, she couldn't think of anything more horrible.

* * * *

As she followed Jeremiah up the stairs and into the lobby of the Barbizon Plaza Hotel, her sleeve slid back revealing her watch. Her heart jumped as she caught the time. "You've got a plane to catch. Go, collect your bags. I'll check you out." Janice turned toward the carved front desk with a handsome young man behind it.

"No one's ever gotten me an interview with either the *Today* show or *Weekly News*." Jeremiah touched her arm more gently, his eyes earnest.

"We'll see what the story's like," Janice said, already nervous about him making his plane, ready to catch her train to Albany, a chance to finally see her mother and Caleb.

"Thank you for taking care of everything." Jeremiah's voice was so appreciative. Janice was relieved, hoping he'd forgotten their disagreement back on Madison Avenue.

"We won't say our goodbyes just yet. Bring me your key, so I can check you out, pay the bill, and you can be on your way."

The elevator opened and Jeremiah stepped in. He poked the number of his floor like he'd poked her. The doors closed with a soft whoosh like blankets snapped free of dust.

Janice told the young man at the front desk, who she was and how she would be paying for Jeremiah on her card. "Ah, you have some messages." He looked startled for a minute and quickly turned his back to pull the slips out of her box.

Five were from her brother to call home, spaced fifteen minutes apart. Four spaced on the half hour. Then nothing for the last few hours. Janice's heart banged like when she had stepped her foot into a noose and shoved off over the Normans Kill, the rope burning the arch of her foot, the only answer to let go at the farthest arc because the rope wouldn't return you back to the bank, but would swing you back over shallow water. Her one chance would be to let go at the farthest point, to land in the deep water where she'd be safe, and she was terrified she wouldn't let go at the right moment.

"Miss? Here is the bill." She looked over the charges: the lingerie from the hotel store, the room service, two hundred and fifty dollars in calls. She handed him her company credit card and looked toward the pay phones at the end of the desk.

"Could you tell him I had some important phone calls and couldn't see him off? He'll be dropping off his key. The man with a limp who just got in the elevator," Janice said as she signed her name, her hand sliding off the "l" in her last name like someone had pushed her wrist. Brian nodded, ripping the paper apart and handing her the copy for her expense account.

She walked away quickly, her head up, her feet burning in those new shoes, the weight of books she'd not given away, burning the meat of her palm, the shoulder strap dragging on the floor, the elevator doors finally closing, the floor lifting her to that desolate ridge she'd climbed all by herself. By the time she reached her floor she was soaked, her body, her face, with the grief of those pink slips, what her brother would tell her when she called home.

It took three tries to punch the familiar number. Janice breathed to steady her voice. Her uncle picked up the phone. "I'll get your brother," he said, his low, quiet voice like water gurgling around stones.

"Where were you? I called before dawn. Who goes out before the sun comes up?" Janice heard the accusation in his voice, not unlike her mother's when she accused Janice of cattin' around, when she was driving off to ride in Caleb's tractor.

"The *Today* show." Her voice was loud, pushing past a lump of grief.

"Mom died this morning. Alone. Dad walked out when we

got the call."

"I'm sorry," Janice said apologetically, as though her being in New York had caused her mother's death; as though she
should have been the one to sit that last night with her.

"When are you coming home?" He sounded more gentle.

"The next train." Janice reminded him of the time they'd
already agreed on when she'd made plans to slip upstate after
her New York appointments. After she hung up she grabbed the
bedspread and hugged it tight like a shawl.

Hard knocking on the door. Had someone on the other side
of the walls complained about her noise? Stopping her grief was
like pulling a shade over a window, that once it was pulled down,
she couldn't let up slowly. It would only snap open at the wrong
time, an unexpected time. So Janice splashed water on her face
and wiped it off with a towel. The person kept knocking.

She slid the chain latch and cranked open the brass knob.
Jeremiah stood outside the door. "Didn't you hear me?" he said
impatiently.

Janice nodded and let him in the tiny room where there was
barely room to squeeze past the bed to the table and two chairs
overlooking Avenue of the Americas. She heard horses' hooves
clopping from the carriages and broughams of the Central Park
horsemen. Jeremiah squeezed by and sat down in the chair
propping his feet up on the foot of the bed. "I'm taking a later
flight home. I'll take you to your train." He explained how he
called his travel agent who promised to make the changes.

"I can manage." Janice shivered as the cool hallway air blew
in when she shut the door.

"The clerk said you looked a fright when you got your messages." Jeremiah looked as pale as she looked, his cheeks blotchy
as though he'd been crying.

"My brother said she died this morning around four. They'd
put her in the hospice last night and didn't expect her to go this
fast. No family member was with her," Janice said with a dead
calm, her tears, the pain that had split her, closed over. In the
dream her mother had stood next to her as a train slowed, then

stopped. Then she stepped toward the train and that was it, Janice had awakened.

"Why didn't they call you sooner?" Jeremiah asked.

"They did," Janice said, nodding at the pink slips, "but I've not been back to my room since this morning."

"I mean before. You could have left the tour."

"They knew I was coming home anyway." Janice buried her face in her hands.

"I'm so sorry. Losing my father was the worst thing, part mixed with relief and part mixed with sorrow that verged on desolation. You have a tough road up ahead."

Jeremiah took her hand, held it so tightly that it cut off her circulation. He squeezed his eyes so tightly, they looked like squeezed lemon wedges. "Dear Lord, please be with your dear servant Janice as she returns to her family today. Grant her journey mercies. Comfort her. And Lord, help her return to her work able to promote my books and the other books written for Your glory. In Jesus' name, amen." His words limped as badly as he did. At least he tried to cover her with God.

"I'll call Pete while you pack your bags," Jeremiah said.

"That's all right." Janice clutched the bedspread with one hand and punched in the numbers. Jeremiah pulled her suits off the hangers and hung them in her garment bag. They didn't have long to get to Grand Central.

Before she could say anything, Pete congratulated her on the *Today* show. "We convened chapel early to watch the show. This is beyond our wildest dreams. Thank you Janice."

"I wanted to tell you," Janice paused, "my mother..." she couldn't say the rest.

There was a long silence, filled with emotion, as though Pete choked up. "Take all the time you need. You've earned it."

"Thank you."

"All of your friends here at Godspeed will be praying for you."

"Thank you."

Jeremiah signaled for her to give him the phone. Janice

handed it over, vaguely listening to his comments as she wad-
ded her dirty clothes and stuffed them in a zippered pocket. She
slipped her painful shoes in another pocket as he talked.

"Let me carry these." He hefted the garment bag over his
shoulder and picked up the briefcase. "Haven't you learned to
travel light?" he tried to kid her.

Janice shook her head vaguely and looked under the bed, in
the bathroom, for anything she'd left and switched off the light.

Jeremiah clapped her on the shoulder and shut the door behind them. His face looked so full of compassion and humanity,
he almost looked like someone whose shoulder she could cry on.

When they were standing in Grand Central, waiting for her
train to be called, Janice looked up at the travel poster of China
high up on the walls. The stubby mountains looked like they belonged on another planet. What would they look like up close?
What would the air smell like? Here it smelled like diesel and
urine and air that was trapped for a hundred years. She looked
at the ceiling where she was surprised to see faded stars underneath grime. This place was like being inside a mountain range.
She felt small, but honored that such a building was built to ac-
commodate people's travel, her travel. She walked back to Jeremiah who stood straddled over her garment bag and briefcase,
his own duffle slung over his shoulder. A disheveled woman, her
hair straggling out of her pony tail, her shirt tails pulled out of
her jeans, stepped away when Janice walked up.

"That was a lawyer's wife my folks knew at Joyful Rest. Her
baby daughter drowned a few days ago in a pool. Then her husband had a heart attack and is in intensive care. Alice looks like
she's aged twenty years. She went through that in one weekend.
It's terrible the tragedy people go through." Jeremiah looked be-
wildered, awed.. "It's amazing how life could switch from being
the good life to something hellacious in a matter of hours. What
if something happened to Elizabeth? Or my son Allan? I'd be
torn limb from limb."

"Grief does that," Janice whispered, looking at the clocks in
the center of the terminal—white moons speaking the time in

four directions. In two, three hours she'd face her father and brother. Her grief and their grief would roll at each other, likely to meet in a huge splash and crash.

"Just imagine, the Lord put me here at Grand Central to comfort them when they needed me. Amazing, isn't it?" Jeremiah said. He'd given the woman his card, telling her she could call any time.

"Yes, Jeremiah," Janice said, not sure how much of a blessing Jeremiah could be. Just then the Lake Shore Limited was called, departing for Croton, Albany Rensselear, Schenectady, Utica, Syracuse, Buffalo-Depew, Erie, Cleveland, Elyria, Sandusky, Toledo, Bryan, Waterloo, Elkhart, South Bend, Hammond, Whiting, Chicago. The words were tinny, bouncing somewhere between the glorious dome of the ceiling and the floor.

Janice pulled out her ticket and held it cocked off to one side as she picked up her garment bag and briefcase. The muscles across the top of her shoulders pulled. Jeremiah looked at his watch. "If I catch a cab and the tunnel is clear I can make my original flight," he said.

"Thanks for bringing me here," Janice said, feeling supported by his presence.

"You'll be all right."

"I always am."

Before he left Jeremiah grabbed her arm, "I know it's hard beyond belief. But fathers and mothers die. Losing them is one of those refining fires God promised. You'll walk out the other side of this a stronger woman. And life will be richer." Jeremiah stood on tip toes to kiss her cheek, then was off. Janice watched him hop, skip and jump, his fastest lame gait as he walked across the floor, dodging people and up the stairs until there were only the stairs and strangers. Janice turned to the arch in the wall, the cave leading out to the train, the engine idling to pull them out of the city. She shuffled with the crowd toward the darkness of the platform, the air even more stale than in the station. The old Bible song rattled through her head in her father's voice, belligerent.

The Lord knows the way through the wilderness. All I have to do is follow.

Follow like fallow, the ground left to rest, but Janice saw the humps of plowed earth waiting to be harrowed, waiting for the seed. *If a seed falls in the ground and dies, it springs up to everlasting life. That's how your bodies will be seeds. The Lord knows the way through.* God, Janice hoped so because she sure didn't. Janice stepped into the darkness and walked along the lit windows of the train until she chose stairs to stumble up, a seat on the Hudson river side. And the irony was, it was Janice pulling herself aboard the train, not her mother like in the dream.

CHAPTER FOUR

August 1983, Amtrak: Albany Rennsselear

Janice caught of glimpse of Lucian standing with a woman she'd never met before, both of them looking straight ahead, not up at the windows as the train slowed and finally stopped several train lengths past them. *That must be Marcel*, she thought. *My brother's newest conquest.*

As people stood up and gathered their things, Janice sat back and closed her eyes. She wanted the train to pull forward to carry her backward up to Schenectady, across the Hudson and Mohawk, the black bars of the iron bridges marking the miles she wished she could put between herself and her mother's death. She'd be happy to step off at Union Station in Chicago, take the bus home, and skip this part— the hugging and I'm sorries and the tears that wouldn't come, no not since she'd pulled them down like a shade when Jeremiah stood at her hotel room offering to see her safely to Grand Central.

Janice reached into her briefcase and pulled out her bottle of Normans Kill water. A tiny bit was left in the bottom. She uncapped it and poured the rest on her hands and rubbed them together. She could almost feel the real stream, warmed by the sun, the water moving over stones coated in river weed. It wouldn't be long before she sat down beside it. *By the waters of Babylon, we sat down and wept, and wept.* She sighed wrapped her hands around her garment bag, around her briefcase and hauled the garment bag in front of her and the briefcase behind her. A porter waited to take her hand as she stepped down, but her hands were full; she was balanced. The pavement hit her feet so hard her blisters broke. Even though she was dressed in her best work clothes, she felt sweaty and ragged going to meet Lucian and this new woman. *How many fiancees did this make? Four? Five? Would she be wearing the same ring Cindy wore? Or was the woman before Marcel, Antoinette?* Janice couldn't keep them straight.

She caught herself. These were unkind thoughts. But she'd been looking forward to riding home with him alone. No one else. So he could tell her what happened. So she could ask what will become of them without Mother? And he could say, "We'll go on just like always." So they could be brother and sister to each other, comfortable as family.

Lucian's face warmed when he saw her. Marcel's face held that blank stare like someone searching the crowd. When she saw Janice, her face broke into a wide smile that was frightening, it was so bright and naked and friendly. And she was beautiful, her skin pale and translucent as porcelain. Her jet black hair was pulled back in a bun. Janice averted her eyes glancing at a gum wrapper on the pavement. She touched the unicorn necklace at her throat. But she couldn't keep her eyes down when she saw the tops of Lucian's muddied Timberlands. He looked like a man with a glass shard poking into some soft, tender place. *Had he been there when Mother died? Had it been too hard to bear their father's grief? Or his own?*

"Hi, Sis. I want you to meet Marcel, my fiancée." Lucian stretched his arm out to present her.

"I wish it were under better circumstances." Marcel leaned into Janice for a hug before Janice could set down her bags. Her arms came around her, light and polite. Janice noticed she was wearing paddock boots flecked with horse manure around the soles. Her Oxford shirt had pictures of brown horses jumping over fences.

"Lucian didn't say you loved horses."

"We have a surprise at home," Lucian said.

"A surprise?" Janice didn't want any more surprises. Her mother's death was enough.

"We're boarding Marcel's horses while she goes to college."

Before Janice could react, Marcel said, "I'm so sorry for your loss. In the short time I knew her, your mother was like my second mom."

"I can't believe she's gone," Janice said.

"We didn't know she was this close to dying, or we would have called you," Lucian said. "Here let me take your bags." Janice handed him the garment bag. Marcel took her briefcase.

"What happened?"

Lucian explained that she'd asked to go into the hospice facility at St. Peter's Hospital because she didn't want to be alone, with it so hard to breathe. The nurses sent them home early last night, saying she was doing well and not at all close to dying. Their father left as soon as he got the call. He didn't bother to wake Lucian. He was driving out the road by the time Lucian knew what was going on.

"That must have been so hard," Janice said.

Lucian shrugged. "She's in a better place." He said it like the cliché it was.

"How's Dad holding up?"

"Better than expected."

"We think he did a lot of grieving when he left this morning," Marcel said.

"He's a private man." Janice paused and added, "We all are."

They fell silent as they stuffed Janice's things in the back of the Pink Panther, Lucian's Triumph convertible. Janice climbed into the back seat, shutting her eyes and feeling the warm sun on her face. Road noise and wind would make it hard to talk.

Janice thought about the last time she'd seen her mother, who was admonishing her daughter about falling for Caleb.

They'd been in the kitchen, her mother making macaroni and cheese for the special meal she'd planned for Janice before she flew back to Chicago.

"Don't you have any self respect? Don't you have a clue as to how I raised you, to conduct yourself like you're to the manor born?" Her mother had cut pieces of cheese, dropping them into the white sauce for macaroni and cheese. She was smaller than Janice, and wearing slacks and a man's dress shirt, untucked. Her swollen ankles ended at a pair of worn Hush Puppies. Her wig was cut in a gray pageboy.

"It's something deeper. In here," Janice had poked at the space between her breasts. "You wait for a good man, who loves the Lord, and you, a man who loves the earth and is simple. What Caleb seemed at first but isn't. You be sure to wait."

"How can I wait for a good man, when they are so hard to come by? I've come across a lot of Christian men and none of them, I tell you none of them, holds a candle to Caleb."

"He makes my skin crawl."

Janice knew what she meant. Caleb's girl was a naked woman sprawled on sand, pinned over his desk. But still, something about him. It was the machines and the ground and the wheat or corn or bean seeds, he laid into the ground. "He makes me feel beautiful. He tends our land."

"You're not going to marry him." Her mother added more milk to the double boiler. She stirred the spoon scraping the bottom of the pan.

"No I am not."

"But he asked. And you said yes. And then he stood you up. And you cried for hours. Do you remember how you cried?"

"Of course."

"Then how can you go back there?"

"He said he was sorry."

"You forgive way too easy."

"The marriage thing. It was a joke between us."

"It's a reckless game you play."

"He's my friend."

"I didn't raise you to cat around," Barbara ripped open the box of macaroni and poured it in the boiling water, the sound like a shallow brook thrashed by cobblestones.

"I have to go now," Janice had said gently. "I have to."

She'd gone to Caleb and found the comfort she always found when she sat behind him while he worked the fields. She'd stepped away from the terror of her mother dying and that had been enough.

The wind felt like cat paws batting Janice's face as the little car made its way out of the station and onto the Dunn Memorial Bridge over the Hudson River. She didn't open her eyes as she felt the car tip back a bit and the wind become colder. Off to the south she heard the low horn of a freighter making its way to the Port of Albany. She heard Marcel murmur to Lucian, "Oh she's asleep." Janice opened her eyes and saw Lucian's hand was strumming Marcel's shoulder, as if each finger were tugging on a string, a fine intimacy for a guitar, but too personal for Janice's eyes. She felt like she were back on tour, forced to make nice and think of good questions to ask like how did you meet Lucian, and tell me about your horses, instead of coming home to family, where she could walk around in pajamas if she wanted. She forgot to look whether or not Marcel was wearing Cindy's engagement ring, or a new one, or any kind of ring at all.

* * * *

Her father was grilling hamburgers with Uncle Steve and Uncle Merle who were standing to the side with their arms crossed and looking awkward because he couldn't use their help. For a few seconds Janice thought this was just her relatives getting together to celebrate Labor Day, her father looked so intent. He flipped a burger and pressed it against the grill, flame leaping up. He was wearing the dress pants her mother had bought last Christmas, and one of his white dress shirts, the cuffs rolled back and the neck unbuttoned.

"Hi Dad," Janice said kissing his cheek. His arms barely

touched her shoulders as he hugged her. His beard prickled her lips, and he smelled like old coffee. Her mother and dad used to sit across from each other, steam from their coffee rising, saying a few words here and there about their day to come. Instead of collapsing on his shoulder, weeping at the thought of him facing no one on the couch, Janice stepped back.

"I saw that Jeremiah Sackfield on the *Today* show. I was so proud you made that happen." Her father's eyes looked heavy, like he was having a hard time staying awake. He turned back to the burgers, flipping them.

"We never thought she'd go this fast." His upper lip trembled and his eyes filled with tears. Where Lucian puffed up when his emotions came on strong, her father seemed to wilt before her eyes.

"Oh Dad, I'm sorry." Janice put her hand on his shoulder, which felt big and round like turned over dirt. She wanted to hug him, but too many years of standing back, keeping a respectful distance, stopped her.

"She's 'absent from the body, present with the Lord,'" he said, flipping the burgers again and pressing them down against the fire, which roared up with fragrant smoke. "If I didn't have that promise from the Bible, I'd go right to bed and lie down and not get up. But your mother is in good, good hands, the kind and warm presence of Jesus himself. She is safe now, drawing deep breaths from Heaven's fresh air."

"I know," Janice said, taking the platter of burgers and setting it on the dining room table full of food the Community Church deaconesses brought them—platters of cold cuts, macaroni and cheese casseroles, taco salad, noodle salads, cookies, lemon bars. Then she swung back outside and took her father's elbow so she could steady him. He patted her hand and smiled, as she opened the door and led him into the dining room. Uncle Merle invited everyone to hold hands around the table, which meant about thirty people counting the children, grandchildren, and women who were helping. He was a tall, dignified man, his compassion mixed in with austerity in such a way the family looked to him as their minister.

Janice stood between Aunt Denise and Aunt Sarah, her mother's sisters. They took each hand and squeezed gently. They were like having Mother standing on either side of her. They'd known her the longest of anyone.

"Father," Merle spoke like he was on speaking terms with the Almighty. Well, so was Janice and everyone else in the room. The screen door slammed. Merle stopped and looked up. Everyone stopped and looked up. Lucian walked into the dining room and stood between Aunt Sarah and Uncle Steve trying to look like there was nothing wrong, but there was something wrong. Where was Marcel? They heard a scratching at the door, then the screen door opening and shutting with King and Arthur nudging their way in, wagging their tails, finding Kurt and lying down next to him. Aunt Denise squeezed her eyes shut as tears pressed out.

Uncle Merle resumed his prayer. Both aunts squeezed Janice's hands hard like they were telling her they loved her through how fervently they pinched her fingers. Aunt Sarah frowned and wiped her eye.

"She's happy now," Janice said and excused herself for the bathroom. She'd forgotten she needed it until now.

When she returned to the dining room Janice watched everyone fill their plates with hamburgers, corn and the church food. Uncle Merle and Aunt Denise walked through the buffet together looking more like actors than her aunt and uncle. Uncle Merle was tall and stately, with his voice like a cello, deep and resonant. As a young woman Aunt Denise's features were sharp, accentuated by her cat's eye glasses, but now, she had grown into a beauty. Her face was the sort to welcome a person home. She pulled her hands out of her pleated navy skirt and white blouse to pick up a plate and silverware, Barbara's good silver. Oh how her mother had loved Aunt Denise and Denise her mother, the two of them talking nearly everyday. Her face looked rinsed clean.

Janice waited until everyone had walked out of the dining room. She picked up her plate and began spooning the various types of macaroni and cheese onto her plate. She would sample each and see if any rivaled her mother's. She would let the food be her friend, take her away for the time it took to eat it. The hot corn bit her fingers as she dropped an ear on her plate. She picked up the most shriveled burger but ignored the bun.

Suddenly Marcel was standing beside her as Janice was focusing on stabbing an olive with a fork. Janice could smell the coffee smell of horse. "I don't feel good," she said.

"What's wrong?" Janice asked looking at the other woman's face. She looked more pale than when they first met, her hair in ropey knots, her hands smeared with horse dirt. The yellow shirt with horses had a streak of green across the front.

"Migraine." She touched her head and stomach. "Tell Dad and Lucian I'll be over first thing."

"You could tell them," Janice said. "Dad's outside here. Lucian's in the parlor."

Marcel shook her head and swallowed. She blinked hard walked outside through the kitchen door, holding her head up like nothing was wrong, but Marcel was not the kind of woman to let her hair look that straggly and sweat dampened even after a work out.

Janice followed her, hoping she could help and then walk out to Caleb's tractor, when Aunt Sarah called her. "Sit next to me," she called, her voice demanding like the frown she wore on her face. Next to the redwood lawn chair was an empty plastic chair.

Janice looked at the beautiful machine with four large tractor wheels painted red and white like the barns, and floodlights like eyes, that she'd seen flashing against hedge rows, catching deer poised to run or once an owl staring down at them.

She sat down, holding her plate in front of her, not sure she was up for a talk with her aunt, because she wasn't afraid to hurt a person's feelings. She looked so much like her mother before she lost her hair that Janice wanted to hug her and say goodbye, but all she could do was hold back her tears with this woman who was not safe or kind.

"Your brother's got a nice girl." Aunt Sarah folded into herself and stirred her macaroni salad with something pink and suspicious in it—crab or shrimp, Janice couldn't tell.

"I guess," Janice replied. The first macaroni and cheese she tasted was the pee yellow stuff out of a box, fine for hotdogs at lunch but not now.

"I hope he stays with her." Aunt Sarah's eyes followed Marcel's truck backing out of the parked cars and driving out the road.

"Who knows?" Janice said, her stomach feeling hollow as Marcel's truck passed the arbor for bittersweet. "Someone should be happy. It might as well be Lucian."

"She'd be crushed if he leaves her." Sarah scooped a cold pea salad onto her fork, the peas dropping off one by one.

"Who would take care of her horses?" Janice asked. That was the question that bothered her since she saw Marcel's horses, a Roman-nosed Thoroughbred mare, a buckskin Marcel said trotted like a daisy cutter, and a blood bay colt, the mare's baby just now broken to saddle.

Did she love Lucian for Lucian or for a free place to keep her horses? A woman could love her horses like babies and do anything for them. Yet, Marcel couldn't fake that kind of look, that kind of devotion and love when she looked at Lucian.

"Aunt Denise and I would feel very comfortable with her in your mother's kitchen." Sarah stuck her fork tines down into a piece of turkey and cut, the plate shifting on her lap.

"That's nice." Janice hadn't thought of Marcel that way.

"Where did Marcel go?" Lucian walked out of the house and stood in front of Janice, his hands on his hips, his feet splayed like he was waiting between softball pitches. He looked startled, and not a little afraid.

"She didn't feel good, and told me to tell you," Janice replied as matter factly as possible. "She'll be back in the morning."

"What about her horses?" Lucian asked.

"I don't know." Janice shrugged her shoulders.

Lucian flapped his hands looking lost and walked away. "I'll bring them in after awhile," he said over his shoulder.

CHAPTER FIVE

Janice was glad when Marcel didn't show up first thing to feed her horses. She was looking forward to spending some time alone with her father and Lucian. They ate their breakfast in the parlor, the TV running game shows in the background.

"We met at the hospice and the therapist asked what your mother wanted for each one of us. I've never heard anything so beautiful." Her father's eyes welled up and his upper lip quivered.

The air between them became thick. The house groaned. Lucian picked up his plate and walked out.

"What did she say?" Janice suddenly felt unworthy, afraid of her mother's blessing.

"She loved you so. Here, she wanted you to have this. Her father picked up an envelope and handed it to her."

He waited expectantly for her to open it, but she set it down on her lap, afraid to look, afraid of how her emotions might burst forth when someone needed to be strong. She needed to be strong.

After awhile, Janice took the envelope to her room. She could almost hear the walls whisper, "Quit your job. Come home. They need you." Janice felt like someone was placing a wet cloth over her mouth and nose, pressing hard. She walked outside.

Janice could see how well bred Marcel's colt was, a blood bay that glistened in the wind, the product of an accidental breeding to a nationally ranked jumper, whose bloodlines ran back to Northern Dancer. She walked up to him to pet him, to listen to his tearing grass with his teeth but he picked up his head, like someone picking up their bags and moved three seats down.

Janice wondered where Caleb was, but with a thousand acres spread throughout Albany County she had no idea where to look. Would he even be glad to see her? Or would another woman be riding in her place?

Lucian walked up and asked if she would like to see a cave he discovered at the Clear Mountain Study Center. Sure, hard exercise sounded good to her. He explained how he'd taken Marcel for a walk to show her the school his mother had started. They'd climbed up the side of the Helderberg escarpment and walked along the base of the cliffs. He felt a cool breeze blowing into a crack, the tell tale sign they'd discovered a cave. He brought his caving buddies and some shovels. It wasn't long before they realized they'd discovered a whole cave system running through the escarpment.

Marcel had some errands to run and would meet them at the land.

* * * *

Lucian wasted no time leading the women along a logging road that followed a dry streambed, where they fell silent. The trees themselves looked layered like the cliff face they were walking towards. Devonian, Ordovician, Silurian were the names of epochs these rocks represented. Janice didn't remember which was oldest, and closest to the bottom. She just remembered that there was an immensity of time and age they were climbing. She'd forgotten how marvelous it was to see a huge boulder the size of a house, sitting there in the woods, trees grown up around it. She'd forgotten how brachiopods, small shells, and crinoids, stems of ancient plants, that looked like dimes stacked on one another marked these stones and were something of a miracle from millions of years ago. Or how good the slow burn in her calves felt as she climbed.

She pushed against the mountain, her back soaked with sweat, her arms and legs limber from stretching up to balance herself and lift herself to the next boulder. She caught her breath as she watched Lucian scale the very steep, very large boulders without ropes, using tiny ledges to balance his feet, so he could pull himself up. Marcel followed close to the bottoms of his boots, lifting herself as though she were mounting her horse. Both swung up the wide, steep boulders like they were nothing.

All Janice could think of was the air behind them, the steep pitch of the mountainside and how long it would take to call an ambulance. She sidestepped, pulled herself up the bank and onto the steep slope of the mountain.

Lucian and Marcel looked down on her, their hands on their hips. Janice admired the pillars of their legs—Lucian's short and very strong, Marcel's long and very graceful, a slight bow in the middle because she rode horses.

Then they disappeared. Janice felt the thrill of abandonment, as if they were saying she wasn't good enough, because she couldn't keep up. Only she was balanced against a steep slope, trees only as wide around as her forearm holding her from tumbling backwards.

Janice looked down to see where she was planting her feet. Then she looked up. Lucian touched Marcel's lips, then cupped her head and slowly, deeply kissed her. Marcel's arms swung around him as she pressed her body against his. The cliff bulged fifty feet over them, a silver gray block.

"Oh sorry," Janice said, when she planted her hands on the path and crawled onto it, slowly standing up, her eyes averted.

Marcel stepped back, her eyes soft and dreamy. "I love your brother."

Something about that look, the nakedness of it, made Janice feel more lonely than she'd ever felt in her life and that was saying something. She was in woods where she could howl her own grief, but Lucian and Marcel were standing in front of her, waiting for her response. She looked down at her damp boots, water spreading from them.

"We've decided to marry Christmas Eve," Lucian said, his cheeks flushed.

Janice leaned against the cliff, feeling dizzy. Of course Lucian should find happiness. Of course Marcel was the kindest, prettiest one of them all, but she just couldn't find it in her to look up and smile, or even step forward to give them a hug. What kind of a sister was she, not even happy for Lucian, who had to have suffered, watching their mother fade?

"He makes me happy," Marcel continued, that moony look on her face. "He told me, 'Babe I'm here. I'll take care of you the rest of my life.' There was a full moon that night as he held my hand. I felt so safe, so protected."

"You're the first person we wanted to tell," Lucian added.

"Everybody knows. You were the talk of the party last night."

"What did they say?"

"They're comfortable with Marcel in Mother's kitchen. And I'm happy for you both," Janice mumbled, her chin quivering, the tops of the trees blurring, and there was nowhere she could hide her tears. She felt the heights behind and in front of her—the cliffs looming, and the steep slope the rocks making all that air, all that distance so empty, that Janice shivered. It would be easy to sit down and slide to the bottom, her face smeared with tears. But here were Lucian and Marcel waiting for her blessing, a blessing she had to give.

"You don't sound happy," Lucian said.

"It's not about you," Janice said to Lucian's back as they walked around the cliff, the trail narrowing to a foot wide, the limestone scooped out and sheer to a mass of rocks below.

"What's wrong, Janice?" Marcel asked.

"Please, please, I can't talk about it." Janice's tears seeped. She pressed her hands to her eyes and cried. "You go on ahead. I need a few minutes to collect myself."

"No way am I going to leave you here in this state."

Janice felt ashamed that she was openly weeping in front of her brother and Marcel who squatted down and rubbed her back. "There, there, there," she said like Janice was some sweaty horse with rolling eyes. She knew she needed to grieve, but why did her tears have to come at the wrong time?

Janice wiped her face and smiled weakly. "I think I'm better. I don't like to do that in front of people, kind of like leaving the door to the bathroom open."

"Which you do," Lucian said nudging her with his elbow, trying to get her to laugh.

"What?" Marcel asked.

"We don't have many secrets," Lucian weakly smiled.

They stopped where a dry streambed folded away from the cliff face. The trail narrowed to three inches until there was a five-foot drop to the dry streambed. A house-sized block had tumbled down to a locomotive-sized block with a crack down the middle that was so big a person could walk through it. That crack looked more inviting than the narrow crevice Lucian pointed to, his pride blowing him up to twice his size. A person would have to crawl belly down. A narrow crevice and a fresh pile of tan and blue clay marked the entrance to the cave. Janice's heart began to thump. All she could think of was how heavy the rest of the mountain was sitting over that hole. "Pretty impressive, huh?" Lucian said, more like a question than a statement. "I haven't reached the end."

"I don't think my hips would fit," Janice said.

"It's only a small opening. Then it widens into this beautiful room."

"There's this wall that's so crowded with fossils, you can almost feel how full of life these oceans were. Your brother could barely contain himself after he found it. He even had me up here digging and we'd barely started dating. Isn't this just so beautiful?" Marcel swung around and waved her hand at the view.

"Of course," Janice said. Every inch of her—from her toes to her scalp—felt terrified. She began to shiver even though it was a warm day. The sun had gone behind the mountain. Would they walk down after dark? "No. I can't go in there," Janice whispered. The mountain seemed to shift from one buttock to another.

"You've come this far," Lucian said.

"Absolutely not," she said. "I don't like tight spaces, so why should I lie down and crawl into a space where I don't think my body would fit?"

"The Janice I knew a few years ago would have gone in."

"No she wouldn't," Janice said quietly. Her right leg started to bounce up and down like she'd seen boys' legs bounce under desks in school. A breeze rattled the leaves down the mountain. She could almost hear the path it skipped from treetop to treetop to the bottom.

"You were always willing to try," Lucian's voice cracked. He shifted from one leg to another. "Beauty is good for the soul when times are hard."

"Yes Lucian. I'd dive off the beam in the barn because you said it would be fine. But it wasn't, my wind was knocked out. I didn't know if I'd breathe again."

"This is perfectly safe," Lucian argued.

"You two go on ahead. I'll enjoy the view and wait here." The view was a clear shot to the Berkshires, cloud shadows on their backs, Albany with its white towers, the nearer farms and tree lines. Didn't people tell her if only she'd remember to breathe she'd calm down? Instead, the more she breathed, the more terrified she felt.

Marcel glanced at Lucian as if she were telling him, "I'm with you, but I need to be with Janice in this." She put her hand on Janice's shoulder and squatted down as if she were talking to a child. "We're losing sunlight," Marcel said kindly.

"I should have known you'd wimp out on me."

"I'm not feeling so hot," Janice kneaded the back of her neck where a headache was blooming. "Go on ahead. I'll wait. Though I'd like a drink."

Lucian dropped his pack to the trail, and pulled out a canteen, handing it to Janice.

She gripped the top, trying to unscrew it, but the metal burned her hands. "It's too tight," she said as she handed it back. He untwisted the cap, taking a drink first. Then he handed it to Janice, who drank sloppily, letting water run down her chin. The water tasted metallic and warm, almost muddy. She handed it to Marcel, who wiped off the cap and sipped.

"We'll go back," Lucian said with something resigned and relieved in his tone.

Janice wished she could have pleased him in this, especially now that Mother was gone, but she just could not. The terror, she could taste the terror at the thought of lying down in all that darkness and with all that rock squatting on her.

CHAPTER SIX

"I called you at your hotel, but they said you checked out," said the voice like a bullet snapping through the trees over the Normans Kill. "It's Jim Sanders. Your assistant said to call here. I'm sorry for your loss."

Janice rubbed her eyes, disoriented, sweaty from sleep, naked under her night gown, sitting in the chair next to her mother's side of the bed, the faint smell of cigarettes and her mother's perfume lingering. The phone had rung, two, three times before she dove out of bed to get it. "Thank you."

"You sound tired." Jim's voice was full of compassion.

"I am." Janice rubbed her sore thighs from climbing yesterday. Just outside, the pump was hauling water out of the ground.

"It'll get better," he said, his voice turning kind as bedroom eyes.

"I feel like Dante lost in the dark wood," she said. "And you know where his walk took him."

"Remember what I said. Your God is near the brokenhearted. He's near you."

Her father appeared in the doorway, whispering the words, "I'm going to arrange her grave. You stay here." He held his hand up like a policeman holding traffic. Janice held the mouthpiece to the phone. "I'll be there in a minute," she whispered.

"You don't need to." Her father waved her off and walked away. He was dressed in the same suit he wore yesterday, with a fresh dress shirt and knotted maroon tie.

"I'll make a lead out of the dinner party Sackfield attended with the leaders of American Evangelicalism, how they are looking for Billy Graham's successor."

"Can I call you back?" Janice interrupted him, pulling on the cord, but it wouldn't let her stretch far enough to grab her clothes or call her father back to the room.

"I'll check my facts with George Will. I'm surprised they're friends."

"Jeremiah said they go back to when his parents ran Joyful Rest."

"The connections in that world never cease to amaze me."

"Can I call you back?" Janice was at his mercy. She couldn't just hang up if she wanted him to write about Jeremiah.

"I found mistakes in Sackfield's *The Christian Bestseller: Why Not?* His presuppositions on the marketplace are off kilter," Jim continued, as if he'd not heard her request.

Janice heard the screen door slam.

"Can I call you back?"

"John Updike, Andre Dubus, Annie Dillard are Christian writers who have done quite well in the general marketplace," he continued.

"I see where you're coming from," Janice managed to choke out, tears running down her face. Most likely her father was trying to protect her from the pain of going to the cemetery and the church. But she'd rather hurt; she'd rather know her mother dead by going through these rituals, and know she was part of the family, than be left out. Sure as shooting he would have let her sleep. The pump slammed off.

"I've got three columns, so it won't be as long as you like." Jim sounded apologetic. "Sure, you can call me back."

"Thanks so much." Janice dropped the phone on the cradle and ran through the door in the bedroom. The hard wood of the porch smacked her bare feet. Then the cool grass soothed them as she sprinted across the yard, waving and shouting. King and Arthur barked, nudging her calves, then surged ahead of her and circled. Billows of dust swirled behind her mother's Chrysler as her father, or maybe her brother drove it up the road. Why couldn't her father wait? By the time she reached the mountain ash her parents had planted to honor her birth, the brake lights came on and the car slowed and began backing up.

She ran up to the car, the stubble on the side of the road and the gravel bruising her feet. "Don't leave me," she panted, the air burning her lungs.

"We've got an appointment at the cemetery in half an hour," Lucian said. He was driving, the dress shirt he was wearing open at the collar. Marcel sat in the back, her hands folded in her lap. She wore a khaki skirt with a black blouse.

"It'll only take a minute to throw on some clothes."

"Hop in," Lucian said looking over his shoulder at the door.

She felt sweaty and grimy. The dogs jumped in and climbed on the seat next to her. The sound of panting filled the silence until they pulled up to the house.

"They can wait, if you want a shower," her dad said. "We won't be the first people to show up late to their gravesite."

* * * *

Albany Rural Cemetery was beautiful with old growth maples and oaks creating shade for the graves. Hundreds of stones speckled the hillsides. They drove down into the valley and stopped at a tiny limestone building that struck Janice as too small for such a big cemetery. The sexton pulled out a card catalog and looked for the record of the Westfahl burial site. Her father's family's birth and death dates and cause of death were listed. Janice saw how her father's mother, father and sister died within a few years of each other. 1955, her birth year was nestled right in the middle of all those deaths. Her brother was born three years earlier just as the first, her father's sister, died. Her mother's father died the year after she was born. With all that grief, how much did her parents have to give to her and her brother? She didn't know how she would grieve her mother and carry on with her job, let alone have a newborn to tend.

After they made arrangements for the burial, her father, Lucian, Janice and Marcel followed the sexton out of the valley and around winding curves past President Arthur's grave, along winding roads, past beautiful monuments and large maple trees. The sexton stopped alongside a ridge where the cemetery opened up in a small meadow. He walked right to the gravesite and pointed.

"There's room for you to be buried, one on top of the other," he said. "I'm sorry it's not side by side."

Kurt ran his hand over the carvings marking his parents and sister's birth and death dates. He explained how it had been at least twenty-five years since he'd been here, since he'd laid them in the ground—first his sister, then his mother, then father. "What a hard few years, all of them dying close to each other, but I've not come back to visit their graves. They weren't here any more, so what was the point?"

As they stood at the plot where her parents would be buried, the wind blowing through the trees, the sun racing clouds in the sky, Kurt said, "I'm going to sell The Farm. Son, I don't want to tie you and Marcel down." He looked Lucian in the eyes first then Marcel. "You both deserve independent lives. Janice, I don't want you coming back here to help me take care of the place. Under no circumstances do I want you," he looked at Janice in the eyes, before he finished, "coming back home on my account."

Janice felt like he was making a covenant with them, not unlike the patriarchs in the Bible, making the other put his hand against his thigh, to seal the deal. This was not how she feared he'd be. No, she'd feared he'd guilt trip her into coming home, when she could not come back.

Lucian's eyes widened with fury, and he puffed up, resembling a tomcat whose territory was challenged. He opened his mouth. Then he shut it, and ran his hand through his hair.

"Dad you can't," Marcel said.

The sexton glanced at Marcel with such compassion he must have thought she was the daughter. He said, "If you'll pardon me, but it's never a good idea to make decisions at times like these. I've seen more people than I can count stand by the grave of their loved one, promising changes they regret later."

"I won't regret this," Kurt said. "It's been on my mind ever since my daughter left for college. I only waited out of respect for my wife."

"But The Farm is your home. All your memories are here," Janice said.

"Honey, they're not in the house, they're here," he said tapping his heart. "They're with me wherever I am."

"You have to do what you feel is right," Janice said. "Just sell it to someone who will let me walk the land anytime I want."

"I can do that," Kurt said.

"Are you sure you want to do this now?" she asked.

"Give it a year. And if you feel the same way, then sell The Farm," the sexton said, his hands crossed in front, respectfully.

"That sounds good," Lucian said. "A year. A lot could happen in a year."

"I'll be happy to help in any way I can. It's the least I can do since you let me keep my horses there," Marcel said. "I'll mow the lawn, clean house, cook Barbara's recipes. This must be so hard for you." She hugged Kurt as if holding him tightly could ease his pain.

Kurt patted her back. "You don't have to do anything. It's my pleasure to board them."

"I'll pay for the roof, and put new siding on the house," Lucian said. "It's better than pissing rent money down the toilet."

"That's kind of you Son, but you should spend your money on you and Marcel. The Farm was your mother's and my dream. I don't want to impose it on you."

"It's my dream too," Lucian said. "I don't know what I'd do if I couldn't live at The Farm."

"Son, you need another bedroom," Kurt said.

"I put my waterbed in the room next to my room."

"You and Marcel need your own place. You don't need me hanging around," Kurt said.

"We don't mind," Marcel said.

"Janice?" Kurt turned to her.

"I can't imagine how painful it would be for you to give up your home so soon after Mother died," Janice said.

"She didn't die. She went home to be with the Lord." Kurt made like he wanted to sit down on the ground and ease the pain in his knees, but they were too stiff to let him. "I don't think I can bear to live in her house without her." He leaned on the Westfahl headstone.

"I can't bear not to," Lucian said.

"Son, I don't want to be a burden; I don't want The Farm to be either. You and Marcel deserve your own lives together, starting out, building them, making your own dreams come true, making your home your very own. The Farm was your mother's and mine; we made it our very own. Now it's your turn to start new, and build your own dream."

"But Dad, you don't understand."

"Lucian, I understand more than you know."

"But The Farm is my home too."

"You can't expect Marcel to change your mother's decorating in order to make it her own. There's too much. It's too hard."

"We don't want to change it, do we?" Lucian looked at Marcel.

"Or course not. I love your house. It's more home to me than mine."

"She deserves to start new, with her own place, her own ideas, without your mother overshadowing her. You deserve it. Haven't you from the time you were born, wanted to get out from under her control? Now is your chance."

"I loved Mother. You have no right to say I didn't."

"Of course you did, Son," Kurt said.

He turned to the sexton and said, "Others have told me to wait a year, but I'd like to get it done as soon as possible, so that if anything happens to me, my children will be taken care of. Money is easier to divide than land."

Janice interrupted. "It would be a hard loss for me too." Janice's eyes welled up in tears. She couldn't imagine losing The Farm just now because she had been as much or more mother to her than her own mother. It was the ironwood trees by the Normans Kill that had been steady as she'd leaned against them weeping. The wind through the treetops, the wood creaking had been voices that comforted her with as much frailty as wood that might break. She loved them.

"Then I'll wait."

"Give us all a year to get used to the idea."

"All right," Kurt sighed.

Marcel looked at her watch. "Weren't we supposed to meet Pastor Ted?"

"Thank you, Marcel." Kurt pushed himself off the Westfahl headstone and walked back to the car.

"Let's go see Mom before we go to the church," Marcel said brightly.

"She'll be fine," Kurt said as he reached for the passenger door. Marcel put her hand on his shoulder.

"It might be good to get over the shock without everyone there." Marcel said kindly. "My mother always said she was happy to say her goodbyes in private, before the crowds."

"I've already seen my wife as a dead person."

Lucian gave his father a killing look that reminded Janice of the straight-lipped stares Barbara gave any one of them when they'd not pleased her. Kurt shrugged and sat down, not saying anything else as the car hurtled towards Delmar, Lucian driving like her father had driven when they were children, going fast and swerving, despite their delighted but frightened screams.

There had been time before their meeting with Pastor and Madeleine, so Lucian pulled into the funeral home parking lot. Kurt pulled himself up from the car, using the door like a cane to stand upright.

"Dad, are you okay?" Marcel asked.

"I'm fine," he said. Janice stepped to his side to take his arm.

"When we get home, Lucian will you go upstairs and look for my father's cane?"

"But I have to mow the lawn."

"I think I know where it is," Janice said, remembering the tiny rooms under the eaves where her parents had stored odds and ends. She used to dig through there when she lost something, hoping it would turn up. She'd seen the cane there.

Janice was afraid to walk into Tebbutt's Funeral Home. She was afraid it would smell like death or worse the chemicals they used to preserve a body. It was the same fear that had kept her from hugging her mother goodbye that last time they were home. But the funeral home director was dressed in a suit and acted like an ordinary business man. Sure he expressed his condolences but they were plain, not overbearing and dripping with sympathy. Right now that was the last thing she wanted. The place looked just like a house furnished with chairs and very deep blue carpet. There was a stand with a guest book and fountain pen.

"Let me be alone for a minute," her father said bravely. He looked pale and caved into himself.

Standing was the most tiring thing you could do, so Janice sat.

"Thank you for telling Dad not to sell The Farm," Lucian said, rocking back and forth on his feet. He'd worn sneakers and jeans with his dress shirt and sport coat.

"I couldn't stand to lose it just now," she said.

"You and me both," Lucian said.

"When we get married we are thinking of asking Dad if we can build an indoor arena and cut trails so we can start an equestrian center. Beaverwyck has been sold, so they can build a mall, and my trainer is looking for another barn." Janice swore Marcel looked all moony when she said that.

"How would you get the money?"

"We'd take out a home equity loan on The Farm. It's a ready-made business."

"We could make enough hay on the fields."

"I used to dream about that when I was a kid. Where's your ring?"

"We're picking it up tonight. We had to get it sized."

Janice bit her tongue. Like always her brother was going too fast. They'd met what? About the time she'd started Jeremiah's tour?

When Kurt came out of the room he said, "I don't like how she looks." He explained how she had been beautiful right after she died. Her face had been young and clean like had been when he'd first fallen in love, and they'd hoped to buy a farm someday and have five, six children and start a day camp for needy kids. "All those dreams came true," he said. "Even the Clear Mountain Study Center."

"I thought I was the reason she started that," Lucian said.

"You were a good part of it."

In the casket, her mother's hands had been crossed over the low spot between her hipbones, and Janice couldn't shake thinking about how that hollow reminded her of the low spot that flooded first on the Normans Kill. Janice felt her own round belly, like her mother's had been until this last year. She felt her fingers, the blood and muscle pushing against her skin. She focused on each one, then her palms, her wrists, her forearms. "It's a good way to ease pain," her mother had said. "Feel your body, finger by finger. That's how I had you and your brother, naturally." Janice had looked away feeling her skin tingle like she'd touched an electric fence when her mother said her birth story, always ending it with "I saw you crown in the mirror."

She knelt by her mother and felt her hand. Cold. Like cardboard. And stiff. But the cold didn't seep into her hand and up her arm, as though death were some power that slid from the dead to the living. She remembered the delight her mother took in showing her that last house she'd fixed up, across the valley. The original farmhouse had burned because the owner fell asleep while smoking. He'd died. Her mother's eyes had smiled the whole time she showed Janice the cherry cupboards and windows overlooking the Normans Kill.

Janice had stepped out the back door looking across the valley at the low spot down on the flat that Caleb never planted. Her father had shown her an ooze of water he said was a spring. "What will happen to us?" she'd asked aloud and was surprised her mother had stepped outside with her.

"Watch your brother," her mother blurted, looking startled at her own words. "Don't you dare let him pressure you out of your inheritance if something happens to your father."

"He won't do that. He's a church elder. We're closer than we've ever been," Janice said.

"I'm afraid for you, that he'll cheat you...I'm out of time. Your dad and I could not think how to divide things between you. You'll have to sort it out if your dad's heart fails.

Janice never dwelled on those words of caution. But now her mother seemed prophetic; Lucian and his bride-to-be definitely had plans for keeping The Farm—for themselves.

That Marcel; I don't trust her, Janice thought.

Janice thought about a bisque vase her mother had given her right after she had warned about Lucian.

"This was the only thing your great, great grandmother was able to bring from England because her husband gambled away her inheritance, on the boat no less. I want you to have it and keep it in the family."

Janice had thought it was rather ugly and held it while she felt the Normans Kill running hard down below, lines of rapids across the surface from the snow melt. The vase sat on a shelf in her apartment. She now wondered if her mother had chosen that one thing as a reminder that people you love, and to whom you are bound, could squander everything that is yours.

Funeral arrangements were set; everyone seemed to agree on hymn selections and a eulogy. Everyone—even Marcel— seemed subdued.

After a round of hugging and handshaking, the Westfahls and Marcel climbed back in the car. Lucian asked if they could stop at the jewelers and pick up Marcel's ring. It'd only take them a minute.

"A little good news won't hurt. Marcel we're glad to welcome you into the family," Kurt said.

"I'm glad to be here."

Both Lucian and Marcel were glowing when they walked out of the store. It was like this island of happiness in all their grief and loss. The round cut stone was as big as a piece of gravel, not like any of the other stones Lucian had given his former fiancées. It had to have set him back a few bucks. Two other stones, shaped like triangles framed it and was the kind of ring a woman would wear when she was dressed to the nines, not mucking stalls in the barn. Would Marcel take it off for her barn chores? How would she ride without running the risk of breaking her fingers, if the reins got tangled or her horse pulled hard?

Kurt kissed her on the cheek and admired it.

"I'm happy for you," Janice said, as she hugged Marcel, smelling her rose scent, but she did not hug Lucian because he stepped back from her. "Good for both of you."

On the outside of the store there was a glass display of rings with colored gems. She saw one with an emerald that looked so pale it reminded her of the fields around The Farm; of the days when she was little and she'd run into the hay and throw herself down to look up through the grass at the blue sky and clouds.

CHAPTER SEVEN

Back at The Farm, a warm wind coasted between the big barn and little barn, the aiming hairs for storms. If Janice saw the sky between them blacken, she knew they'd get a bad one. But today, it was plain blue. Nobody needed her, not Jim for his story, not her father and brother to mow the lawn, not Marcel who went home for a few hours. Janice walked out between the barns, following the horse trails until they disappeared in the lush, uneaten pasture. Marcel's horses swung their heads up, chewing, tails swishing, then dropped them back to grazing. The dogs ran underfoot and away in the surging uneven circles of border collies, their bodies breaking the weeds and grass.

She walked over the small hillock at the far end of the field. The people who built their farmhouse were buried where she stepped, the gravestones plowed under by an earlier farmer tired of keeping the plot trimmed. She walked, but with each step, the ground dropped from her feet. That's how losing her mother felt, like she was stepping onto air without a safety net. On top of the hillock a round apple tree spread its branches, fat red apples bending down. Janice walked up to a lower branch and pulled one off, her hand barely reaching around it. Arthur and King nudged her in the back of the thigh with their noses and flopped down in the shade. Janice took a bite, tasting the sweetness of an heirloom apple.

Janice wasn't hungry enough to keep eating, so she tossed it in the field, both dogs diving for it, King reaching it first and tossing it up in his mouth. Then he circled back at Janice, holding it in his mouth, dropping it, stepping back for her to toss it again. She shook her head and walked past the tree to the taut barbed wire fence, pressing her foot down, bending the wire as far down as it would go. She slipped between the strands, a barb catching her shirt. She stopped, thought about it and slipped back, unhooking the barb. She tucked her shirt tight into her jeans and tried again.

When she stood, she stood on the cow path that would take her down to the Normans Kill valley. Legend had it the Normans Kill was named after Albert Bradt de Noorman. She wondered what the community would remember about her mother or any of them three hundred years from now. What stories would be passed down?

She looked up at the Helderbergs, the escarpment resembling a small blue wave on the horizon. How many would remember the school she started and how the Clear Mountain Study Center taught them a love for learning or the land or the arts?

Janice walked down the hill, swinging her arms to the hill's downward pull. She looked at the valley to her right, maple trees and a clear forest floor with nothing but leaves down there. The Greens, who owned The Farm before her parents, said Native Americans camped in this bowl, and that they had to chase them away.

A voice that seemed to rise from the land itself ran through Janice's head. It sounded like wind running through hay just before it's cut. "Keep The Farm no matter what. It's the most beautiful place on earth and you are the daughter. You are an heir."

What about Dad? What if he needs nursing care? How will those bills be paid?

The voice ignored her questions. "Build a house at the head of the road or fix up the upstairs into an apartment."

What about this work I'm called to do?
"You belong here, taking care of us."
And who might we be?
The voices went silent, the wind crackling over the dried grasses that made Janice think of snakeskins.

Didn't Marie Antoinette's ladies-in-waiting settle this valley? Did they bring their memories of bloody rivers when they watched the Normans Kill flowing quietly, full of sturgeon, bass, clams, its currents voluptuous and brown, the memories leaving their minds, drifting into the fields, settling into the timbers of these houses as the men and women notched them together? Did they haunt the valley, keeping it wild, long after it had been settled to the fine tune of electric wires, gas lines, telephone poles? Is that what she heard just now? The voice that her parents called the fierce Normans Kill people, possessive of their land.

The wind circled her throat, squeezed her rib cage. She panted. *Who's owning who?* It scared her. Walk. Walk. Let those feelings out. Your mother is dead.

But all Janice felt was her grief plugged behind a calm that deepened as she walked.

Janice ducked around a thorn-apple tree, the branches full of inch long thorns. To her left the ridge dropped down to a farm road and shale cliffs. The cow path she was following would eventually join the road, leading to a foundation hole, built by the same family that built the house Janice grew up in. She looked down at the mud trail for clay rings that were shaped by the rain and a pebble, but the ones she found were broken in half. She stooped down and picked one up, felt the half moon edge, stuck her finger through the hole. Even as a kid, when she could pick them up any time, these clay rings seemed as mysterious as this valley.

When the ridge flattened and widened to a pasture, she picked mint leaves and smelled them, then followed the stream to the Normans Kill where two mallards lifted off. A huge willow grew in the bank—the willow she'd wished for when she put her arms around her mother and she wasn't there, wide and healthy. Janice spread her hands as far as she could reach around it. It would take two, three more people to make fingertips touch. The river whirled around its roots. There was the crackle of the river, fat and sassy, and the trickle of the water playing by the bank. Chips of light flickered on the opposite bank. The river caught sunlight, tossed it back in the weeds. She dipped the perfume bottle into the water, feeling the coolness run over her hand. She capped it and sat down to watch the light, the sand molding to her bottom, cool. Arthur and King lapped the water, bounding away into the dense growth of reforested pines that her parents planted to hold onto the hillside. Then they came running back.

Janice tried to grieve because this was the perfect time and a very private, beautiful place. No one would hear her sobs or shouts or coughing, but all she felt was calm, an inexplicable knowing that death is dead. She felt it in her bones. It didn't make sense because she'd not felt close to God these days. Her mother was about to be buried, but Janice felt like she had already jumped out of the grave, that Jesus was calling the dead to rise. It was a trick of time Janice didn't understand, but she felt it as real as the cool sand she was sitting on. Death was not the last word on her mother or any of them.

She fell asleep and dreamed her mother stood in front of an assembly in heaven, holding a bouquet of yellow roses. There were no straight, grim lines on her face, only a wide smile that made Janice sigh over how radiant her mother looked. Her mother turned to a man whose back was straight and sure, who was dressed in a white linen suit. Was it Janice's father, who by that same trick of time, was there already? Or was it someone who was more husband to her mother than Kurt? The man reached up with his thumb and wiped her cheek. Janice felt like a rose, her own yellow rose, bloomed in her chest.

The breeze rattled the willow leaves waking Janice. It was time she got back and made supper for everyone. She stood and leaned against the wide willow, her cheek scraped by the bark, hugging hard. She pushed away from the tree and walked back up the trail, stepping on the clay rings, feeling them crunch under her feet.

* * * *

At the wake, Janice stood away from her mother's body. She stood by the door because she felt trapped all the way at the end of the room with her relatives sobbing and all those people walking in to pay their respects. Her father guarded her mother, surrounded by the men who prayed with him every Thursday night. He was holding up well enough. Pastor Ted and Madeleine circulated through the room, checking on every member of the family, and then wandered back to her father. Lucian and Marcel stood by her father, helping him greet the people who paid their last respects to a woman who'd worked hard for her community. Janice was proud of how her mother had touched so many lives through her work as a realtor and starting the Clear Mountain Study Center. Her face ached from smiling and her feelings were all mixed up from grief, but also from the celebration of seeing people she hadn't seen in years.

Her heart skipped when Caleb walked in, his face blank until he saw her and he smiled, opening his arms and pulling her close, holding her with all the sincerity of a hug trying to tell her he loved her. Well, of course, he was her friend. Her mother had died. They'd known each other for several years. All those hours she'd spent riding behind him on the tractor, all those cloud shadows she'd watch run across the land, all that presence of sitting with him while he worked were wrapped up in those arms around her. Why wouldn't he hug her that way and fill the air around them with his presence? He smelled so good, like mechanic's grease and curing hay. His body wrapped around her like the woods by the Normans Kill. Lord knows he felt good and she felt safe enough, relaxed enough to close her eyes and sleep.

"You've changed," he said stepping back from her, holding her by the forearms, a thrill running through her from the firmness and gentleness of his touch. His voice reminded her of that old farmer's saying, sheep running through grass, which described wind blowing through a field.

"Of course." Janice felt the emptiness of mother's body lying across the room, how they'd argued over this man the last time they'd been together.

"Chicago agrees with you." He grinned, while his eyes were sad. She saw admiration in his face.

"A little."

"You've grown up since we last saw each other."

"You think?"

"I've never seen you so poised. How's that for a fifty cent word?"

"Pretty good."

"You should use that in one of your poems."

"I already have." Janice thought about the poem she'd written about his disk harrow, and how it floated to the ground, ever so slowly, how it smoothed the lumps the moldboard plow had turned over.

"Shall we go see your mother?"

"Sure."

He took her hand and walked up to the casket to look at her mother. He held her hand, his fingers light on hers. Janice noticed how the pancake foundation clumped in her wrinkles, so many wrinkles, as if the sun had baked her skin, like mud dried too fast.

He glanced at her set face, then turn back to her. "She was so furious when I took down that phone line with my combine. She threatened to sue because I interfered with her real estate business. I was just picking the wheat."

"When did that happen?" Her mother hadn't said anything during their phone calls. She was surprised her mother hadn't taken the opportunity to run him down.

"About a week and a half ago."

That had to be about the time Janice heard about Matthew's scheme to bring violence into Jeremiah's revolution.

"I was afraid to finish off the fields."

"I'm so sorry."

"Your dad stopped me on the road and said he'd calmed her down. Of course I could pick my crop. He's a good man, your dad."

"He's missing her terribly.

"I could tell they were close.

"I hate that I have to go back to Chicago in a week. But he's got Lucian and his fiancée, at least."

"Why don't you stay?"

"I'd love to but I'm not sure that's God's will." She'd felt there was no one else who could do the job she was doing, that somehow God wanted her there, even though it was driving her to become a woman she hated—two-faced—a gossip. One minute she was promoting Jeremiah and his revolution. The next minute, she told journalists behind his back that they'd better pay attention because he wasn't far from trying to blow up the country. If the sleeping evangelical giant got riled up, watch out. Isn't that what Jeremiah said? Even so, maybe she was doing some good warning the media, bringing the secret to daylight.

Was this another proposal? If you come home, we'll get serious? But he'd asked her to marry him last winter and she'd said yes and he'd stood her up. Why would she set herself up for that kind of pain, yet again? Why would she gamble on her independence for a man who'd not kept a simple promise to show up when he said?

"We could ride around the county like we used to."

"And how would I earn my living?"

"You'd find something."

"I'm not so sure about that."

"It could be like old times."

"But I'm not a kid anymore with summers off."

"I miss you sitting behind me."

"I miss you too."

Just at that point her father walked up. Caleb shook his hand and offered his condolences. He thanked him for calming Barbara down. "We were just saying how good it would be if Janice came home."

Janice's father looked even more stricken than he had that afternoon. "Did you know Janice arranged for an author to be on the *Today* show?"

"No, she didn't mention it."

"Opportunities like that don't come along every day. My daughter is having the time of her life. She doesn't need to come back here," he replied so abruptly even Janice was startled. She'd always thought her dad wanted her to stay home, that his love would trap her. But no, she'd been wrong. He wanted her independence.

"But don't you miss her?"

"Of course," her father turned away to talk to a man in a dark suit. Then he turned back, looking pale, like he could not lie about his true feelings any longer. "Her mother made me promise not to pressure her to come home, but if that's what she decides, I guess that's up to her."

If her mother could, she would have rolled over in her casket then and there. She'd always told Janice to finish what she'd started. Just a few days ago, her mother had said, "this is that something special God has in store for you. It is why God made you." Her mother's last words. But her father had said coming home was up to her. She could decide. Coming back home was possible. That terrible decision yawned like one of Lucian's caves, a great emptiness in her soul. She did not know what to do. Her father had always said it was her choice, even when she was too young to make those kinds of decisions. Somehow that left her feeling more insecure, and more dependent than if they'd said she had to do what they wanted or else.

"Walk me out?" Caleb asked.

"I'd like that." Janice was relieved to breathe in the cool evening air and be around the dead metal of people's cars. She didn't have to smile or take their hugs. Her skin was sore from everyone's reaching for her. She was tired of how sorry they were, of tears that came easily to them, but not to her. They stood by his Chevy two ton, a pile of wheat in the back. She stepped up on the running board and dipped her hand in the seed, raking her fingers through the pale kernels. "I wish I had a jar to put some in, to keep by my desk," she said, then stepped down.

"I'll bring one tomorrow."

"I'd better get back inside." Janice looked at the lit windows of the funeral home, the well-dressed people going inside. Caleb tipped up her chin to his soft and electric lips. His thighs pressed against hers. She felt him. Pleasure rolled between her legs, all the way to her lips, all the way to her toes, so all she felt was tingling, as if Caleb's lips were two wires lightly touching her. He wasn't letting go. She felt fenced and safe from all her troubles.

She touched his forearm, feeling the rock hardness of muscle, to her way of thinking, the sexiest, most powerful part of a man's body.

He wiped the hair out of her eyes, whispering, "I'll see you tomorrow."

"You don't need to come," she protested. He had fields to bale, and she'd seen the weather—rain was on its way from Ohio.

He put his finger, his calloused finger, dirt driven deep into its lines, on her lips, on her lips like a pastor giving communion. "I'll be there."

Then he was off behind the door of his truck, starting it, the engine turning over, his arm working the double shift. He waved. He smiled. He backed away. Janice watched the mound of wheat piled up as it turned and drove down Kenwood Avenue.

* * * *

Back home, Janice rinsed her mother's Pfaltzgraff plates from that day's meals and put them in the dishwasher. She stared out at the flat while the water ran over the dishes, but only saw her reflection back in the window—the peaches and cream tones of her face and the stark white of the kitchen behind her.

"Leave those." Her father had come into the kitchen. He sounded hoarse.

"I'm watching the view." She looked up at his reflection

standing behind her. His feet were spread apart, his hand in his pocket, his eyes half awake. "Only a few to go. Then we'll be ready for tomorrow."

"Your Caleb's been cleaning up the fields." Her father sat down in the chair next to the cherry table, the rushes creaking underneath him. "Your mother was furious he left them so unkempt."

"She didn't much like him." Janice rinsed off a plate, feeling the water warm her hands.

"I told your mother to leave you alone, especially with your boyfriends, but also with other things. She was too hard on you."

"I talked too much."

"I told her to stop. I thought she'd drive you crazy; you were no different than any other teenage daughter my friends talked about. Maybe more careful."

"I wanted to obey her, but it seemed the more she said to stop, the more I talked. She used to say no one was interested in all that detail, but I found people liked my stories. It was her that wasn't interested."

"She had so much on her mind, it was hard for her to listen. I know we shouldn't talk ill of the dead, I loved your mother, but I love you too, and I wanted you to know she loved you the best way she knew how."

"I realized that one day when I was walking out on the road. I wrote a poem and even memorized the first line. Here it is, "Wait until you find your best love is the wrong love, a love that cripples your daughter with the lameness you hate."

"Honey, maybe now you can strengthen those weak knees, and walk soundly again."

"I hope."

He reached in his shirt pocket and pulled out her mother's rings. He cupped them in his palms as though he were holding water slipping through his fingers, offering her a drink. *Drink quickly before it's gone.* "I want you to have these."

Janice took the dishtowel and wiped her hands. She could feel the valley open behind her back, behind the wall of the house. She could feel her own sense of unworthiness open along with it. "Don't you want to give them to Lucian and Marcel?"

"Give me what?" Lucian came in the room, holding the dessert plates.

"Mother's rings," Janice said. He was her mother's favorite, and the oldest. He was the one in love.

Kurt's eyes were magnified through his glasses. They held the same look Janice had seen in Lucian's eyes, too wide, shocked. But then they looked alike, small men, more wide than tall, solid. "I want you to have her rings," he said firmly, holding them out to her. "Marcel got her ring. You should have your mother's rings."

"All right." She held her hand flat like she was feeding sugar to a horse with great, yellow teeth. Her mother's rings, simple gold, her engagement ring a solitaire diamond. Her father tipped them in her hand. They felt cool in her palm. Janice slipped them on. Her mother's ring felt loose on her ring finger. "Oh Dad, thank you," she said.

Lucian set down his plates on the counter and walked out.

That night, Janice didn't have the energy to walk to the pines, let alone all the way out to the fork in the road, where the manure pile from the Genovese's dairy used to heat up and burn. She didn't walk past the lawn, before she turned to the mountain ash standing smack dab in the center of the best softball, soccer, riding yard. She picked up a stick and threw it for King and Arthur, who charged after it, playing tug of war in a long circle around her. She hugged the tree, her arms around it and then around themselves again.

She squeezed her forearms and pressed herself against the tree, thinking about Caleb's kiss, about how he'd wrapped her in his arms and she'd felt like she could sleep right there, standing up in his arms. Blessed sleep. How long had it been since she'd slept a good night's sleep? She thought how her mother wouldn't even look at her that last time she was home. She looked the same way in the coffin that she looked when she was furious, like Janice had failed her and always would. But wasn't it normal for daughters to displease their mothers as they grew up and became their own person? And now she wore her mother's diamond. *Oh Lord have mercy. On me. A sinner.*

She could not catch her breath. She heaved at sighs, and heaved again like she was hefting Caleb's bales, bumping them against her legs and then up to the pile, her thighs burning from the stalks, her hands burning from the rope. Tears would not come.

The tree felt hard against her breastbone. She turned her back and looked at the house, the lights out, except for the parlor, which she could see through her brother's room.

Up on the Helderbergs the TV towers blinked. The stars quivered.

How could she belong in the world, if her own mother's face was set against her? And always would be.

But here was her tree planted in her honor when she was born. It was a slender tree, with a long, narrow crown that looked elegant and would bend nearly to the ground when the wind roared. She reached up and shucked orange-red berries off the stem and rolled them around her hand. Funny how this was the first year the tree had ever borne fruit. Maybe another mountain ash had found its way to The Farm, pollinating this one.

She patted the bark and slid down to the ground feeling the bark scratching her. This tree rooted her to this place, standing in for her, reminding her family that she was family too. The night air warmed her skin. Caleb's lips had felt like an electric fence against hers. His hand on her neck, holding her—well she felt sweet and wet. Maybe it was a sin to feel that. Her mother was dead, how dare she feel anything good?

Caleb hauled the kind of light that flickers through trees, and Lord knows she needed to feel that light on her skin.

King brought her the stick and dropped it at her feet. Both he and Arthur stepped back, their ears pricked. Janice threw it as hard as she could, watching the white on her parents' dogs flashing in the darkness. She didn't get much chance to walk the road, so she stood up and began walking.

She kicked a piece of gravel. Arthur dove for it, picking it up in his mouth and bringing it back to her, dropping it at her feet. King danced around him, wanting to play. Janice took it out of his mouth and put it in her pocket. No sense in their breaking a tooth. She looked at the white pines up ahead. What a marvelous sight they were, tall, graceful trees standing like sentinels watching over the borders of their fields.

Bees hummed in the hollow of the first white pine as she walked up. The branches sounded like cellos in the breeze. She used to think angels sang in those trees. She stretched out her arms to fly, just like she had when she was a girl, the wind catching her armpits. It was good to walk by those trees again, but she startled when she saw a fresh killed snake in the road. Had she run over it when she'd arrived home?

That night when Janice pulled off her clothes, the diamond caught on her sleeve, a barb, around her middle finger, an ache crawling up her arm as if her mother's loneliness bled onto the ring. Janice remembered the letter her father had given her. She opened her briefcase and pulled it out of her Bible. It was written on yellow legal paper, like the letters her mother used to write when she was in college.

My dear Janice,

It's been a lesson in trusting the Lord for my physical being. I've had to trust Him for every breath. I wish I had six more months to fit the pieces of my life together, to tell you some things that might help guide you as you sort out your life. Please know I've made my share of mistakes as I explored who I am as a woman. Some didn't even seem like mistakes at the time, but looking back, I wish I could have avoided those relationships.

You'll be with people and later you'll wonder, 'Why did I do that?' Your tears will feel like they'll never end, and sometimes anger will take hold of you, and seem like it will never end either. (I think about you and Ca-

leb and wonder if he's one such person.) Don't ever give up. Keep walking. Keep turning to the Lord, even if it doesn't seem like He's there. Mistakes, missteps, the wrong people, are part of growing up and becoming the full woman God intends you to be, making you wise. There is a good man waiting for you. I know it as surely as I know I can't stick around any longer. I am so sorry for this, honey. I wish we could have had one last weekend, better than the last one, when we argued so. But my body won't have it. I am so sorry. And I couldn't let you quit your job and come home that night you called, even though I desperately wanted to see you. It would have ruined your life.

I've already taken a dip in the great river between here and the Lord's full, unadulterated presence. It's cold, it's muddy. I didn't know you could pee in the river, but you can. I dreamed you met me at a train station, the lights of the train roaring in and it was my turn to get on board and finally go west. You saw me off with all your love and that was enough for me to let go of this life.

Honey, I know you'll be sad, but try to appreciate the good things along the way.

With all my love and prayers that won't stop when I go home,

Mom

Janice pressed the letter against her heart and finally, the tears came. She had seen her mother off at that train. They'd been together one last time, if only in a dream. Her mother had given her best wisdom to Janice, here in this letter. Now at least now, she could grieve the woman who'd often told her which way to turn. She'd blessed Janice in the inevitable mistakes she would make. King jumped on the bed behind her and Arthur nudged her arm until she had to pay attention to him. On the other side of her door, her father's radio played Larry King quietly. She buried her face in the dog's rough, hoping her father wouldn't hear and switched off her light, so he'd think she was sleeping.

CHAPTER EIGHT

When Janice followed her father, brother, and Marcel out of the pew after the funeral, she was shocked to see Jeremiah and Jim sitting in the congregation. How wonderful these men came to offer her their condolences. It wasn't just about work. They were her friends.

A beautiful woman sat next to Jeremiah, with red hair swept up in a bun that should have made her look severe, but instead she looked very kind and patient. She wore a white cardigan over a black sheath. No wonder Jeremiah looked for lingerie in hotel catalogs. His wife was slender, her body barely touching the fabric. Jeremiah glanced at her and smiled his broad make-you-feel-like-you're-the-most-important-person-in-the-world smile. She smiled back. He looked like he was wearing the same Polo shirt and khakis he'd been wearing when he put Janice on the train.

Jim's navy pin stripe suit fit him so well, Janice guessed it cost at least a thousand dollars. He looked like a different man, like he belonged at Chase Manhattan instead of scratching out lines for *Weekly News*. His rugged jaw and hooked nose and stern demeanor reminded her even more of an eagle.

Lucian turned around mouthing the words that he was impressed. Janice nodded, afraid to speak. Neither one belonged sitting in the blue chairs that sighed every time a person stood or sat. Neither one belonged here at her church, or in her childhood places. But they were here. She sighed the sigh of a woman finishing a well written book.

And there was Caleb sitting in the back corner of the church, wiggling his fingers at her, as if to say, "Hello, hello, please notice me; see I came." His thighs stretched his clean and pressed jeans and the balls of his arms rolled out of his short sleeved shirt. His golden hair was still wet from the shower. Her womb rippled, remembering his kiss from last night.

Janice twisted her mother's ring with her thumb until the diamond dug into to the palm side of her hand. How would she introduce him to Jim and Jeremiah? As her parents' farmer? Her muse? Janice turned the corner behind the pews and stopped at the foyer to wait for Jim and Jeremiah and Caleb, to invite them back to The Farm after the committal. She twisted her mother's ring so it faced outward. No barbs for shaking hands, not even diamond ones. Marcel nudged her asking if that was Jeremiah.

"It is," Janice said.

"He's hot."

"He is, but not the way you think."

Janice watched her mother's casket float into the back of the hearse as if there were an inch of air instead of rollers in the floor. Her father watched, his chin jutted, a line of moisture ran down his face. Lucian talked to a man whose hair looked dented from wearing a construction hat who smelled of carbide and stale dirt.

"I am so sorry for your loss," Jeremiah said, his eyes tired and sad. "Your mother was gifted to accomplish all that in her life. You come by your talent honestly."

Janice blushed and thanked him for coming and shook his wife's hand. Janice liked Elizabeth's handshake. It was less forceful than Jeremiah's, yet still there, showing she was glad to meet her.

Jim stepped out of the church and leaned into Janice to give her a hug. He smelled like a log cracked open in the woods, with all kinds of new things growing in it. He whispered, "All will be well, all will be well, all manner of things will be well. Don't forget that."

"Thank you," Janice said, tears brimming her eyes.

"We meet again," Jim said to Jeremiah, as he shook his hand, looking down at the shorter man with laughter around his eyes.

"Sad times," Jeremiah said, letting go of Jim's hand, rubbing his fingers.

"She'll be fine," Jim said looking into Janice's eyes with such utter kindness that her heart lifted as in the liturgy: *Lift up your hearts. We lift them up to the Lord.*

"She's the best in the industry. I hope we don't lose her," Jeremiah said.

"You won't lose me," Janice replied too quickly.

"I'm running your story next Monday," Jim said.

"Great, great," Jeremiah said. "What are you going to say in the article?"

Janice was about to say, "Can you stay? I'd love to show you where I grew up," when Caleb walked up and kissed her cheek. "Dear Janice, another hard day for you."

Janice nodded. Caleb filled the space in front of her with the faint smell of mechanic's grease and curing hay. She glanced at Jim and Jeremiah shaking Marcel's hand and Marcel, acting feminine, and humble, and admiring like a groupie. Elizabeth touched Jeremiah's arm.

Aunt Sarah walked up and shook their hands. Janice overheard her saying she owned a Christian bookstore and she sold many of Jeremiah's books and would he, could he, come back to The Farm afterwards? She admired him and his works and would love to talk more. "Of course," Jeremiah said.

"And this is Jim Sanders, a writer for *Weekly News*," Jeremiah introduced Sarah. "He's working on a story about me and the Cause."

Sarah turned to him, folding into herself, like she did when she greeted people. "It's so nice to meet you. I enjoy your articles even though I don't agree with you when you say there's no such thing as a personal devil."

"I'd like to take you out tomorrow," Celeb said, holding Janice's hand, his calluses rough against her palm.

"I don't know how any thinking person can question the fact of a personal devil any more than they question the fact of a personal Savior," Jeremiah said.

"Are you some kind of Manichean believing evil and good are perfectly balanced?" Jim returned, his eyes flashing.

"Gentlemen!" Janice chimed. "Perhaps we can resume this discussion another time," she admonished. "I'd like you both to come to the family farm after the service."

Jeremiah nodded in agreement, but Jim begged off, saying he needed to get back to New York. He had some deadlines to meet.

"Janice?" Caleb asked, his eyes looking at her, beautiful as a clear sky after a hard hard shower.

"Yes. Of course," she said blankly. "You're coming up to The Farm?"

"I have the headlands to bale." He slid his hand into his pocket and pulled out a jar with a red rose on the lid, full of wheat.

Janice wanted to open it, and run her fingers through the seeds, creased like long, narrow bottoms.

* * * *

The funeral directors pulled the hearse forward and parked it in front of the two limosines—one for Kurt and Lucian and Marcel and Janice, the other for Aunt Sarah and Uncle Steve, Aunt Denise and Uncle Merle.

Janice walked to the limosine and her father waiting. She slipped her mother's ring back against the meat of her hand, and clenched her fist, feeling it bite into her palm, feeling it catch like the rusted barb wire fence caught her shirt and her back yesterday when she walked, walked out her grief. She tried to unscrew the lid to the jar, but it was on too tight. She had to satisfy herself by looking at what the ground and sun and rain had made.

* * * *

"I see you have a ring," Marcel said as they turned into the mile long road finally, leading to The Farm, after a long morning of services. "I saw you with Caleb last night. Did he ask you to marry him?"

Janice shook her head.

"My daughter should have her mother's rings," Kurt said defensively.

"Let's see," Marcel leaned forward to look. Janice held out her hand as though Marcel were going to kiss it. Marcel took her fingers and looked. "It's beautiful."

"Dad has good taste," Janice said looking down at her mother's diamond, a single solitaire on a simple band that reminded her of a water droplet suspended off a pine bough.

"Yes, Dad does," Marcel echoed, her voice unsure and wobbly.

"It reminds me of what Mother said about dinner parties. 'Keep it simple and elegant.'"

"Your mother's ring is what I imagined wearing one day," Marcel said. Lucian stared his angry cat stare at her before he turned back to the window. "But I will always treasure this one."

"Lucian bought you a grand ring, bigger, and prettier than this one," Janice said, leaning forward and touching Marcel's diamond.

"At the check out the other day a woman told me, 'Barbara Westfahl helped me find a house after my divorce. She's so wonderful.' When people talk about her, they're grateful."

"She liked you," Kurt said.

"I am so blessed to be a part of your family," Marcel said.

When the limousine drove up the hill and The Farm was visible, Janice saw Caleb's truck parked in the field, but the tractor and baler were gone. Jeremiah and Elizabeth were sitting in the redwood chairs under the maple tree. They stood up when Janice got out of the limo.

They looked so regal and dignified. "What a beautiful place to grow up," Elizabeth said.

King and Arthur trotted up to her wagging their tails. They greeted everyone and then trotted around the car looking for Mother. They came back to Janice, leaning against her legs.

Janice thanked them and wondered if Jeremiah and Elizabeth would like anything to eat. They shook their heads saying they would have to be going. "Has your father ever thought about donating it to Joyful Rest as an American retreat center?" Jeremiah asked. "He could stay here the rest of his life, without having to worry about upkeep."

"It hasn't crossed our minds."

"This has to be more than he can manage."

"He's got my brother and I."

"You're not thinking of quitting and coming back here are you?" Jeremiah looked stricken.

"No."

"I can't imagine going on tour with anyone else."

"Neither can I," Elizabeth said. "I know he is in good hands with you."

"Let your dad know about our offer."

"I don't think he'd be interested." Janice thought back to how he'd insisted on selling the place, and being done with it. She and Lucian had barely talked him out of it.

"You never know."

"I think I do. But thank you for the idea and thank you for coming. Elizabeth it was nice to meet you." They exchanged hugs all around and Janice watched them get in their Volkswagen.

Janice turned to her family's guests, thanking them for coming and catching up on old news, until she saw Caleb's tractor and baler and hayrack come up the road. She shut the dogs in her room, so they wouldn't follow, excused herself and, walked towards the headlands between the pond and the ravine that set the border with Genovesi's fields. The straw was cut closer than a lawn. The stalks crunched underneath her feet and she stepped over the windrows he'd already raked. She hopped over the tiny gully that had been grand fun when she'd galloped her horse and made her jump.

He pretended not to see her and drove up a row, the baler spooning the loose straw into compact bales and then kicking them into the wagon. They were like little explosions, those bales as they flew into the air. In the old days, a farmer had to drive through the field slowly, as someone on the ground picked up the bales and heaved them into the wagon. Another person stacked them.

Janice felt exposed, standing in the field, waiting for him to see her and stop. The thump and grind of the baler sounded a beat she could almost dance to, something sexy and pumping, but she stood in the middle of the windrow, the straw fragrant and scratchy around her legs. The entourage of machines turned next to the grove of pines somebody must have planted to mark the field borders. She crossed her arms, the sun warming her, but just on the surface. She felt cold way deep, like the bottom of a pond, because she was so tired.

He flashed his headlights at her, six bright suns, that moved slowly. Janice waved exuberantly as though she were in the spotlight. The lights were so bright, she saw them floating in her eyes after he switched them off. Janice didn't care that she was wearing a maroon jumper with black t-shirt. She didn't care that her nylons had just run because of the straw. Or that she was being rude to her family's guests. She just wanted to be with Caleb. He swung the door open. "You're looking like you could use a friend."

"I could always use a friend."

She pulled herself up the ladder, taking the first step as if she were stepping onto one of Marcel's tall horses. She slipped into her perch behind him, pulling her dress down over her legs. Caleb looked around her to the equipment behind them and leaned one arm on her knee to balance his looking at the straw, to see how it was feeding into the baler and then popping into the wagon. Her belly warmed with the goodness of feeling his

weight and his arm warm against her knee. Caleb took his arm
back to turn the tractor, the baler, the wagon at the end of the
field. Pine branches swiped the window.

When he faced the tractor down the row, he looked at her
with compassion in his eyes, "Your mother was loved by a lot of
people."

"That she was."

"I never cried so hard when my father died. I don't much like
to think about those times."

"Me too."

"Not to change the subject, but who were those men talking
to you at the church?" He turned to look at her and then looked
away at the straw gathered into the baler. "They're from work."

"I thought you lived in Chicago." He pronounced it "Shy. Ka.
Go."

"One's from New York. The other by Boston."

"You must be Somebody."

"I never thought of myself that way, no."

"You didn't introduce me like you were too good for your
friend. But hey I'm just a dumb ole hayseed."

"It's not that. I was trying to keep track of them and my aunt
and Marcel. I need a job to go back to."

"My God Janice, you were burying your mother. I don't
think they'd care."

"You don't understand the work I do. When I'm around
those people I have to be 'on'. I apologize for not introducing
you. I have no excuse."

"I don't like the way the Suit looked at you."

"How's that?"

"Like he had the hots for my dear, sweet, Janice."

"Him? He's writing an article on the other one—Jeremiah,
who is more than I can handle."

"He makes passes at you?"

"That's not what I mean. He's too radical. He says you can
stop paying taxes if you don't like what the government says."

"I'd like to get out of paying taxes. I could make a living if I didn't pay taxes."

"He says that if the federal government pays for abortion, and we feel they are killing people, we should have the right to withhold our taxes. He says violence is the last resort." She shuddered at the memory of Matthew and his eyes lighting up when he mentioned bombs. Fortunately Jeremiah placated him.

"I wouldn't want any wife of mine hobnobbing with men like that. She'd have to quit her job."

"Wife?"

"Yes, wife."

"Caleb, we talked about that last year, so don't even go there. You scared yourself and broke my heart, remember?"

"That was then. This is now. You're different."

"Besides we haven't even gone to a motel," Janice said, trying to return to an old joke, the joke that had turned sour last year.

"How about tomorrow? I'll pick you up at 1:00?"

"I'll believe it when I see it," Janice said.

"Then you'll be surprised."

"Shocked."

"Flabbergasted. You'll see."

"All right. But I won't hold my breath."

They rode in silence while he finished the field and the sun moved over to the west and her family's comforters began to leave one by one by one. When he pulled up and parked the tractor, baler, and wagon, he asked if she wouldn't mind following him in his truck, so he could put his equipment away and roll the wagon into the barn to keep it out of the weather over night. She agreed, happy to help, as she always was when Caleb let her take part in working the ground.

CHAPTER NINE

The day after the funeral, Janice was raiding the refrigerator for Louisiana Ring Cake and butter pecan ice cream when she saw Marcel drive up in her truck, but instead of coming into the house she disappeared into the barn. By the time Janice dressed and went inside the barn, Marcel was tucked under Johnny's saddle, pulling the buckles tight. Johnny was holding his breath with a mischievous look in his eye. Martha stuck her head over the stall door and nickered.

"Hey," Marcel said.

"I saw you come in, and thought I'd come out." Janice patted the mare who was so light bay she was more yellow than brown, with a black mane and tail.

"Why don't you take Martha out? It's a beautiful morning for a ride and Johnny could use some schooling on the trails."

"It's been awhile since I've ridden a horse."

"Just stay relaxed. Martha's pretty steady. But don't grab her mouth or she'll think she's racing."

"Relaxed isn't my forté," Janice said rubbing the mare's cheek. She'd forgotten to bring a carrot.

"You'll be fine. I used her for my more advanced beginners."

Marcel clipped a lunge line on Johnny's bridle and ran it over the top and through his snaffle bit. She picked up a whip with a long tail on the end. "I'm going to work the itch out of his legs, so we can have a nice ride. Martha's saddle and bridle are right there." She pointed at the barn wall as if Janice didn't know how she'd set up her own barn as a young girl.

Janice buckled the mare's halter on and brought her out of the stall. It felt good to run a currycomb and brush over the sixteen-hand mare, who dropped her head and dozed, her lower lip hanging down and relaxed. The saddle was Janice's old Stubben Siegfried, a hunt saddle with padding for her knees and thighs that she'd left at home when she took the Godspeed job.

Janice and Marcel rode side-by-side, mostly in silence. When they reached the bottom of the hill, they walked along the tree line alongside the Normans Kill. The river was so swollen from recent rainstorms, lines on the surface reminded her of cauliflower and cabbage etching the water for a few feet then disappearing. A plate of cloud hung at shoulder level. Janice could duck underneath and see corn everywhere.

"I've decided to marry Lucian," Marcel said unprompted, breaking the silence her back and hips moving in the smart rhythm of Johnny's walk.

"Yes, I know; we all know that's what you said."

"No, no. I mean this week." Marcel looked so earnest when she said that. "As soon as we can get our blood tests."

"We just had a funeral. Why not wait for a happier time?"

"Now's as good a time as any."

"But your desires are as important as his."

Marcel hesitated. "Maybe."

"Marcel, there's no maybe about it." Janice noticed tiny drops of dew on the corn leaves and black bubbles that looked like mature puffballs nestled in the corn stalks. She let Martha walk a few steps and added, "But isn't committed love about working out what you want and what he wants and figuring out how you both can be happy?"

"Sometimes you have to put the other person first."

"True, but what made you change your mind?"

"I know what it means to have someone hold you in your

skin. Lucian needs me to hold him through the night, Marcel said. "And Dad could use a woman's cooking in these lonely days...Why wait?"

"You're asking a lot of yourself," Janice said softly.

"Don't you think I am up to it?"

"I'm not saying that. What I am saying..." But Marcel didn't let her finish. Johnny grunted and took off in a dead run, his ears back, his hooves pounding the sand. Martha leaped forward to keep up. Janice's back almost hit the mare's back she was so off balance. Janice grabbed the reins to stay on, which was enough for Martha to take off at a dead run. She was a racehorse and racehorses leaned into the bit to find their speed.

Corn leaves whipped Janice's legs. Stalks bent and snapped up. Her heart leapt in her mouth when she saw the freshly dug woodchuck hole. Johnny jumped it. Martha swerved around it and came even. Johnny dropped his head and kicked back, twisting. He almost caught Martha in the jaw but Martha pulled ahead. Marcel looked horrified. Janice dropped her weight into her heels and leaned forward, feeling the mare's power and speed. Goosebumps ran up her arms as the morning air chilled her. Martha's joy bubbled around Janice, so she couldn't help feeling: *Lift up your heart. We lift it up to the Lord.* The mare pulled away from Johnny by one, two, three lengths. She was out ahead running hard along the edge of the field, tree limbs brushing Janice's face. She had never been first in anything, not one thing before this. It felt good to have a clear track ahead of her.

Martha pulled ahead by ten lengths before Janice looked back and saw Marcel had pulled Johnny back to a canter. She had such a hold on him, he nearly cantered in place.

"I didn't mean for you to race," Marcel scolded.

"Then what did you mean?" Janice kept her voice quiet, too quiet.

"I've spent months trying to convince Martha she's not a racehorse and here you turn a friendly canter into a head to head match up."

"It didn't seem friendly to me."

"Listen, Janice." Marcel looked fierce. "I'm tired of you questioning whether I'm capable of loving your brother."

"Somebody needs to question it," Janice said.

"Can't you just be happy for us?" Marcel nearly shouted.

"You're young," Janice pleaded. "You don't know what you're up against."

"And you do?"

"No. None of us know. But I can predict there will be some terrors and stomach-twisting loneliness."

"Lucian needs me now," Marcel said heatedly.

"But he has you now."

"Not all of me."

"But why not wait?" Janice admonished. "Why rush things?"

"I don't think I can."

"Do I have your blessing or not?"

Janice paused, knowing Marcel was resolute. "You have my blessing and my prayers."

They climbed the hill in silence, the early morning dampness drying out, so the horses' hooves found better purchase on the grass. Janice watched Johnny's hindquarters bunch and push and his tail swish as he climbed the hill. Marcel leaned forward, her heels dug deep down low. They rode behind the house, past Lucian's Japanese larch tree, the one that was planted to celebrate his birth, planted after her mountain ash was planted, to even things up.

Speak of the devil, Lucian was walking out to his car when Marcel nudged Johnny to trot up to him. "Lucian, I have something to tell you."

"What is it? I'm late for work," he sounded brusque, not happy to see her, which surprised Janice. Besides why was he going in for work the day after his mother's funeral? But then again his job at the Software Group in Ballston Spa was intense, absorbing work.

"Yesterday was your mother's funeral."

"So." He rattled his keys.

"I was hoping we could spend some time together, alone." Marcel looked back at Janice and smiled.

"Not now." Lucian paused at the pink Triumph, like he was going to say something, then slid inside.

"Yes," Marcel blurted, throwing her arms wide like she was welcoming the world.

"Hi Janice." Lucian acknowledged his sister and then slammed the door and pulled away, leaving them in a billow of dust.

"Don't I get a kiss?" Marcel said dropping her hands and picking up the reins even though Johnny's head was low and relaxed.

"I'm sorry," Janice said. "But this is what it will be like."

"But I love him."

"I know you do."

"It's not your love I'm worried about, it's his. He's been engaged before. More than once. He gives her a diamond and she's history."

"He's told me about the others."

"You don't need me telling you, then"

"No, I don't."

Martha stepped forward and then back. She didn't much like standing still. Janice gathered up her reins to walk her down the road.

"Listen, my friend boards horses at her place. Pretty cheap I think. Her name is Judy Bradley. She's in the book. Lives in Westerlo. It's not as long a drive as you'd think in case things don't work out."

"Don't worry. They will," Marcel said as she hopped off Johnny and ran the stirrup up. "You're welcome to keep riding."

Janice walked Martha up the road, listening to the mare's hooves rhythm. The sun warmed her face and inhaled the coffee smell of Marth's sweat. She was horrified she'd become her mother trying to talk her out of Caleb and she couldn't stop her words, as they slid out of her. *Is this what it means to be a prophet? That words run away with you and you blurt the*

God's honest truth, so much so that you become cruel? But why can't I do that with Jeremiah?

She let the reins slide through her fingers as the mare stretched her head down. Janice guided her along Caleb's manicured wheat fields along the pines and up through the opening Consolidated Gas had cut years before. They'd cut a trail on the survey line, that Lucian claimed he and Marcel had opened. This was the overgrown trail she'd stumbled down when Caleb stood her up, just before she left for Chicago.

As she headed down hill she braced herself against the stirrups, feeling each of Martha's legs stepping down the long grade. The soft needles of the tamaracks brushed her shoulders. Her mother said this was the only place in the state they grew naturally outside of the Adirondacks. The valley smelled like crushed leaves, and it was as cold as if someone had switched on air conditioning.

Janice turned the mare towards the open space where she knew the sink holes were. Lucian said he'd read in the records from the 1700's that there was a salt lick down here, but they'd never found one. Oh, how she missed the valley and trees rising over her, blocking out the sky so it didn't bore down like it did in the Midwest. Maybe Janice could resign, and come home. She could buy a horse and ride with Marcel and fix up the upstairs. Surely one of the colleges would hire her with her MFA and maybe Caleb would mean what he said about marrying. Or she could find a job in New York publishing, coming home on weekends. She could shoulder some of the burden Lucian and Marcel were hauling.

Martha snorted and stopped. A deer skull, long and narrow sat on top plates of mud. The sinkholes were like they'd always been, round plates of mud in the middle of the valley. Nothing grew on them. Martha backed up fast. Her feet sucking out of the soft ground. Janice didn't understand what she was seeing. She nudged the mare forward but Martha kept jumping back in a motion like flying. Janice's eyes focused. Right in the middle of the largest sink was a deer skull, long and narrow. Tiny leg bones were scattered in front. A rib cage arched halfway over the surface like a small animal trap. She could almost hear the animal's screams when she found out she couldn't wave her white tail and jump free of danger.

A breathlessness came over her like when passion comes, only the thing rising through her belly, up her chest and out her mouth wasn't pleasure, but the grief she'd waited so long to feel, but now that it came, she didn't want to step into it. No she didn't want to be like that deer, stepping forward for a drink and finding no way of escape.

Her mother was right. *I don't belong here.*

"Come, come," she said to Martha as she turned her away, turned her back towards the hill and Caleb's wheat fields.

* * * *

Janice returned to the house, sitting folding her arms on the dining room table.

Kurt glanced at his wife's ring on Janice's middle right finger. "I'm glad you're wearing it."

Janice twisted the ring on her finger. She still wasn't sure she felt worthy enough to be wearing her mother's diamond, marking her parents' love for over thirty years. "How are you doing?" she asked, looking him square in the face.

"I'm holding up."

"If I were in your place, I'd be beside myself."

"When that time comes you'll have the grace to bear it."

"You're right." Janice remembered her dreams: the one about her mother getting on the train and the one about her mother as a bride. "I dreaded this time my whole life, but it's not so awful."

"She's in a better place. And we both would like you to have some things for your apartment."

"You don't have to," Janice murmured, feeling like the Prodigal Daughter taking her inheritance before her father was even dead, which was like wishing him dead. "I don't want to take the things you need to remember her."

Her father's hand felt like dry leather as he touched her. "Janice, she's right here in my heart, and my memories, and the life we lead together, and you and Lucian. Those things only make the remembering more painful than I can bear."

She could feel his eyes trying to meet hers, but she studied the grain in the table instead because it was too painful to look back into those eyes. "Janice, what do you want?"

"I haven't thought about it," Janice said.

"I want you to have the cannonball bed," he said.

That was his marriage bed. It was a beautiful old thing with perfectly carved balls on top of four posts. They were the size of cannonballs, and carved when there was such a thing as cannons. Beneath them were carved hollows that looked like an eaten apple, and then a round that looked like a jug until the bedrails joined the posts.

Her father leaned back against the chair. She put her fingernail into a black spot where the rust of a nail had bled into the wood. Then she smoothed it over with her hand, the wood, the black spot all one smooth piece.

"Where will you sleep?" she asked. Her father and mother had always slept in that bed. "It's time you stopped sleeping on that couch you bought from your boss." He laid his hands flat on the table and rubbed his fingers, pulling at the joints.

"It was yours and Mother's."

"And now it's yours. It's useless to me without my wife. I'll have Lucian move a bed down from the upstairs."

"I want you to have the original picture of the ship," he said quietly, changing the subject. Janice looked into the living room at the picture of the ship her great grandfather Jacques LeGere piloted, the waves blue and storm clouds pale white domes. "Her sisters think it belongs to them. It doesn't. Besides who would I give it to without causing a fight? It's best I let you take it."

"And this dry sink." Her father pointed to the beautiful pine one that held her mother's flow blue collection. The drawers held the family odds and ends. On top were the pillar and thumbprint glasses her mother used for special occasions.

Marcel walked in and stopped. "I see this doesn't concern me. I'm going home. Janice could you bring the horses in this evening? Their stalls are ready for them."

"Sure," Janice said, watching Marcel's back straighten, seeing her hair flick back off her shoulder, that old girl's sign that Janice used to think said, *I'm better than you.* "I'd like you to have mother's silver and half her flow blue dishes and half her pillar and thumbprint glasses." Her father wrote a note on a Post It and walked over to the dry sink, pushing it on the wood.

Together, they agreed on a list of furnishings and valuables Janice would take: a cedar chest; plateware; a rocker; vanity; spinning wheel....

"Dad, I appreciate all of this, but I really don't want to take things from you and this house; it doesn't feel right."

"Could I have that table?" Janice stood and ran her hand on the Shaker Settle where her mother had set her flow blue tea service on a table top that flipped up to make a seat. "I remember when that girl leaned on it, and everything slid onto the floor, broken. Mother said if I'd been home playing with the girl it wouldn't have happened."

"That girl's mother did not offer to pay for it. Of course you can have it."

Janice's father walked into the living room. The dogs pulled themselves up and followed him.

Janice saw her mother's porcelain doll sitting in the corner of the spindled cradle.

She picked it up, her porcelain head and chest feeling as firm and dead as her mother had felt when she patted her hand that last time. She put her hand under her cloth legs, smoothed her green skirt, and saw dust spilling from a tear in the feet. "When I was a little girl, I remember how Mother loved her. She'd had her as a little girl, but lost her, and you found her at an antique store," she said, holding the doll close.

"It was on our first date. Your mother was so delighted we

found her," Kurt said. "I'd like to keep her."

"Of course." Janice set her back in the cradle. Janice glanced at the place on the couch where her mother used to sit, half expecting her to be sitting there, her legs tucked underneath her. "Oh Dad, the house should stay the same."

"I want to honor your mother's final wish. She planned to do this before you went home to Chicago. They walked through the house and Janice picked out a ceramic doll he'd brought back from California, a carved wooden ship from Nova Scotia, her own picture of the Godolphin Arab she'd brought back from England. She took a cast iron hunting dog and a plastic dog her father played with as a child.

Her father finished tying a ribbon around the bed and walked over to the door leading to the upstairs. He pointed up. Janice heard his uneven gait, the pain in his knees as he followed her. Together, they inventoried the bedrooms and when they were done, Janice's inheritance list had doubled.

They turned and walked back down the stairs ending in the bedroom. Janice couldn't imagine the room without a bed or the two side tables or rocking chair or cedar chest. It would echo it was so empty. Already she felt the loneliness of it, but her father had been adamant. She went in her room and picked out her clothes and headed for the shower.

CHAPTER TEN

Caleb's Dodge Ram pickup drove in the road five minutes before he said he would be there. He pulled onto the gravel next to the Little Barn, and Janice was out the door, pulling the strap on her purse over her shoulder. She was glad to get away from her father's generosity.

Caleb smelled like Irish Spring soap, his hair was damp and he was wearing the same thing he'd worn to the funeral—a western shirt and jeans. She sat next to the car door, but he reached over for her and pulled her next to him. "I've got an errand to run," he explained looking down at her with the same kind of attention he gave his windrows. "Then we can go to a motel."

"Sure that's fine," she said, looking at his mouth, listening to that wind in the grass voice. They could almost kiss, but he didn't lean forward, and she didn't think it was her place to kiss him first. "Thank you for calling this morning."

"I didn't want you thinking I was going to forget you."

As they drove towards the Hudson River they chatted about how farming was a gamble because a man could never predict the weather—whether there would be enough rain or too much.

As a boy he'd wanted to go to college but his father said he could learn all he needed to know by working with him and reading *Farm Journal* and *Farmers Weekly*. He asked about Janice's job, and she filled him in on the parts she loved and the parts she hated. It felt good to be independent and feel like her talents were being used well. She found the job rewarding, but it divided her against herself. Right now she felt she should finish what she started because that's how her mother raised her.

Albany shot up with its old buildings and Rockefeller's South Mall set on the side of the hill. She'd never realized before what a steep city Albany was, the streets pitching up in the sky. The South Mall with its tall white buildings and egg shaped auditorium and blocky State Museum looked dated despite the fact Rockefeller built them to be futuristic. He would have been better off making office buildings that fit the Dutch architecture of the rest of the city. Even as a young girl she'd resented the cost and how the deep holes dug for the foundations disturbed historic remains of the early settlement.

They drove along the Hudson, wide with tall bridges spanning it, and blue as the sky. Sunlight caught the cups of the waves rocking. If the river had never been polluted it might have been the caviar capitol of the world, historians saying it had once been full of sturgeon. They turned off the expressway and drove through an industrial neighborhood past the art deco Montgomery Wards building.

Caleb pulled into a driveway in front of a low slung brick building with "International Harvester" written over the door. This looked like some kind of business, and she wasn't sure it was any of hers. "Should I come inside?" Janice asked.

"I'd like that."

They walked past an open area with cubicles barricaded by frosted glass. A tall thin man with horn rimmed glasses, and a washed out look that comes from working the land introduced himself as Russ. He was dressed in a light brown business suit but would have looked better in coveralls and grease. He was so businesslike Janice felt uneasy. Inside his office, she stared up at pictures of red tractors with closed in cabs plowing wide, flat fields like the ones surrounding the suburbs in Illinois. The place smelled like sharpened pencils. Now Janice felt like Caleb's wife, not his friend, and all she wanted was to be his friend because her job, her life was back in the Chicago area.

"I can't give you any more extensions. I need the money or I'll repossess the tractor," Russ said quietly.

"I don't have the money."

Russ stood up and extended his hand. "We'll be out next week."

"I can't farm without a tractor." Caleb did not shake the other man's hand. Russ walked over to the door and stood there, tucking his hand into his pocket, jangling the keys. "For what it's worth, I called Corporate, but they refused me, said the tractor comes back."

Caleb heaved himself out of his chair. He threw his stained International Harvester cap on the man's papers. Janice cringed when she passed Russ, his smell like wet, moldy wood. Her eyes stung with the knowledge that farming wasn't just about plowing and planting and harvesting. There was the crushing debt, where one tractor cost as much as a very fine house.

Caleb backed out of the parking lot without looking. Janice jammed her foot against the floor when she heard a squeal of brakes as a woman driving a Mustang stopped to avoid colliding with them.

"Janice, Janice. I won't get us killed. Now for that motel." Caleb put his truck into drive and signaled left. They followed the Hudson until he found the ramp that took them to a bridge across the river to Troy. "You have any Rolaids?"

Janice dug in her purse for a roll of Tums. "Here." She handed them over. "I had no idea." She didn't know what else to say as she looked ahead at the stop light and leaned against the seat, his truck pitched back on the steep hill climbing out of the Hudson valley.

"I gambled and I lost." Caleb ran his hands along the bottom of the steering wheel. "The wheat straw off your parents' land will pay my taxes for the quarter."

"What happened?" Janice felt her weight push back against the seat as he put the truck into gear and drove ahead.

"I owed Agway a hundred grand for lime and fertilizer to get my fields in shape to plant. To cover it I built those grain bins and planted twice as much corn. They put down the wrong application, and it's been rainy at the wrong times. I've got the corn to harvest and a cash flow problem." Caleb pulled up to another stop light and shifted down to wait.

"You going to sue Agway?" Janice asked looking at the smile creases along the side of his face that were deep and curved.

"Can't prove anything." Caleb rubbed his palm around the stick shift. "It's been a good run, but I've got ulcers from the pressure and asthma from the dust."

"I'm sorry." Janice touched his arm. She watched old houses bunched together, cars pulling alongside, then the city fading to the rolling hills in front of the Green Mountains.

They passed a motel with a gravel driveway and a few cars parked in front. Janice sucked in her breath. She could almost smell the mold in the rooms, and hear the creaky bedsprings. The sign said $20 a night. He pulled into the gravel drive and grinned.

"I don't think so." Janice swallowed hard. She wasn't Marcel. She didn't want to comfort him in his grief. She didn't know how to touch a naked man.

Caleb patted her knee and drove out of the driveway, the gravel spitting underneath his tires. "I'm not in the mood anyway," he said as he pointed the truck towards the Green Mountains.

"Me neither," Janice whispered, her heart racing. Caleb had never come this close to calling her bluff. All she felt was comfort like a huge mattress stuffed between her and her feelings. She watched the dairy farms tucked into valleys, cows walking slowly to the barns. Trees were tipped with yellows and reds. Cloud shadows raced along the mountains.

He pulled into a yard where gorgeous red tractors with two

tires on the back and climate controlled cabs and long, cigar like augurs and disks folded like butterflies lined up along the road. There was a long show room with lawn tractors in the window. The truck knocked and shuttered for half a minute.

Janice reached for the door handle, but Caleb touched her and shook his head.

She nodded and sat back without even a book to read. He left his keys in the ignition, so she could play the radio.

Caleb heaved open the door to the dealership and disappeared inside. "He will be failed from what he should have been. He will be failed. Look at the mess he left our fields in," her mother had said with such scorn, Janice felt her face heat up with shame.

But the Farm Crisis made Nightly News with farmers losing their farms because the price of land bottomed out, but not before the farmers had bought more land or equipment at high prices. Interest rates on loans were high. A farmer would borrow against his land when it was worth something and end up with huge debt when the value of his land fell. A bad year could wipe out anyone who'd borrowed to the limit. And the government limited how much their corn was worth.

Janice didn't know it would touch Caleb because he'd not bought land, though she'd asked him when she first met him how he could afford all these shiny new machines. "Credit," he'd said, "I've got good credit." What would happen to him? He was his farm. Unlike the Midwest where a farmer could go out his front door and work the land next to his front porch, Caleb had to drive his machines to a field here, a field there, until he worked a thousand acres around Albany County. His work was a kindness to people whose fields would disappear in sumac and goldenrod.

She pulled the fist-sized clump of keys from the ignition and filed through them, wondering what machines and buildings they opened. The International Harvester key opened the door to his tractor; the John Deere had to run the combine. She ran her finger along the jagged edges of the IH key. Sometime next week he would hand it over to a man driving a flatbed.

She filed through the keys to another one, brass colored, that probably opened the machine shed where he parked his equipment, his office with the picture of a topless woman lying on a beach, her plastic flesh gray with dust, a picture that made Janice's breath catch because it said he didn't think much of women.

Was Caleb someone she could show her body? She flipped through the keys. He had more than one house key that didn't match.

Caleb wasn't just a man making the ground submit, making the ground bring forth corn and soybeans and wheat. For years Janice had sworn he was a god of the earth. Who would she look to now, who would carry the glory, and tilt her chin up, bidding her stand the pain and stay alive? She wanted him to stay a farmer for her sake. But Caleb was a man who made mistakes, not a god of the earth.

She picked out the John Deere key and pushed it against the crotch seam in her jeans, drawing it up and down, up and down, the fabric too tough to be ripped, but she felt no joy down there like she'd felt as a girl walking up the road under stars the tight seam pushing against her woman's parts, making her passion rise to her desire that God send her a man. But not Caleb who once had given her hope there was more than the pain. But today he'd showed her his own grief. She fingered the keys back to the Dodge truck key and pointed it back into the ignition.

Finally he walked down the steps, watching his feet take each slab of concrete.

He opened the door, slid into his seat, looked straight ahead. His silence was like a hand pushing her against the door, hoping it would spring open and shove her onto the pavement. She held still. Once Troy started to rise around them in old rickety buildings, and the road pitched downward towards the Hudson, Caleb sighed. And with that sigh the silence stopped pushing her against the door. "They can't help," he said.

"What are you going to do?" Janice asked.

"Bale my hay. Pick my corn. Sell it. Pay as much as I can. Declare bankruptcy."

"I'm sorry." Janice patted his tightly muscled thigh. His hand didn't leave the steering wheel to hold her hand or even to pat it.

"It might be a relief to go to a job I don't have to think about. I'll try to get on full time at the quarry. If that doesn't work I'll go to work for an over the road company or a moving company. I know I could come visit you." He tried to smile, but his face cracked in a grimace. "If I took up trucking, I could pull my rig into the parking lot where you work, tell you to climb into the cab, and we would wander together. When this settles maybe we could make a life."

"Maybe so," Janice sighed, not believing him, not like she had when he asked her to marry him last winter. Besides, Caleb was the kind of man who didn't leave the county, let alone cross four states to see her.

"I could tear up the check I made out to the IRS and pay off my tractor for a few months."

"Don't be crossing the Feds."

"Why Janice, you gave me the idea."

"Me? When did I do that?" Janice's heart pounded. She wanted no part of encouraging someone to break the law.

"Didn't your preacher friend say that sometimes a person is justified not paying the government?"

"He's a nut case. Don't listen to him."

"But you're working for him."

"That's different. That's my job."

"To promote fools?"

"Yes. I promote others, good men and women, with good books."

"That doesn't sound like the Janice I knew."

"You're right."

"If you're hungry we can run through McDonalds."

"I'd like that." Janice covered his hand with hers until he had to downshift at the first stop sign, the first crossroads offering a choice, this way or that, east or west, north or south. "Could we go to the quarry, see if they're blowing up the mountain?"

Caleb looked at her, with a little fear in his face. "I don't have time for that."

"It might make you feel better."

"I have hay to bring in before Monday," Caleb said too patiently. Caleb drove through the intersection, headed the same way, back home, where the news would not be good for either one.

* * * *

She walked in the house just as Lucian was driving up. A cloud of dust blew over the lawn. Her father had added green ribbons to the Post-it notes on the furniture he was giving her. She could smell meat on the grill and saw the corn was boiling in the pot. She found her father gleefully pouring water on the fire that had roared up around the London broil and began telling him about Caleb losing his tractor.

"Dad what are you doing?" Lucian asked as he slammed out of the dining room.

"Your mother and I decided Janice should have some things to remind her of home," Kurt said, spearing the meat and dropping it on the platter. "How was work?"

"Do you know how much the Shaker settle is worth? If you sold that, you could pay for the roof on the house."

"Janice asked to have it." Kurt pulled out the silver carving knife and silver fork and began carving the meat—the knife slicing like it was cutting butter.

"Why didn't you do what Mom and Aunt Sarah and Aunt Denise did when Grammy died? Let us choose what we want. I get one choice. She gets the next," Lucian said reasonably.

"That's not what we're doing today. Your mother and I want Janice to have some things."

"What about me? Do you want me to have some things?"

"You live here, Son."

Lucian opened the dry sink and saw notes stuck halfway through the stack of flow blue plates, their smeared cobalt blue colors mocking him. "You can't be giving her half the flow blue plates and half the pillar and thumbprint glasses. How will I set the table for Christmas?"

"As long as it's here, what does it matter? I can enjoy this when I come home," Janice said.

"Please don't make me break my promise to your mother." Her father jutted out his chin, locking Lucian, then Janice with his heavy, sad eyes. "Please." There was the other part of the word in his voice, plead.

"Dad, don't do this to me," Lucian wailed.

"I'm not doing anything to you Lucian," his father said patiently.

"Mother always hated me."

"That's a lie from the pit of hell. A lie. Lucian, if I ever hear you say that again, I will kick you out of the house, and throw your computer and bed and all the rest on the lawn. And I will change the locks. Every decision we made concerning this family centered on you."

"The house doesn't have any locks," Janice whispered, her heart thudding.

"I will install locks."

"You know how Mother was," Lucian continued, his eyes shocked and furious.

"Don't test me, Son. Don't." Kurt slammed down the knife and fork.

"You can't manage The Farm without me."

"Then I'll sell before the year is up."

"Dad. Lucian. I don't need any of this." Janice pressed her ears with her hands and shut her eyes to press back her tears. "Keep it please."

"No Honey, those things are yours," Kurt said quietly.

"I need to pack," Janice said backing away. The boards squealed under her footsteps as she walked in the living room. Her being within earshot didn't stop Lucian from saying, "I'm glad she's leaving, so things can go back to normal."

Janice turned back and leaned her head on the doorway. She wanted to vomit. She knew she should leave, but she could not make her legs move. All this grief. And Marcel wanted to marry into it? No she was not sorry for warning her.

"They'll never go back to normal. Ever," Kurt whispered.

"I'm glad she lives in Chicago," Lucian hissed.

"Son, you'd better get one thing straight. She's your sister and you might need her one day. The world's an awful lonely place without family in it," Kurt said.

"I'm not saying anything Mother didn't say."

Lucian walked out and backed his Triumph around the parking area and stepped on the gas, pushing it as fast as it would go. Dust exploded behind it.

"I'm sorry you had to hear that," her father said gently. "He'll get over it in time."

"I hope," Janice said.

"Your mother never said anything like that."

"I don't believe you." Her mother had often said she was glad to see her come and glad to see her go. She had often said Janice talked too much, that people weren't interested in all that detail, and it was her mother who wasn't interested, not people. Just before she left for Godspeed she said she was beginning to like her as a person. What about all those years before? Had she not liked her then?

"Look at that ring on your finger."

Janice glanced down at the clear silver stone.

"Don't let him make you question her love or mine. You're welcome to come home anytime you want."

"Oh Dad," Janice hugged him. "I am so sorry for the trouble we're giving you."

"Mourning lasts for a night. Joy comes in the morning. Remember that. Everything will be fine."

He wasn't saying anything different than Jim had told her. Here were two men, older than her, who believed in the hope of the future. Maybe she could hold onto that.

* * * *

Since this would be the last night she could walk out the road, Janice hoped she would cry all the tears she had to cry for her mother's dying, so she could be done with grief, lay it down, right here, right now on this road she walked, so she could fly back to Chicago, cleansed, clean, whole, wholesome, ready to work for Jeremiah and Dennis and all the other authors at Godspeed. But all she felt, all she felt, was quiet, that calm that had fallen over her when she stepped off the train to meet Lucian and Marcel. What would happen between them?

Janice walked by the white pines when she heard Lucian's Triumph hit the mile long road to the house. She heard rocks hitting the car, and saw the dust whirling up behind it like a cloud set on fire. She bit down on fear like dust, pushing into the brush under the grove, and huddling behind a tree. The dogs were sniffing the dead snake in the gravel. "King. Arthur. Come." They looked at her and dropped their noses. "King. Arthur. Come." She called louder seeing Lucian's headlights top the rise one hill over. They trotted farther down the road. King lifted his leg and peed. Lucian's headlights looked like St. Elmo's fire hurtling up the hill. The dogs lifted their heads, their coats puffed out, the sign of dogs at attention. They backed up and began barking.

No way would she be able to hide. The lights turned the bend and caught the three of them, making them cast long shadows. Janice ran to King and grabbed his collar and pulled him off the road into the field. The car seemed to speed up. It seemed to swerve towards her. Arthur ran towards it barking, his herding instinct taking over. Janice screamed, sure he would be hit, but the car blew past him, the dog nipping at the tires. Then it skidded to a stop. Arthur jumped away, barking.

The door opened slowly. Lucian got out very carefully. "Janice come here."

Janice stood holding King's collar. He was pulled so hard, she could barely hold him.

"I have something to give you." His voice sounded sweet, almost gentle.

Janice let King go. He ran up to Lucian wagging his tail. Arthur swirled around his legs, lifting his head to be patted. Lucian absently touched his head. Then he walked up to Janice, so puffed up, his eyes so furious, like a rooster ready to haul back and strike with his pinons.

"What happened?" Her fear caught in her voice.

"She broke it off," he spat.

"Lucian, I am so sorry."

"No you're not. You're not sorry at all. You didn't want us to be together."

"Oh Lucian that's not what I meant."

"Yes it is. You win. You take this ring," He squeezed her fingers over the diamond so hard it cut. "With this ring I thee wed. Isn't that what it says?"

"No, Lucian." Janice tried to pull away, but he had her hand firmly in his. He pulled her to him and kissed her hard on the lips, bruising her. Then he pushed her down so hard she fell onto the gravel. The dogs lunged forward barking.

She opened her hand, her palm bleeding from the sharp stone. She heard a car door slam and the motor rev. Lights flashed into her eyes. The Triumph was so close she could feel the heat coming off the engine, feel the bumper graze past her, smell the exhaust. The dogs darted out of the way, barking. Gravel pinged as he hit the accelerator, stinging her cheek. Blood trickled. Janice could feel the dust drive down to the roots of her hair.

She wept for the diamond like she'd always wept for objects nobody wanted. She wept for how mean she'd been to Marcel and Lucian because she wanted things to stay the same. Why not let them be happy?

When she walked in the house, she dropped it in a bowl on the dining room table where Lucian would be sure to find it. It would come in handy when he asked the next woman to marry.

CHAPTER ELEVEN

On their way to the airport, early the next morning, Kurt sat solemn. "The house is going to be awfully lonely without your mother around. I'll miss how she cooked lima beans and Lobster Newburgh." He turned onto Font Grove Road and drove slowly up the hills that bent around Furman's fields.

"I could come home," Janice whispered, even though Lucian didn't want her anywhere near him. But her father needed her, even though she was sure that if she came home she'd be trapped like the deer trapped in the sinkhole. A shiver of fear rippled along her ribs. She found it hard to breathe.

But the Bible said a person was worse than an infidel if you didn't look after family. And her father was good to her, even though that goodness frightened her, and Caleb was treating her like his wife. It was clear he wanted her back home.

"I need to know you're out there doing something worthwhile in the world, something you were born to do," Kurt said quickly. "You'd help me more by doing your work there in Chicago than by staying home and keeping me company. Just call me every week. Collect is fine, like you've been doing."

"Are you sure you're going to be all right?" Janice asked. He'd seemed too brave, the tone of his voice too hearty, but if he didn't want to talk about it, or call her home, who was she to argue?

"You go back there and do what your mother and I raised you to do. Finish what you started." He turned right onto Krumkill Road and stepped on the gas. Janice felt the Chrysler Brougham lift with speed, down the mile long hill to the Normans Kill valley.

"I work with a bunch of radical fundamentalists. Just before I came home they were talking about bombing abortion clinics." Janice sighed, feeling very tired as she looked at the fields and houses whipping by as the car accelerated. She wasn't even afraid like when she was a girl and he'd driven recklessly. Let him have his speed. They flew across the steel bridge over the Normans Kill and the car slowed as it hit the steep climb out of the valley.

At the airport, Janice stopped at the newsstand and saw Jeremiah's picture on the cover of *Weekly News.* He looked even more fierce and scary than he did in person. The headline read: "Jeremiah Sackfield: Evangelical Rabblerouser." Her heart leapt up. Jim hadn't said anything about a cover story, but here it was, the biggest success of her career. "Look, Dad, look," Janice handed the magazine over to him. "Here's the article on Jeremiah."

"Honey, I'm so proud of you I could burst." He looked happy and serene and better than he'd looked in days, which filled Janice's heart even more.

She took another copy and flipped it open. There was a picture of the book and another one of her author speaking in front of the Coral Ridge Presbyterian Church in Fort Lauderdale.

Jeremiah Sackfield is the point man of a growing movement to involve evangelicals in a social, possibly anarchistic, revolution. He has recently published An American Treatise, *a manifesto urging Christians to get off their prayer benches and out of their Bible studies and become actively involved in American life.*

"It's time to stop retreating from our culture while our culture decays into sexual filth in our airwaves, godless journal-

ism, and we are murdering our children before they escape the womb. We believe in becoming involved in all of life, art, the media, and politics. This culture won't make it unless Christians infiltrate every aspect of it, unless they salt the meat so to speak. When Jesus prayed 'Thy kingdom come,' He meant that we are to usher in that kingdom by taking a prophetic stand and by being salt and light in the world."

This might be the mere ravings of a radical fundamentalist, someone on the fringe of mainstream evangelicalism, were it not for the fact that Sackfield has sold 300,000 copies in a month. He just finished a ten city tour that began in Hang 'Em Up City, home of the Upright, Downright, Just Plain Right Americans for Social Justice who say they are going to use the book as a study guide for their members. Already evangelicals have begun picketing abortion clinics and staging protests.

The book also has an anti-government flavor, quoting the Declaration of Independence, 'That whenever any Form of Government becomes destructive to these ends, it is the Right of the People to alter or to abolish it, and to institute new Government...' Sackfield states, "An American Treatise *urges Christians to disobey the laws of the land if the laws of the land continue to support injustices like abortion on demand."*

Throughout he urges the reader that if peaceful protest and legislative means don't work, then violence is justified. Like his namesake, Jeremiah, Sackfield challenges Roe v. Wade. He says, 'After all a million babies a year are being slaughtered. Who will speak for them? A million babies a year is this nation's Holocaust. Who stands up for them if we don't? A baby in the womb is utterly defenseless. Anyone else, even a small child, has the opportunity to run from their murderer. An unborn baby has no such chance.'

"How will God judge this country with a million a year dead? Pragmatically, look at the people who won't be coming into the work force, who won't be contributing to society. Social Security won't be able to support our generation because there won't be enough children to pay into it. What if this genera-

tion's Martin Luther King or Winston Churchill were aborted?"

There are 42 million evangelicals in this country. If even a small number gets involved, we could see a revolution as significant as the Civil War. For example The Upright, Downright, Just Plain Right Americans for Social Justice are going to send their people into libraries to see if An American Treatise *has been shelved there. They are not planning on leaving any facet of society untouched.*

Janice's father stepped up to the counter and paid for both magazines. When he came back to Janice, he said, "That is something. That is really something."

"I can't believe it either. Jim said he only had three columns but instead we got the cover."

"You're making history. Not many get that opportunity. Promise you'll tell me the stories."

"Oh Daddy, I will. I can't believe this." She waved the magazine around.

"I will live to hear them."

When they walked up to the ticket counter, the agent said, "I can get you on the earlier flight if you want. It's boarding now." He looked over his half glasses at Janice.

"That sounds good," she said. She could stop at the office, and find out what Jeremiah thought of the article and maybe brag a bit. This news might offset the first day back sympathy that she dreaded because work was not a place to break down and cry.

"I guess there won't be time for brunch." Kurt looked disappointed.

"I'll get something on the plane."

"I understand. I wanted to tell you Lucian said this morning he hopes you come for Christmas." Kurt's eyes flicked away and his face went slack.

"He does?" Janice held her ticket close, her briefcase looped over her shoulder, cutting into it as she stepped away from the counter, her garment bag already swallowed by the conveyor belt. She wondered if he was lying, but her father never lied. He couldn't lie, a trait she'd inherited somewhat.

"Madeleine said anger is a normal part of grief." Her father put his hand on her arm to lead her to the metal detector. She felt his grasp, light and firm, a guiding touch that would not stuff her into the box of their home, asking her to take care of him, a touch that was nudging her towards that door, the jet waiting outside, her own life, hard as it was, that was her very own.

"Of all of us, I worry about Lucian, as bottled and brittle as he is," Janice said, feeling the door behind her like the emptiness of her mother's casket.

"He'll be fine because he knows how to work it out at his work, or with a woman or digging out those caves," Kurt said.

"How about you?" Janice asked.

"I'll take it a day at a time, just like I've taken the rest of my life." Her father looked down, his eyes hidden by his hat brim.

"When I come to New York for Jeremiah's next tour, I'll book it so I can come home."

"That would be very fine," he said looking up. Tears stood in his eyes, but her father didn't wipe them away. The gate attendant called for rows in the back of the plane.

"I'm watching for publishing jobs in the City, so I can make you proud but come home more often." Janice swung her briefcase in front of her. "I read the ads in *Publishers Weekly*; I know people. Once I finish my first year in this job, I can seriously look. This article and the *Today* show are making my reputation."

"I'd like that." He took off his hat and ran his hand through his hair. They heard the gate attendant call for her row in the front of the plane.

"I'll call you tonight."

"I'll put your furniture on the van before the end of the month, so you can have a little bit of home and know how dearly your mother and I love you," he said.

"And maybe when I fix up my apartment, you can visit and see where I work."

"That would be very fine," he said. "You finish what you started."

CHAPTER TWELVE

As Janice drove from O'Hare to Godspeed Books, it felt good to be in the maelstrom of Chicago traffic, speeding up and slowing down to find her place. Even though her Firebird was gutless with four cylinders, she still felt power when she slammed down on the accelerator to keep her space flying at seventy miles an hour as she followed the arrow toward Indiana. She glanced down at her mother's engagement ring. It looked like the ice on the pond that cracked, not unlike a shotgun she could feel beneath her skates, the clip of the skates on the ice, her toes bitter and numb, her mother waiting up at the house with hot chocolate and popcorn.

As she swung past O'Hare she saw three 727s hover on their approach. They looked like stair steps leading back into the sky, back east, back home to her father and brother, back to their grief, back to her own as well. Janice wished she could feel something more than a calm she couldn't kick through if she tried.

She looked over her shoulder and merged to the right hand lane. In a few minutes she'd be back at her office that was just as messy as Jim Sanders' office, with papers lining her desk and floor, books lining the bookshelves. On the seat next to her was the copy of *Weekly News*.

She'd felt pure joy and the thrill of accomplishment when

she had flipped to the cover story about Jeremiah while she had waited to board her plane. She thought the coverage had been fair. But there was no predicting what Jeremiah would think.

When she pulled into Godspeed's parking lot, her face prickled with the weariness of the flight, of saying goodbye to her father, tears brimming in his eyes, of having to walk away, climb up the stairs to the plane. "You finish what you started," he had told her and patted her on the back to push her off like she was a boat from the dock.

She looked at the chain link she parked behind, the gray diamond mesh, and beyond, the neighboring one story factory with blinds in the windows. She didn't even know what they made in there. *Finish what she started?* She slipped the *Weekly News* in her briefcase and hauled it across the gravel parking lot out to the sidewalk into the one story yellow brick building in the industrial part of Westwood. It was the kind of building that made her feel bored to look at—long and flat, as if the sky sat its rump down again and again, squashing it, until it was one story, close to the ground. She looked out her window at a factory just like it. She felt embarrassed for all the condolences people would offer. She wanted the forgetfulness of the work itself.

She set down her briefcase and looked at the pile of mail on her desk with pink phone messages scattered throughout. It would take several days to read it all, though sometimes the mail could be like Christmas for the surprises it brought. But the rest of her office looked too neat. She wondered where the manuscripts and press releases and notes were—the ones, she'd left to work on when she returned. How would she pick up where she'd left off if where she left off wasn't there any more?

She took out her bottle of Normans Kill water and Caleb's bottle of wheat seeds and placed them on her desk.

"Pete couldn't stand the clutter of your office, so he asked us to straighten it up," Ron said, looking sheepish. "The work you left on your desk is in that file drawer." He pointed to the bottom drawer with his blue pencil.

"Pete, Pete, Pete," Janice sighed. "If I know where everything is, why does it matter?”

“How was it? How are you? We’re so sorry,” Ruth, a telemarketer, stood by Ron in her doorway.

“The funeral was more like a wedding. I didn’t know it until then, but yes, the Bible’s right.” Janice felt that knowledge sparking along her bones. “I’ll see her again.”

“How’s your father doing?” Ron took off his half glasses and wiped his eyes from copy-editing. He looked like he was about to cry because his eyes burned with pain he never talked about. His shirtsleeves were rolled up; he stuck his hands in his pockets and rattled his change.

“His faith is sustaining him. He misses her. My brother is there to keep an eye on him.” Janice began sorting her mail, putting magazines on her typewriter, neatly typed envelopes on her blotter, bigger envelopes and junk mail on her credenza. She picked up a pile of pink phone messages. She noticed several from Jeremiah. He’d called every hour on the hour.

“How is your brother?” Ruth asked, a beautiful blue-eyed blonde with soft curves who would happily take over as Janice’s mother if she let her. She was shaped like her mother—the healthy, over weight, bosomy version of her.

“He’s having a tough time.” Janice said, ripping open an envelope with her name typed across the front.

“You might think of volunteering to teach Sunday School. Give you something else to think about,” Ruth said, her blue eyes sympathetic and earnest at the same time.

“This job is my Sunday School,” she said trying to be funny. Most of her authors’ personalities changed once their book was published, and they demanded she promote their book like it was the only one on her desk. She pulled out the *Weekly News* she’d stuffed in her briefcase. “Did you see this?” she asked.

Ruth nodded to the pink slips. “Jeremiah’s been calling all morning. It’s almost straight up on the hour. He should be calling again.”

The phone rang—speak of the devil—and Janice picked up. But no it was Dennis Manley, the vice president of the Upright types, a tall, stark looking man. "I just read in *Weekly News* that we're going to send people into libraries looking for several books including Jeremiah Sackfield's anti-government book, *An American Treatise*." He pronounced "anti-government" loudly, angrily.

"I was pleased to see they gave us the cover," Janice said, startled that Manley would be so unhappy. What did he expect when *An American Treatise* advocated violence if nothing else worked to sway the government? What more could he want? She'd gotten the Upright types free publicity. This book was crossing over to the general market. It could be a million best-seller in no time.

"You can't let them get away with this, Janice. You write a letter to *Weekly News* in your boss's name saying that the book isn't anti-government and that Jerimiah is not an anarchist. That's libelous and could get us into deep trouble with the FBI, the IRS and create an audience we don't want."

"I didn't know." Janice had no idea that telling Jim all this could result in the feds getting involved. She did not want to talk to the FBI, IRS or any government agency about what she knew. She watched a semi pulling a flatbed piled with huge rolls of paper for Jeremiah's *A Christian Bestseller: Why Not?* and *An American Treatise*. A flatbed would be pulling into Caleb's yard today to take his tractor. Her throat tightened. He'd described how his father's tractor ended up in someone's antique collection in Gloversville. Would Caleb track the whereabouts of this tractor? Or drink himself numb this evening?

"Someone bombing an abortion clinic in the Upright name, or Jeremiah's would harm The Cause, by driving away our people. Our donations will drop," Dennis said.

"People have told Jeremiah that might happen."

"It can't."

"I see that." How would she feel if someone were hurt as a result of her publicity?

"Jeremiah wrote that was a last resort."

"Some people might read it otherwise."

"We can't be responsible for illiterates who read things out of context."

"Then who is?"

"Who's side are you on?"

"The Lord's." Janice wasn't so sure about this, but it was an answer he would accept, and vague enough that she could avoid the lie that she bought into the Upright credo.

"You don't sound it."

"Somebody is going to ask these questions. It might as well be me. Besides, then I know the answers you'd have me offer, when I'm asked." Janice said thinking so quickly her words tasted like bacon grease.

"I've got another call," Manley said, his voice impatient.

"I'll see what I can do," Janice said and put the phone down. The phone clicked into a dial tone, so she wouldn't have to answer another call. Her skin felt bruised. She began tearing open envelopes and packages from that morning's mail, the dial tone humming in her ear, until the fingers-across-a blackboard-tone and the nasty words "If you would like to make a call, please hang up and try again." Janice listened to six of those before she hung up.

The phone rang again. Before Janice could even say hello, she heard Matthew Sparks' high, uncentered voice, "So, is Jeremiah taking me up on my offer?"

"What offer?" Janice asked. She knew exactly what he was talking about but she wanted him to spell it out. How could she forget the blasting caps in Sparks' hand, the flash of terror that drove her to excuse herself to the bathroom?

"I read the *Weekly News* article. He sounds like he's hopping the radical bandwagon."

"No more than when we spoke in March."

"Tell him that I've started fifty groups in the Southeast who are reading *American Treatise*. They're not just reading it, they're strategizing ways to implement it. Tell him I'm happy to help him make some barns go pop in the night."

"Barns?"

"I'm afraid of skeeters."

"Skeeters?" Janice began to wonder if he'd gone off his rocker. She hadn't been able to read him when they'd met back in March at the Crab Shak.

"Janice, Janice, how did someone so dense get a position as important as yours?"

"My parents said it was God's special calling," Janice whispered. "And I wanted to leave home."

"Surely you realize our phones are being tapped."

"With Reagan in the White House? He likes us." Janice wondered. *What am I dealing with, a paranoid schizophrenic, who knows how to set off bombs?*

"The Feds watch anything that smacks of revolution."

"I don't believe you."

"Notice your surroundings. I bet Godspeed Books is under surveillance even as we speak." Janice reflexively looked outside for a black Suburban. Reagan had been guarded by black Suburbans at the National Religious Broadcasters Convention, and caught herself, wondering if she'd gone off her rocker as well. She uncapped the bottle of Normans Kill water and brought it to her nose for a whiff of the muddy, wet smell of a river up and running in the spring.

Just because she worked with Jeremiah didn't mean she needed to hear his conspiracy. *But if I heard it, shouldn't I report it? Is it real or just bluster? Is he nuts to worry about the Feds? Or onto something real?*

* * * *

Ruth poked her head in the doorway, saying that Jeremiah was on the other line. Janice mouthed thanks.

"Listen, Jeremiah's on the other line," she told Matthew, relieved.

"Tell him."

"Why don't you tell him yourself? You have his number."

"Channels. I believe in going through channels and you're it."

"I need to run," Janice said.

"Tell your boss I'll be ordering another ten thousand copies." This was on top of the twenty thousand copies he'd ordered at Tybee Island. Thirty thousand copies of *An American Treatise* in the hands of people set up in cell groups being taught how to stage a revolution. What could that mean for the country?

If this is Christianity, I want no part of it, she thought. But what was she doing playing Judas by telling Jim and any other journalist that would listen? She pressed the second lit button on her phone to hear Jeremiah's voice as angry and frantic as she'd ever heard him.

"Watch Jim Sanders. He pretends to be your friend when he isn't. I called to ask what he meant."

"What'd he say?" Janice hugged the phone up to her ear. She rested her elbow on the space bar of her typewriter, shutting her eyes, trying to calm herself.

"I complained that he portrayed me and the book as anti-government. And Jim said, 'Damn straight I did....You want to start a revolution and topple the government. I'd say that qualifies as anarchistic.'"

Janice started sketching a cartoon of her sitting crouched between two desks. The longhaired, eagle-beaked Jim throwing a typewriter at Jeremiah who pitched his book back at him. She looked up and saw rain spitting her windows. She drew a stick straight up from Jeremiah's head and then a circle to make a halo. Above that she wrote an explanation point and then a question mark.

"Janice, I was shocked," Jeremiah said. "Even the most vitriolic journalist doesn't insult a man."

"Yes they do," she quipped, "all the time."

"Everybody reads *Weekly News* and once these guys brand you, there's no escaping," Jeremiah protested "The IRS could audit my taxes. They could audit Godspeed's. They could audit yours. The FBI could put us all under surveillance like they did Martin Luther King, and there's no telling the trouble. I wrote to Jim's boss. I will pursue legal action. I called my lawyers, and they said calling me an anarchist it's libelous. The book is not about the government. It's about defending the helpless, in our case the people who are babies in women's wombs being flushed out. They can't run or speak up for themselves."

Janice rubbed her eyes because this was the second time she'd heard about the Feds watching them. She looked out her window to see if there was a black Suburban sitting on the street.

Jeremiah continued. "I am a scholar. Janice, he practically shouted at me that Jeremiah Sackfield wasn't a scholar."

Janice started filling in Jeremiah's figure with black ink on her blotter. Her eyes burned.

"Janice, I wanted you to know this because the publisher will be named in the suit.

Your company is in the middle because people will think it's an anti-government company."

Janice took a quarter out of her wallet and set it under her index finger, flicking it so it twirled around her desk like a top.

"What should I do?" Janice's voice cracked. "Will I be called into court?" she asked wondering whose side she'd be on. Her quarter wobbled and she set her finger on it again and snapped it, watching it spin across her pictures of houses and the fight.

Jeremiah's tone filled up with hurt. "Why doesn't he like me?"

"I don't know," Janice lied, catching the quarter and snapping it into another spin. Her finger stung. She thought she knew—Jim had listened to her whine, cry, and complain about Jeremiah for nearly a year and contrary to what Jeremiah said, Jim was her friend.

"This is the worse example of what *A Christian Bestseller: Why Not?* is about—how the liberal media doesn't give the conservative mainstream a fair chance."

"What do you want?" Janice said it softly, the words back in her throat, insistent.

"I want my letter to the editor printed and *Weekly News* to retract its statement. If they set the record straight my lawyers will drop it. He suckered me. If I'd known this was going to happen I never would have told him about my life."

"When did that happen?" Janice asked, remembering the bland tone of the interview.

"After you left for your mother's burial. We talked by our cars at the church. I was impressed that he came. You must be a very good flak to have that kind of relationship."

"Here I thought I did good," Janice sighed. She slammed her hand down on the spinning quarter before it ran off the edge of her desk.

"Janice don't talk to Jim. Stay out of it. He's using you."

"What else is new?" Janice watched a steel grey jet pushing west and felt the cold quarter under her palm.

"It was real bitchy hatred. I've seen nothing like it. Did I do something to Jim?"

"I don't know," Janice said.

"You still drinking Diet Coke? I figured out if you started at seventeen by the time you were eighty years old drinking nine Diet Cokes a day you'll have spent about a quarter of a million bucks. I started to worry you would be having it on breakfast cereal."

Janice lifted her warm, nearly empty cup of Diet Coke she'd bought at the airport in a mock toast. "It's half my grocery bill." Jeremiah could do that, switch subjects so fast her head swam. She wasn't sure if he was trying to keep her off balance or that was how his brain worked. Now was her cue to tell Jeremiah about Matthew.

"How is Pete treating you?"

Janice set her cup down on the ring it had already made on her blotter. She had to be careful. "He gave me the time off I needed."

"I told Dennis that he should give his book to your company because Janice Westfahl is working there." Jeremiah sounded so proud she could see the thumbs in his armpits.

"He called this morning. He wants me to write a letter." Janice uncapped the jar of wheat Caleb had given her at her mother's funeral. She stuck her fingers in the grain.

"Good idea."

"I'll get right on it, but we have a problem. Matthew Sparks called just before you."

She felt like she'd ridden a stiff, unbroken horse diving this way and that, jarring her. She smelled her own guilt mixed with a sense of pride.

"He's all talk, no action. Don't let him trouble you."

Janice repeated what he said.

"That's great news. Those fifty groups will tell others to buy the book. And then they'll all want *A Christian Bestseller*. What are you worried about?"

"The revolution might happen," Janice whispered, her heart thudding against her chest at the thought of it. She pinched a kernal from the jar and put it in her mouth. She bit down on it, tasting the nutty, gravelly texture.

"That's right," Jeremiah said. "That's what we're here for."

"You said it was all," she dropped her voice, "bullshit."

"I'm not responsible for what people do with my books. God told me to write them and I did. He's responsible for the rest."

"I don't know what to say," Janice paused then said, "but you just said you were suing *Weekly News* for calling your book anti-government."

"Janice, you worry too much. "

"I'm too young to be one of the first ones shot." Tonight she was buying a *Chicago Tribune* for the want ads. She'd had it with this job. Had it. Hell, they couldn't even be happy with one of her biggest accomplishments—this *Weekly News* article. Phones had been ringing on the other side of that door with orders.

"It won't come to that. I've got to go now," Jeremiah sighed, sounding distracted, papers rattling in the background.

"Promise me you'll call Matthew after you hang up."

"Janice, I will. Promise. Maybe I'll order cherry cabinets instead of oak, and Italian marble for my kitchen."

"Cherry. Order cherry. Oak is boring."

"All right. Cherry, it will be."

CHAPTER THIRTEEN

Janice was relieved when she saw her co-workers returning from prayer meeting, the weekly half hour where the company sang hymns, heard a sermon and prayed for their needs. They were held in the print shop that separated the marketing and editorial departments from the rest of the company. She capped the water and the seeds.

"We missed you at prayer meeting," Ruth said as she paused by Janice's door. The phone rang. Janice rolled her eyes, and pointed to the rest rooms at the back of the office. Ruth picked up. "Hi Pete." Ruth listened and put her hand over the mouthpiece, "He wants to know if you can stop by his office in a few." Janice nodded as she backed towards the ladies room. It felt good to close the door and relieve herself, which was the best language for peeing Janice could think of because relief, even the humble relief of going to the bathroom was a blessing from God.

Pete's eyes squinted above his full black beard with a merry expression. He wore a dark blue pinstriped suit. Even though it was late afternoon and warm, he still wore the jacket. His tie was loosened which made him look casual when Janice knew he micro-managed everything. Most books were late because of it. He shook her hand and asked her to sit down. She folded her hands in her lap, concentrating on how each finger felt against the other.

"I talked to Dennis Manley and Jeremiah this morning. They were both upset with the *Weekly News* article that came out today."

"Yes, but Matthew Sparks is ordering ten thousand more copies," Janice shot back before Pete could ask about her role in the article.

"I've written a letter to Jim Sanders' boss. Here's a copy. It's already in the mail." Pete held the paper across his desk, the paper slightly bowed in the middle.

Janice took the letter, glancing down at the typescript, grateful she wouldn't have to write it. That was one more lie she didn't have to tell.

"I can only put them together—our author and the journalist or producer. What happens next is out of my control." But a crackly voice chattered in the back of her mind that said, *You didn't have to tell Jim how awful Jeremiah was; you didn't have to tell him the emotional dirt.*

"We're very proud of the work you're doing, Janice. Both Dennis and Jeremiah spoke well of you. We'd like to give you a bonus." He handed her an envelope. "I think you'll be pleased." His lips pushed back his beard in a warm, toothy smile.

Janice took it and held it there, the paper dry against her hands. "

"You've opened doors beyond our wildest dreams. You'll also see a substantial increase in your paychecks," Pete said pushing back from his desk with both hands and standing up. Janice stood up and held out her hand. Pete's hand felt slightly sweaty. "Jeremiah insisted we do this." His eyes dropped to the envelope in her hand. "He says you're the best in the industry and worth every dime."

She'd never been the best at anything before. Ever. All her life things she loved came hard—riding horses, writing poetry, finding a man—they all came with deep struggle. Never before had she been so successful so easily. Yes, she'd just listened to how her best work upset people, but she'd also been thanked. Yes, she was caught in the middle, sometimes betraying her authors to honor her sense of herself—that she just did not buy Jeremiah's cause, yet she fooled them into thinking she was on their side.

What if the pebbles of Matthew's small groups began snowballing? What if he convinced them violence was the only answer? Would their protests outside abortion clinics turn violent? Would they use guerilla warfare, shooting abortion doctors? Maybe bombing their clinics as Matthew predicted? Should she call the Feds and tell them? Was the danger real?

What's more she felt like a whore, taking Pete's praise, the extra money, which made her life affordable, and gave her independence for something she did not believe in. She didn't have to ask her father or Lucian or Caleb to support her. No, she didn't have to be caught in a sinkhole, left to die without a way forward or back, even though she loved The Farm more than anything, even though The Farm was more mother to her than Barbara ever dreamed of being, and The Farm was still there, when Godspeed's books scared her like a lit cigarette tossed down in a drought.

* * * *

Janice closed Pete's door and walked past the receptionist, a woman with pink hair combed like a cloud, who was sorting book orders. She walked through the doors with Godspeed Books displayed in a lighted glass case, and back outside. The sun had tipped towards the horizon, throwing a red-gold light that wearied Janice. The trees along the sidewalk blazed bright yellow leaves. She walked over to Coletti's, the local hot dog stand, to pick up dinner. She pulled open the glass door, smelling the grilled onions, peppers, and spicy chili she liked so much. She read the menu posted in block letters.

"What'll you have?" Frank asked. He wore a paper cap that looked like two V's put together and a whole bunch of stains on his apron. The food was good here.

"Diet Coke and a chili with cheese, no onion," Janice said. This would do for dinner.

She leaned against the counter and ripped open her envelope. Pete had written that her salary was going up ten thousand dollars. Right now, she'd been given a thousand dollar bonus as a thank you for the bestseller status of *An American Treatise* as well as for the advance orders on *A Christian Bestseller: Why Not?*

Janice felt something loose in her chest. No longer would she have to ration her driving, or groceries or books. Out of the corner of her eye she watched the young man in a stained apron draw her drink as she glanced at Pete's letter to *Weekly News* and saw a historical argument why *An American Treatise* was centered smack dab in American democratic tradition. The Declaration of Independence advocated revolution if the government didn't do right by the people. She was proud of Pete for offering an argument so well grounded in American history.

"Good news?" Frank asked as he handed her the fragrant chili and Diet Coke in a cup that was too big for his hand.

"This time yes," Janice said. She folded the letters and grabbed her food.

Once she returned to her office, Janice closed the door and looked at the phone a minute. Pick it up. Punch in 212 and the numbers she knew by heart. She put her head in her hands. Pick up the phone. Call Jim. Read him the letter that was coming. Only she wanted to go home and stretch on her couch with the books she needed to write about, with no one else, no other personalities drawing on her, draining her. *Lift your arm. Straighten your finger. Punch the number.* Purely an act of her will. His assistant Alan picked up. She liked him almost as much as Jim because his voice was smooth as water on the lip of a falls. "Are you in hot water?"

"It's a miracle I'm not." Janice kicked up her feet, crossed them on her desk, looking at the colorful row of Godspeed Books across the top shelves of her bookshelf. "I got a raise instead.

Enough to stop being poor."

"Things have been hopping around here," Alan said calmly.

"Will Jim lose his job?" Janice smoothed the condensation off her Styrofoam cup.

"No, but off the record, he should have hedged his comments. What he said is defensible but misleading. It may make things embarrassing. It's all regrettable," Alan sighed.

"Why do you see it that way?"

"The next time we do a story on that world, people will be reluctant to talk. They feel what they write or say will be savaged. It makes it harder for Jim to do his job."

"It's silly over something small. Jim did it as a favor."

"It won't damage Sackfield. If anything the controversy will sell more books. I'm glad I'm out of the line of fire. I'll have Jim call you."

Janice hung up the phone and took a long drag on the straw of her Diet Coke, which didn't offer any charge, so she set it back on the water ring over her drawing. She opened her chili and took a deep whiff before she stirred in the cheese.

Janice wanted to throw the phone across the room when it rang, and she'd barely eaten two spoonfuls. The memory welled up of her mother sitting on the couch during suppertime talking on the phone instead of eating and here she was doing the same thing. She'd done it by snubbing Caleb when Jeremiah and Jim showed up for her mother's funeral. All for a story nobody liked.

"Are you in trouble?" Janice asked when she heard Jim's voice. She leaned over her desk, grabbing the door and swinging it shut with more of a bang than she meant.

"My lawyer said there was nothing to worry about. He'll talk to Jeremiah from now on. When boys like him play with the big boys, he can expect some big boy bruises. All he cares about are book sales. The book is patently anti-government, so what's wrong with my calling a spade, a spade? It's a free country."

Oh, there's the sarcasm, the bitchy tone Jeremiah talked about that had lurked in Jim's voice. She was glad his sarcasm had never been turned on her. Maybe that's why his kindness was so powerful in her life. "He's afraid the FBI will shadow him, and the IRS will audit all of us," she said.

"Maybe they need to."

"I've thought of calling them myself." Then she told him about Matthew wanting to bomb some buildings. Janice could almost hear Jim sit up.

"Not unless you see or hear something more definite than this. The creeps you're dealing with are all blowhards. Don't let them frighten you."

"I hope you're right."

"It's when no one knows what they're up to that they get dangerous. Don't argue with any of them. Don't let him know we're friends. See what you can come up with," he said.

"I played diplomat."

"That's what you're paid to do, but still you must feel cursed working on this at such a time." Jim's voice sounded more like an echo than a shot across the Normans Kill.

Janice rocked back in her chair and looked at trees behind the factory across the street. They were crooked sticks scratching the sky. Cursed was putting it mildly. She felt like the devil's tail was wrapped around her ankle, and it was lined with burdocks, and all she could do was keep walking on a road that led to hell, where the trees were gnarled and smoke rose up. "I miss my mother," she blurted, standing up and shutting her door, the phone cord reaching around her desk. "My brother blames me for his girlfriend breaking up with him, my friend is losing his farm, and my father is prone to heart attacks. He tells me to stay put, because he wants to find out what will happen next. I don't love this work. But if I went home, I think I'd die."

"If I lived in Chicago, I'd take you out to the Palmer House, and show you Lake Michigan, and the freighters headed for the St. Lawrence Seaway or Superior, and tell you that, yes, this is a bad, bad patch, but it's only that, a patch. There's a wide, robust world out there. The reality is sitting down to a good meal, with good friends, seeing the sky and the lake, and the freighters in the distance."

"You're married," Janice said flatly, remembering Caleb's sudden jealousy, how he thought Jim liked her.

"Not everyone is looking to take advantage. You're hanging around too many creeps." The authority in Jim's voice sounded like a wood post holding a crazy horse. "I'm also your friend, Janice."

"Thank you for coming to the funeral," she said, wishing he could have stayed with her through the committal.

"You looked like you needed a friend."

"I do," she said.

"So keep your head down on this one. Listen to what they have to say. Stay neutral. It'll blow over, believe me."

"Listen to this." Janice began reading from the Upright newsletter about how the American Library Association was subverting Americans' freedom. "I can't think of any more conservative group than librarians. It felt strange seeing Jeremiah go head to head with the president of the American Library Association on the *Today* show. Whose side am I on?"

"The Upright types need a Satan to fight," Jim said. "That's how they raise their money. It's scary with a president in office who thinks it's his destiny to bring on Armageddon. But you're right, fighting librarians is pushing it."

Janice had been raised on songs about being the Lord's soldier and fighting the devil and people at her office talked about spiritual warfare. But she hadn't connected "The Lord's Army" and prayers about binding the devil, with the fundamentalists' response to the world and how that might play out violently.

"Got to run. Sorry about the piece. Sorry to cause you more trouble."

Janice put the phone down. Her ear was flattened and rang as if she were still hearing the high whine of this morning's jet.

* * * *

The next day, Janice woke with the sun slanting down in the front room of her apartment through four windowpanes.

The apartment felt empty. She'd become used to having Arthur and King sticking their noses in her face when they thought it was time to wake. She'd liked having them lie at her feet, especially after her mother had died. Watching them run circles around Marcel's horses lifted up her heart. Maybe she'd get a dog to ward off the loneliness. Her landlady said she could have one. She wiped her face as if that could wipe away the pain. She walked to the bathroom where her thumb pushed up the cap on the aspirin. Janice put the warm Diet Coke back in the refrigerator and pulled out a cold one. She unscrewed the cap and popped the bitter pill.

When she arrived at the office, several pink slips sat on top of the pile of mail on her desk. She needed to write those press releases; though some days all she accomplished was responding to mail and the phone. One was from Jeremiah. The second was from Henry Babe at *The New York Times Book Review*. Others were from reviewers asking for books. She called Jeremiah.

"Instead of suing *Weekly News* we're going to truck bus loads of Christians into New York to picket *The New York Times Book Review*. My book sold more copies this week than the number one book on the bestseller list, but it wasn't on there. We need to go to work right now planning it," he said, his voice calm, full of authority.

"I'm booking you in Chicago to kick this thing off." She ticked off a mix of Christian and secular media including *Christianity Today*, *Moody*, WMBI, WGN and the *Chicago Tribune*. "Then we can fly together to Hang 'Em Up City to stage the rally and plan for the New York demonstrations, then on to Washington and Dallas and Los Angeles. You'll end up in New York for the demonstration and the major media there. That way we have time to coordinate with the Upright folks," Janice said holding the phone in the crook of her neck and reading her notes on dates.

"Brilliant idea," Jeremiah said, a typewriter pecking the background.

"We could bus people up from D.C., Hang 'Em Up City, Virginia Beach, and descend on New York. Let the media know. It might echo King's marches." Janice set down her notes.

"I'll call Dennis since I have a feeling he's pulling on Thelwell's ear to make this happen as soon as possible. If I were the faithful, the streets of New York are the place I'd want to be at the beginning of November."

Janice hung up, leaned against the wall and opened the paper to the classifieds, paging through, until her eye caught the column for pets. She ran down the list and saw an ad for a male Bernese Mountain Dog, home raised, five months old. Call this number. She'd only seen one Bernese in her life and he was a vision of glory. Back at Wheaton College, a boy walked a dog behind Williston Hall, and he walked like a lion, like a king, like there was something more to him than being a dog. She'd asked the dog's name. Adam. What kind? A Berner. He was big, bear-like with an all black body and deep mahogany mask and socks, with a white blaze sweeping down along his muzzle and then down his neck, widening along his chest hair. The tips of his four paws were white. Adam was so glorious she didn't want to spoil it by petting him.

She picked up the phone and dialed the number not even thinking she'd be leaving on tour in a month, not even thinking she'd be at the beginning of their relationship, starting house-breaking and training, and then she'd up and leave. Maybe a dog could ease the echo in her apartment, and ease how lonely she felt when she opened her door, because he'd be happy to see her, and he'd lie on her bed, his back to hers, and he would bark when things didn't sound right.

A voice trying to hit the high notes came on the line, sounding like she didn't want to talk, like she was sorry she put the ad in the paper, and wasn't selling the dog to anyone, no one at all. Janice explained that she'd had Border Collies as a young girl, learned training in 4H, wanted a good dog for company. She was in her first job, and she might be interested in dog shows if someone told her how they worked.

The woman's voice warmed, giving her the facts: champion

bloodlines including a best in specialty winner back there, seven hundred dollars, all his shots, a good temperament. Berners weren't as quick or intense as Border Collies, but they aimed to please and were very loyal to their owners. They came from the canton in Berne in Switzerland and were used as a general purpose farm dog which included guarding the farms and hauling cheese and milk to market. They were draft animals, built stocky and solid. She'd kept a bitch out of the litter, and already had six dogs, and Joshua needed to be someone's only dog.

Janice agreed to come by that Saturday.

Janice was happy as she pressed the phone hook down. Her raise had come in time.

She lifted her finger and punched in the numbers for Henry Babe at *The New York Times Book Review.* Maybe by this time next week she'd have a new friend. Maybe she would meet new people at dog class who had nothing to do with Godspeed. This pup, this Joshua, might just be her deliverer.

She told Henry Babe about the Upright types' plan to hold a rally there. Henry said he didn't understand why they didn't picket general bookstores for not stocking their books because *The New York Times Best Seller List* was based on the numbers from bookstores. "You and I both know publishers stack the deck with what they think will sell the most, by shipping large quantities to the big stores," he said smoothly.

"That's true, but they're calling attention to the fact that conservative Christian books are ignored by the general market. It's a great publicity stunt, if I say so myself. I wish I'd thought of it." Ruth stepped in her door and handed her a pile of mail. Janice set it on her typewriter.

"Well, the reason I called earlier is to let you know I'm going to review one of Godspeed's books—the one about giraffes. We don't totally ignore you people. Janice thanked him, trying to keep the excitement out of her voice that the book was going to be reviewed. Promoting a beautiful book like *Giraffe Joy,* and having it reviewed in *The New York Times Book Review,* made up for the right wing stuff.

After she hung up, she called Pete to tell him about the change for the tour and the upcoming review. He was pleased about the review and a little apprehensive about the demonstration. He told her to make arrangements to handle the company's end of things and to make sure the journalists weren't alienated. "I'm good at that, " Janice said.

Then, finally she could call Eve, who answered on the first ring, her voice professional. She'd barely said hello when Janice was in a tumble of telling her about the fight between Jim and Jeremiah and how ever could she promote Godspeed Books when her authors were kicking the journalists in the shins? Then there was Matthew Sparks with his big money and bomb threats.

"How would you like to promote Doubleday Anchor?"

"What?" Janice noticed Ruth glancing her way with her eyebrows raised.

"I'm going to Princeton Theological Seminary. I'm recommending you." Eve's voice was calm like a pond on a windless day.

Janice leaned back against the wall and watched white thunderheads mass over the buildings and trees across the street. They were huge and bubbly and something to watch. "I could go home again," Janice whispered. Oh what a good thing, to go home to be with her father and The Farm, to make peace with Lucian. Oh what a good thing, to take the train north to Albany, and walk out her grief on the farm, to miss her mother where she knew her. But not live there.

"Yes, you could go home." Eve explained where Janice could send her resume, and who to call and maybe she could set up the interview when she traveled to New York.

"Are you sure they'd like me?" Janice asked, taking a sip on her Diet Coke.

"You're perfect for the position, with a great reputation," Eve said quickly.

"I'd be two hours by train from home." Janice set it down on the wet ring on her blotter.

"You could commute. People do," Eve said.

Janice stood up; she was so excited. She walked around her desk and began shelving new releases next to last season's books. "This could be a dream come true."

Janice rode that burst of energy and hope the rest of the day, calling journalists and producers, telling them about the demonstration and the tour, following up on the media kit she'd sent before she'd gone to New York. She coordinated her efforts with the Upright publicist whose name was Buck and whose southern accent was so smooth she wondered how journalists trusted him. By the time the sun had set, Janice had written the press release she would copy on company letterhead, fold and put in the mail by the end of tomorrow.

She looked up and saw a jet's landing lights, the lit windows, and she heard the roar. Didn't O'Hare ever shut up? As she reached for two envelopes—one to go to New York, one to go to Freeport—she looked forward to Saturday because by then a dog might be lying at her feet, his breath deep and fast as he slept. By then, she could call her father with some good news.

CHAPTER FOURTEEN

Janice was beginning to wonder if she'd taken a wrong turn or written down right when she should have written down left, when she saw a concrete bridge over the water. A stream about the size and color of the Normans Kill flowed underneath it. Since she was early, she pulled the car onto what looked like a parking place for fishermen. The breeze picked up the smell of dirt and cattle. She walked down to the bottom of the bank, gravity pulling her to the bottom where she almost slid into the water.

Janice felt the sun warm her face, the sun caught by the river and flickering so brightly she looked downstream at cottonwoods lining the river banks until she saw a railroad bridge, the black girders crisscrossing the top. On either side were open fields that rose and fell in gentle hills and sweeping valleys.

Janice yawned, thinking how nice it would be to take a nap in the sun, hearing the calm of the water against the bank. She didn't even know the name of this river, or where it flowed, or where its headwaters began, not like the Normans Kill whose headwaters began back over by the Cobleskill, whose mouth flowed into the Hudson, not far from where Henry Hudson docked.

She stood up and climbed back to her car and turned left

after the bridge, the road rising away from the river. Out of the corner of her eye she saw a For Rent sign in front of a long drive, the second one on the left after she'd turned. It was back off the main road some distance, set in soybean fields. She turned left up the long gradual drive. There'd be no harm in looking in the windows. She liked the looks of the house, even though it was an old stone house with rooms added on both two sides that were sided with wood. It had a porch along the front of an addition, lining it up with the rest of the house. The windows and shutters were green. Behind her the valley stretched in the afternoon haze. Janice could see Connor off in the distance—the grain elevator, the steeples, the trees. She could see the stream she'd sat by, and the railroad bridge and tracks, the two braiding into each other and away. She sighed as she stood on the high point that commanded the entire countryside that rolled like New York, only better because these hills and valleys were culti-vated. Even in the distance the farms looked more like gardens than the grown up sumac and subdivisions that covered the land back east. One step a person would be in the yard, the next their feet would be out in the mud of the fields.

"I saw a car over here and thought I'd better check. Are you Janice?" asked that voice trying to hit the high notes only more resonant than it sounded on the phone. This was a woman who already knew the answer. Her mother's voice had been like that. She swung her left foot to the ground, holding the steering wheel to hoist herself out. It was that little foot, in a gray Hush Puppy planted on the ground that blew through Janice, took her breath and her heart away. Janice wiped the sting out of her eyes. Oh Mom.

"Yes, I'm her," Janice said, stepping forward, her hand outstretched. Behind her a dog jumped out of the Lincoln and dropped his head, sniffing the ground. He looked close to a hun-dred pounds, but what struck Janice was his color, the bright white bib and even brighter copper mask along his face and the dots above his eyes. His tail flared out in a long black sweep ending in a white tip. He looked like pieces of dog that didn't fit together. His rear was higher than his front. His feet looked like saucers, and his legs were long while his chest was narrow. He was completely uninterested in her.

Betty frowned at the dog trotting over to the oak tree and hiking his leg, then quickly closed her face just as Janice's mother might in the same situation.

"I'm Betty Knowles. My family owns the place. That is Joshua, registered name: Connor's Joshua Fit the Battle." She took Janice's hand, the clasp firm, feeling like paper, cold, how her mother's hand felt that last time. She was about as tall as Janice's mother, but this woman's hair was arranged in a bun that resembled a turban squash, the hair billowing out from her head, but tucked neatly into the center. The sandy brown color made her look younger. She wore a green oilcloth parka and blue jeans with a white wool sweater underneath.

Janice squatted and called the dog to her. He looked at her and began sniffing.

"He's his own dog," Betty said as she walked over to him and grabbed his collar. She clipped a wide leather leash to it, giving a slight pop. "Come. Come. Meet Janice," she said quietly.

Janice touched his wide head, which seemed out of proportion to his body. He ducked away like a head-shy horse, and the tip of his tail wagged between his hocks. He looked like he'd been beaten.

"No one's ever laid a hand on him. Trust me. Turning away like that is a characteristic of the breed. They don't warm up to strangers."

Joshua dropped his head to sniff the ground. "I've never had a dog respond to me with such reserve." Despite his broad, round head, and luxurious coat, Joshua left her cold. He wasn't the glorious Bernese Mountain Dog she'd seen back in college, who reeked of presence, who had that *Look at me, I'm grand* conceit that made her think of a king.

Janice ran her hand along his coat feeling its softness and dampness from the bath. Her hand came up with hair on the palm. She dug in her pocket and pulled out a wrapped stick of string cheese. She tore open the plastic wrapper.

Joshua's ears swung forward and he sat down slowly as if what Janice was offering was too good to be true. Janice broke off a chunk and fed it to him, the dog's teeth scraping her fingers. She pulled her fingers back, wiping the dog's slime with her other hand. She put the rest in her pocket. Joshua backed up and laid down like a Sphinx, his body floating to the ground as his front legs extended in front. He almost looked beautiful with his pink panting tongue that looked like a smile, his merry eyes, and his back legs tucked underneath. Clown was the word she wanted when referring to this dog, not king or prince or knight, but clown. He had that glint in his eye that said he liked being alive, but on his terms.

"Bribes work," Betty said. She explained that show dogs had been her hobby, but she was getting too old and Joshua was too much dog for her, especially since her son Fred said, absolutely not, no way did he want to show dogs anymore. "I'm too old to finish another dog. I'd want stud rights, but other than that my contract is pretty simple. You can show him." She handed Janice the typed contract.

"Show him?" Janice repeated, as she took it and glanced over it.

"He's ugly now, but he'll grow into himself. He was a gorgeous pup at eight weeks. If you have patience, train him now, bring him out when he's ready, you'll blow the competition away."

"Could I see the house while I think about the dog?" Joshua stood up and nudged Janice's hand, which she'd stuck in her pocket.

Betty pointed to a chain around one of the trees and suggested Janice tie him while they walked through the house. As Janice reached down and picked up the chain, she felt Joshua's breath on her neck, then his tongue. He backed up and sat, pricking his ears. He wanted more cheese. She pulled it out of her pocket and tore off a piece. "Gentle," she said. When Joshua took it from her fingers, his lips felt like a kiss. Janice hooked the chain to his collar and walked back to Betty. Joshua followed her until the chain stopped him. He whined. Then sat down, ears pricked, begging.

"See, he wants to stay by you," Betty said.

They followed a slate walk to a few stairs at the back of the house. Janice looked through the haze across the fields to a cluster of trees and a gray two-story farmhouse. Across the road was a red barn and big silver grain bins that reminded Janice of Campbell's soup cans. Betty nodded. "That's our place."

"Pretty spot." Janice's eyes followed the fields the other way to where they ended in a grove of trees. She saw how a two-track road going through them hollowed out the trees.

"The bottom land is bordered by the Chicago Northwestern Railroad. They built an underpass so we can work the fields on the other side."

"Could I take Joshua walking?"

"Be all right if you can stand the mud. That long coat makes a mess of a place fast."

While she slid the key into the lock and worked it, she asked, "What kind of work did you say you did?" The window rattled.

"Public relations now. Hopefully I'll be teaching soon," Janice said. "I'm applying at Apple Valley. Job starts in January."

"You have the job?" Betty opened the door and stepped inside.

"Not yet." The house smelled like dust with a tincture of mothballs.

"It's a chore to evict someone not paying their bills." Betty's mouth turned down. She rattled her keys in her pocket.

"Don't worry." Just then she heard Joshua's faint, mournful howl, a voice not unlike the haunting, ancient dog's voice she'd heard in town, and beyond it the bells chiming in town.

"Rent's two fifty, due the first of the month, includes utilities."

"Sounds fair," Janice said. Back in Elmhurst she paid a hundred-fifty more.

The kitchen looked brand new with butcher-block counter

tops and a stainless steel sink looked out on the black fields that ran for at least a mile until they met Betty's farm. The refrigerator looked brand new. On the floor was very thin, indoor-outdoor carpeting that was rust colored with yellow and brown stripes in it.

Betty led her into the dining room that faced the front door. On the left there was a small room with two windows that dropped nearly to the floor. They walked through the dining room to what could be a living room with three windows that also dropped to the floor. The room had hardwood floors that creaked under foot. The varnish was scuffed and chipped. Janice could see how her couch might face the windows and the view.

Like her parents' house this was a house of doors. Doors led from the living room to the porch, the dining room to the porch and the kitchen to the outside. On the wall between the door leading outside to the porch and the door leading to the dining room, there was a wood stove standing on thick tiles. A pipe went straight through the roof. "That's your heat in the winter."

Janice felt the shock on her face. "I told you it was rough. You have a propane pig for your stove and for heat if you need it, but you have to pay for it. The wood's free and keeps the house hot. My son Fred brings it to whoever would rent the place. He also plows out the driveway, but there would be a twenty-five dollar charge. If you move out here, don't you be making eyes at him. He's dating the daughter of the second largest farmer around here."

"Don't worry," Janice said, figuring he was homely as the men her age sitting at the counter in The Pie Shoppe.

"They'll be engaged one day." She pointed to the bathroom with toilet, sink, and shower.

"If I came here, could I put locks on the windows and doors?" Janice asked, opening the cupboard where she might put her linens. The room smelled freshly painted and clean.

Betty said, "There's no trouble here." The other door led to a small bedroom that had one large window behind bushes and one smaller higher up.

"I'd feel better." This would make a great bedroom because it was deep in the house.

"Why not?" Betty walked into the final room with a high window facing Betty's farm, and a lower window facing the yard and the field where it ended in trees, sloping to bottomland.

Betty led her back toward the kitchen. She stopped, looking out at Joshua who was lying down, his eyes bright, watching the door. "Do you want him?"

Janice's heart leapt up into her mouth. Seven hundred dollars was a lot of money, but his lips on her fingers, how he'd listened when she said, "Gentle."

"All right," Janice said, pulling her purse forward to take out her checkbook.

"His papers are in the car. You wait here," Betty said.

Janice watched as she stepped out of the house and trotted to the car. Joshua strained against the chain, panting. Betty stopped by him and scratched behind his ears, saying something to him, her eyes warm, the dog's eyes adoring her.

When they finished filling out the paperwork, Janice shook Betty's hand. "I want to think about renting this place. I should hear about Apple Valley in a few weeks."

"Don't wait too long. I've got others considering it." Betty folded the contract and Janice's check, tucking them in her pocket. She squinted in the sunlight as they stepped out of the house.

Janice touched the arm of Betty's coat. "You remind me of my mother."

"She must be a good woman to raise such a classy daughter," Betty said as she locked the door.

"She was," Janice nearly shouted, a tone of defiance that surprised her. She walked over to Joshua and scratched his ears. His tail wagged slowly like a man's trousers wagging on a clothesline.

Betty looked with a question on her face.

"She passed away a week ago," Janice added.

"You come here, you'll be welcome at our table. I could introduce you to my husband's nephew, Neil. You'd like his looks. Everyone does. He's college educated and heir to one of the biggest farms in the county. You'd be all right together." Betty reached down and unhooked Joshua's chain. She hooked the fat leather leash back on his collar and handed it to Janice.

"I don't want to put you to any trouble." Janice took the leash and was immediately dragged over to the corner of the garage. Her arms ached, and she skipped along, off balance.

"No trouble," Betty said, handing Janice the book *How to Be Your Dog's Best Friend* by the Monks of New Skeet and a bag of Iams dog food. "He'll need classes. I haven't had time."

Janice put them on the passenger seat and slung her purse there.

"I want to hear about him every so often. Send pictures. You're one of the family now," Betty said so definitely that it made Janice wonder what she had gotten herself into.

"Would you mind keeping him while I travel for my company in a few weeks?" Janice opened the car door and pulled the seat forward. She gushed that she knew she should have waited to buy a dog, but she needed company, and Betty knew him, and it would be better than a boarding kennel.

"Be happy to," Betty said. "Maybe when you bring him out I can introduce you to Neil."

"We'll see." Janice looked across the fields at the view stretching back to Connor, the blue haze that had settled over the afternoon. She hated to leave. She wasn't far from telling Betty she'd be happy to write out another check for a deposit on rent. Even if Apple Valley didn't work out, it wouldn't be an unbearable drive to work. And, and perhaps Pete valued her so much, he'd let her work from home most of the week. Maybe the job wouldn't be so terrible if she lived in the country. Maybe not having a refuge was the real problem. She hadn't felt this hopeful in a year.

Joshua leapt across the front seat, landing on the dog food and book and paperwork. He pawed at the dog food.

"It's his feeding time," Betty explained. "But he's better to travel on an empty stomach."

Janice sat down on the wet paw prints and started the car. She backed around Betty's Lincoln, driving slowly down the driveway into that view where the only thing in sight was farms and the small town Connor, where the skies were empty and silent but for redwing blackbirds, robins, crows. Though the fields would fill with the roar of tractors at planting and harvest.

When she crossed the bridge over the river, another river she might come to love, Joshua circled once, twice, his tail tucked under him. Then he lay down, his shoulder shoved up against Janice's thigh, his head over it. She scratched him behind the ears and drove east towards Elmhurst where the air filled with the noise of jets landing.

CHAPTER FIFTEEN

Janice was just about home, her very own home. Apple Valley Community College said they'd be pleased to hire her as a composition teacher for next semester. She'd not often had a day like today. Her father had sent her mother's furniture, the old wood of the antiques warming her apartment. More importantly, the furniture warmed her like her mother's soup on a cold winter day. She felt like her childhood had come home to her.

There wasn't anything she couldn't handle now that she was on her way out of Godspeed Books and into a job teaching kids. It would be hard to keep a straight face around Jeremiah and her contacts until the end of the tour because she needed the job until December, but glory be, she was free. Today she would put down a deposit on the small white house on top of the knoll.

Red warning lights began blinking on and off like two eyes winking. Up the hill stood her new home looking cold, dark, and unloved. She rolled down her window and waved. The engineer let his hand swipe the air. As Janice turned left at the horse farm, towards Betty's place, she could see all the way back to Connor and all the way across acres of farms and houses and barns. She liked the order of this place that was the order of gardens she could watch through the seasons. The fields by her house had been planted with winter wheat, a bright green mat that betrayed the season. Lights flickered in the distance as the day eased into evening.

Janice drove past the huge bins that made her think of Campbell's soup cans and a dryer that sounded like a jet engine. A large grain truck was parked over a grate, grain pouring out of its belly. The place sounded partly like a jet engine and partly like Niagara Falls. Since the driveway to the farmhouse was filled up with Betty's Lincoln, a Volkswagen, and two large pickups, Janice parked in front of the barn. Her heart was pounding because she would be paying her deposit on the house, she would be leaving Joshua, and she would be meeting Betty's family. When she'd called saying she was delayed because of the mover, Betty invited her to come on out and have dinner.

Dark shapes of cattle stood around a metal crib piled with hay. One of them bellowed so loud he hurt her ears. Janice put her foot down on the chunked up driveway, her foot poking the V shapes of a tractor prints.

She let Joshua out and walked in the barn, fumbling for the lights. Joshua trotted through to the grassy area out back, his nose sniffing the ground, his tail circling. Janice blinked seeing the wood floor and three horse stalls. Spider webs hung in the bars. Someone had spent a dime on the varnished oak wood and sliding door fronts.

This had been her favorite time bringing her horses in from the cold, leading them into the stalls she'd prepared, hearing them eat their grain, a lovely shuffling sound, and when they were done, the horses would tear hay out of the section she'd laid down, a rustling sound like wind over snow catching dry stalks.

She vaguely heard a truck door slam, and footsteps, as Joshua pushed past her, knocking her backwards into a man's body, as firm and steady as an ironwood. Janice stepped forward as Joshua curled himself, trotting sideways to the man until he leaned against him and grinned back at her.

Plain as a rail fence would have been a good way to describe his looks, something splintery, rough-hewn, not perfectly even, but natural. And like a split rail fence running along a pasture he was easy to look at. He took off his green Pioneer hat and swiped his hands through his brown hair. "You must be Janice?"

Janice nodded, and batted Joshua's tail, asking him to come back to her. He swirled around his tail wagging so hard it looked like it might swing off his butt.

"They never forget their people, do they?"

"I hate leaving him," Janice sighed, scratching his ear, finding a long, thin mat.

"We will take care of him," the man said gently.

Janice felt the man's blue eyes on her face, the sweeping fullness of them, like she'd felt staring at the ocean, only here was a man who'd probably never even seen Lake Michigan. "You ever been to the ocean?" she asked.

"Lake Superior count?"

"It does," Janice said. "For a prairie jock." She hoped there was enough humor in her voice.

"Saw the waters where the Edmund Fitzgerald went under."

She felt his eyes on her face, her face warming. When would he look away?

"That's something." Janice looked through a window across the street at a man sitting in an easy chair, the light of a television flickering in his face.

"Pretty bleak. Gray sky. Grayer water. Pretty rocks where it met the land."

"My brother used to play that song on his guitar."

"And you?"

"What?"

"Been to the ocean?"

"Yes." How ever could she tell him his eyes had that same kind of blue haze, roar, and calm that came of watching the water roll in, then draw back, a little different every time?

"And?"

"Your eyes made me think of it."

"I don't believe anyone has said that before."

"Your barn reminds me of the place where I grew up."

The wind shifted and she smelled the urine and fermenting grass of the cattle. A couple stood at the gate, their ears forward, their noses snotty and greasy. What she wouldn't give for them to be horses. Maybe Betty would let her keep one here.

Fred looked off at the cars parked at the house. "The whole crew is here—Neil, Beth, Bob. My mother must want you to meet them."

"She reminds me of my own mother," Janice said.

"She said your mother just passed?" He said it like it was a question, like his mother might not have gotten the facts straight, that he didn't want to intrude.

"She did."

"Here, let me show you something you don't see every day."

He tapped her back and leaned around her, opening a door to the grain room. An old bridle with blinkers with a straight driving bit hung on a nail. Next to it was a ladder with the first step, that would be a reach for Janice's short legs, leading into the loft. Up there Janice heard wings flapping from one end to the other, and a clattering.

"After you," he pointed to the ladder. "I'm Fred."

"I figured. Your mother said you were nearly engaged." Janice tried to be arch. It seemed odd he'd warmed to her so fast. And Betty had as much said to stay away from him.

"My mother likes to think a lot of things," he said.

"Mine did too." Janice said, thinking how her wrong her mother had been about her job as a special calling.

"You don't want to get on her bad side." Fred tried to sound like it was a joke.

"They want our lives to be a certain way. Their way," Janice said. "And then we don't turn out the way they wanted."

"It's tough when we grow up and start thinking for ourselves."

"Maybe that's part of being a mother. I bet they started dreaming about who they think we should be when they changed our diapers."

"You got that right." Fred's face lost its light, like he'd come in from fields he'd hoped to pick, but the combine kept breaking.

Janice wanted to ask Fred what was wrong, but didn't want to intrude, so she grabbed the sides of the ladder and lifted her leg, bouncing to haul herself up, feeling the roundness of her bottom grazing the side of Fred's jacket. She pulled herself, one step, two steps, three steps and stepped into the smell of cut hay. Janice's heart turned over with the promise of spring—the pastel colors of new growth, the roiling clouds hauling in rain, the smell of dirt. Fred's face looked happy, expectant as he stepped up next to her. Janice could see the lights of the house through chinks in the wood. Every window on the ground floor was lit up, the light next to the door, two dooryard lights throwing pools of light from the road to the house. It was so bright she could see dust motes floating. One thing she knew for sure, if she and Fred ever became more than friends, she would lose Betty and maybe the house she just rented.

Then the whole loft was shone with the warm brown tones of wood. Something let loose in Janice. It hadn't been long since she'd seen the barn in New York, but this reminded her of years ago when she was a girl, when these same warm, brown tones brought sense back into her world. She followed Fred's finger pointing straight out. Opposite them sat the barn owl, his flat ear feathers pinned against his head, his yellow eyes blinking, staring out at them from the mottled colors of his feathers. A clatter. Then the huge wing span as he glided through the crossbeams. Flapping. Claws out to land at the other end. A clatter.

"Oh," Janice said. "Leave him be." She flicked off the light.

"I thought you'd like seeing him," he said, disappointed. He stood so close she could smell Ivory soap down below the hot corn smell. She hoped he wouldn't climb down first, or ask her to find the ladder rung until her eyes cleared.

"You thought right. Thank you," she said.

"Time for supper."

"Yes, it's time. You all are very kind."

"We're just glad to have someone live in Grandmama's

house again."

Janice nodded. She'd never liked that first step, grabbing a wooden beam too wide for her hands, and sliding her foot across the floor to the top rung and then the next foot and stepping out over the hole in the floor. It didn't matter it was only ten or so feet down. She didn't like stepping over emptiness, on wood she wasn't sure would hold her.

* * * *

The clock read 9:30, just enough time for Janice to call her father before Johnny Carson. She tossed her keys on the counter and walked to the phone, the house echoing without Joshua. She sat on the bed and dialed.

"I heard from Apple Valley," she said, smoothing the crisp letter and contract.

"What did they say?" Her father sounded like he hoped she'd be rejected.

"We'd be pleased if you would join our faculty as a fresh-man composition teacher starting winter semester. You bring a depth of experience that would be an asset to our students and faculty," Janice read as she kicked her feet up on the bed, cross-ing her legs.

"Did the furniture come?"

"Yes it did." Janice said. "I'm sitting on your bed looking at Mother's vanity."

"I know you wanted me to wait, but I couldn't."

"Not even for a few weeks?" Janice asked.

"I don't have all the time in the world," Kurt sighed.

"At least these boxes are already packed."

"What about Caleb?"

"If I came home, he'd turn tail and run. He always has."

"I'd hoped you'd land closer to home."

"I rented a house that's a hop, skip and a jump from the Mississippi. Next to The Farm it's the closest thing I've come to home."

"You're welcome here anytime."

"No I'm not."

"As long as I'm alive you are."

"Lucian won't take my calls," Janice said. How could she explain that she didn't want to be possessed by The Farm the way her parents and brother were? As beautiful as The Farm was, she felt it was a trap as thick and sticky as the sinkhole that destroyed the deer. She needed solid ground. She needed to be free to run and leap and go forward into her life.

"Lucian will get over it when he finds a new sweetheart." Kurt's voice cracked.

"You don't sound good."

"I feel apathetic. Arthur has been sitting in my lap all evening, and King next to me." Her father sounded startled, like a man leaning on his ski poles looking at a long, steep run that ended in a small cliff, that these days, men thought nothing of skiing over. Her father sounded so tired, Janice felt unbearably weary.

"I'll let you get some rest," she said.

"I'm so proud of you I could bust. Don't ever forget."

"I'll be home after the demonstration in New York. I scheduled a weekend break."

"That would be very fine."

* * * *

When Janice hung up she wondered if she should call Doctor Chung, tell him her father didn't sound right, not right at all. But deciding which skirts and blouses to pack and how little underwear she could get away with, filled her mind, until it was time to zip up her garment bag and set it by the door. Then she noticed a small box the mover had placed in her bedroom marked DOLL. She'd not seen it this morning, but she'd been in such a hurry to make the bank before it closed, and drive Joshua out to Betty's.

She tore open the tape and unwrapped the cream paper to find her mother's doll, the one that had sat in the cradle for so many years. Her eyes reminded her of the look Betty gave her when Fred had walked her out to the car, the kind of eyes that followed a person around a room. Janice smoothed down the green dress, feeling how the porcelain head and shoulders felt hard and cold, something that would not bring comfort to a child. Why had she wanted her? Her father had said he wasn't ready to send it. He should have waited, darn it. But oh how good it was to sit on her parents' bed and feel their presence well up around her. Janice freed the doll from the wrapping and set her in her lap, tiny particles of sawdust dripping out of her feet. Underneath was a card, with her name on it, written in her father's hand.

> *As I was packing your things—you need to think of them as your things and not mine or your mother's—I remembered an old story my mother used to tell. It was about a girl whose mother died. But on her deathbed she gave her a doll. As the story went on, the girl finds herself in a witch's house because her family needed fire. The witch sees a slave, but the girl is able to complete each of her tasks with the help of her mother's doll. When the witch finds out, she's horrified the girl has her mother's blessing and sends her home with the fire and her own blessing. I want you to have this doll so that whenever you look at her, you know you have your mother's blessing and my blessing. Who knows? She might just be magic. She might help you with a job as hard as separating wheat from oats.*
>
> *I know you disagree with my doing this. Pastor said I should give it a year. Lucian is barely speaking to me. But I want you to know I've never felt more right about doing something, than I have with sending you these things. My heart is lifted up with joy, knowing you'll have a little bit of home wherever you are.*
>
> *Love,*
> *Dad.*

Janice closed the note and set it on her mother's, no, her bedside table. She tucked herself in the covers and set the doll on the pillow next to her. She'd call her father tomorrow and thank him for everything once she arrived in Hang 'Em Up City.

As she melted into the faint smell of her mother's perfume, mixed with cigarettes, and the faint smell of her father's sweat and dust from The Farm, she thought about her father watching Al's semi until it disappeared down the hill to the dying elm and the fence line that signaled the border to their property. She thought about Joshua standing by the kitchen door as she patted him goodbye and the crescent in the western sky, Fred's hand on the small of her back, Joshua's whine from inside the house.

CHAPTER SIXTEEN

October 31, 1983. O'Hare Airport.

It was noon, Halloween, when Janice turned the corner at O'Hare to walk down to the United ramp that would take her to Hang 'Em Up City. In just a few steps she would be seeing Jeremiah again, and they would begin their tour promoting his *A Christian Bestseller: Why Not?* He'd flown into Chicago to meet with his art director. They'd started his tour here, with interviews at WMBI, *Moody*, *The Chicago Tribune*, *Christianity Today* and Milt Rosenberg's *Extension 720* at WGN.

Carpet held up her feet, but each time she stepped she felt she was taking a step over the lip of a cliff, her heart thumping, her eyes swimming with the speed of the world flying up around her like insects in alfalfa. She felt like nothing could touch her, because she was bound for that little house on a hill looking over farms so well tended, her view would be nothing less than miles of gardens and the wonder of farmers tending the ground.

But she also sighed because the next few weeks would be hard work. Not even her bed would be the same. The only constants would be jets flying them one place to another, Jeremiah poking at her and saying, "You should buy stock in Coca Cola you drink so much of that stuff," and the knowledge that she'd resign her job when the tour was done.

Janice smiled to herself as she walked to her gate. She might as well enjoy the last few weeks of wheeling and dealing before she settled down to grade papers, living in the middle of nowhere. She looked at the gray skies and the gray jet sitting at their gate. Why was O'Hare always gray? Whenever she left or arrived, she could figure on overcast Chicago, full of the restlessness of folks moving from here to there to here.

Janice pulled her journal and a pen out of her briefcase, but she looked into the distance, her eyes resting on a jet leaning down to the runway, strobe lights bright. She wrote about the owl's wings as he flew from one end of the barn to another, and the crescent moon, and the feel of Fred's hand on the small of her back. How protected she felt by him. She had felt accepted by the beautiful woman Fred kissed when they sat down to eat and the beautiful man, Neil, sitting across from her, catching her eyes too often and the two old farmers, Fred's father and Neil's father. But Fred, when Fred looked, she looked back. Betty stabbed potatoes like her mother stabbed them. Already she missed Joshua and how he leaned all his weight against her.

Janice startled. Jeremiah grinned behind fake horn rimmed glasses and a big nose. "Boo," he said. He hefted his garment bag over his shoulder, preferring to carry it the long walk to his gate because he was afraid the airlines would lose it.

"Can I buy you a drink?" Jeremiah slipped the mask into his pocket and slung his bag down on the chair next to hers, the garment bag whooshing against the vinyl seat.

"Sure," Janice said, shifting away from his luggage.

"I know. The usual," Jeremiah said. "We're going into the devil's territory with this book. Expect some major warfare," Jeremiah said as he handed her a can of Diet Coke and poured a wine cooler into a plastic cup.

"How can we tell if we're being attacked?" Janice asked. Sometimes she wondered about the Christians who viewed life as a battleground with the devil under every bush, like they were looking to Satan rather than looking to Jesus.

"Maybe a tabloid will put a blonde in my room and take my picture with her."

"Maybe it's her." Janice nudged Jeremiah to notice the barely dressed woman.

"Right. The ACLU is flying her to Hang 'Em Up City to seduce me. Right. She's not even my type." Jeremiah sipped his wine cooler, watchful like Gideon's men who sipped from the stream with their hands to their mouths because the Philistines might attack. "Be careful what movies you watch in your room. Bad people check."

"*The Black Stallion* all right?" She wanted to lean her head back and close her eyes, but the seats stopped in the middle of her back. She opened her eyes to see a jet taxi across an overpass.

* * * *

The ticket agent opened the door to the jet, and people began walking through it and around where they were sitting into the crowded hallway. "How is your father doing?" Jeremiah clapped her on the knee.

"He sent furniture from home yesterday. I can't wait to unpack but don't look forward to the mess waiting when this is over."

"You must like having things from home."

"I wanted to tear open boxes, but I had to leave."

"Those are more than just things. They are reminders of your parents' love and the good times you had growing up. Don't forget that."

"Last night was the first time I'd slept in a bed since I arrived in Elmhurst. It was like sleeping between my parents when I was a little girl."

"You must have felt secure."

"I felt comforted and safe and slept deeply."

"I keep my father's pocket watch with me at all times. It was his grandfather's watch." Jeremiah pulled out the gold watch and flipped it open. A half moon and sun were etched into the face. The second hand jerked forward and a little back. "My mother was going to throw it away because it didn't work, but I saved it, and repaired it. Now it keeps great time." Jeremiah snapped it closed and shoved it in his pocket.

"Mother's engagement ring is like that for me."

Jeremiah took her hand gently and looked at it. "I'm glad to see it's on your right hand."

"There's no man in my life."

"I saw how your farmer looked at you."

For an instant, Janice thought he meant Fred, who was so kind she wanted to cry. Then she realized who he meant. "Caleb? I used to love him so much it hurt, but now we're just friends."

"Don't be so sure." Jeremiah elbowed her with a smile on his face.

"I doubt I'll go back there to live, so it's a moot point, even if you did see something between us."

"He could follow you here."

"Farmers don't leave their land." Janice caught herself remembering he'd lost his tractor. He could visit. "Besides he's not been in touch. Jeremiah, I'm surprised you're the romantic one today."

"Believe it or not, I'd like to see you happy."

It was all Janice could do not to say she'd just rented a house on top of a hill overlooking the most beautiful farmland, and that she would be leaving this job to teach first year students how to write, that there was a family waiting to take her in as their own.

"How is your brother doing? I didn't mean to leave him out," Jeremiah said twiddling his thumbs. Every so often one thumb would bump the other and they'd go the other way.

"He blames me for his girlfriend breaking up with him, or him breaking up with her. I'm not sure which." Janice watched a young woman with a baby dressed like a carrot, and a toddler dressed like Superman greeting an older couple, throwing her arms around them, then handing her baby off to her mother, her father taking the toddler's hand, the woman shifting her baby bag from one shoulder to the other.

"He'll get over it."

"Ah, but will I?" She felt the scab where he jammed Marcel's ring into her hand, the ferocity of his kiss, the strength of his arms pinning her, so she couldn't escape.

"If you don't, you won't be fit for God's work," Jeremiah said, clapping his hand on her shoulder so hard it tingled. "And we need you fit because we're going into battle. Satan will oppose us, especially since our cause is to make this a Christian country because we are the hands and feet of Jesus, and he's called us to redeem all of society."

"I thought your goal was to sell books."

"That too."

"Jeremiah you switch back and forth so fast you make my head swim."

"I keep you on your toes."

"Do you think God's Spirit is quenched when his people have broken relationships?" Janice asked, her heart beating fast. Jeremiah didn't just want her expertise. He wanted her to be pure in heart, even if her struggles had nothing whatsoever to do with her work at Godspeed.

"Yes I do."

"Then how come He's blessed my work with all these appointments for your tour, and the stories that have already run?"

"You don't let your personal life interfere. I admire your courage."

"My father said being appreciated is a big deal."

"I liked your father when I met him at your mother's funeral. He seemed as godly as my own father. I hope he didn't screw you up like mine did me."

"What?" Janice whispered, feeling something she didn't want to know diving hard from outside her consciousness. "Didn't your father help people work out their relationship with the Lord?"

He punched her in the shoulder again. "Just kidding, Janice. Don't take everything I say so seriously. Though that's what makes you so much fun."

"A barrel of laughs. Ha. Ha." Janice watched the family walk together down the concourse, wishing she were the young mother greeting her parents. She felt so hopeful about her life ahead but saddened and conflicted about her life behind.

Jeremiah leaned over and whispered, "Janice please don't cry. We haven't even begun the tour." The kindness in his voice made the tears roll right out of her eyes. God they felt good, the sweet kind, full of longing and sadness, that always seemed to butt her up to her prayers and a sense of God right there.

"Sorry," she said, closing her book and wiping her face with the palm of her hand.

"People will think I said something horrible."

"I'm tired." Janice slipped her journal back in her briefcase.

He quickly clasped her shoulder and pulled her to him and then released her.

Whenever Janice stepped across the join up between the plane and the gangplank she looked down at the crack of daylight, which reminded her of the wide pine boards in the living room, that had rotted just a bit, so she could see down to the cellar. Lucian had looked up through that crack once with a utility light, his face open and smiling. Why couldn't it be that way between them again? Tears dripped down her face.

When they stopped at their seats, Janice pulled down a pillow and a blanket from the overhead bin. She fluffed it up against the window and closed her eyes. She felt a finger in her arm.

"What's our schedule?"

Janice pulled out her folded schedule and began reciting their appointments.

"I only want to know about tomorrow."

Janice leaned against the window and shut her eyes thinking about how she was seeing the world in ways a person on the ground could never see it, and how places a thousand miles away, that would take a whole day to drive to, were only a few hours off. Janice never came back the same person.

After they were in the air, she noticed Jeremiah had nodded off to sleep. She pulled out the bottle of Normans Kill water and the seeds Caleb had given her. She set them on the tray table looking at the dirty water and tiny seeds that cracked like miniature fannies.

The jet was over Ohio when she felt a finger in her arm. "Don't you sleep at night?"

"Yes I sleep at night," Janice said, her voice tight and cracking. "Can you spell nap?"

"You should sleep at night and be awake during the day. You'll sleep your life away."

"And that would be very fine." Janice turned back to her pillow and pressed her eyes shut, crossing her arms over her chest, thinking how Betty said her mother had to be a good woman for raising such a classy daughter. She felt Jeremiah's finger jab into her shoulder. "What's that?"

She startled awake, "What? What?"

"That," Jeremiah picked up the water. "And this." He jiggled the seeds so they rattled around the bottle. "I've seen you take whiffs of it. Are you some kind of dopehead, sneaking a snort when my eyes are closed?"

"You should be so lucky." Janice explained how the water reminded her of the Normans Kill, a place where she sat and met with God and how the seeds were a gift from her farmer. "What better image of the resurrection than green shoots breaking the ground."

"See he does like you."

"Maybe."

"Why do you carry them?"

"They ground me when I can't walk on The Farm."

"You keep that away from your mouth. Giardia is nasty. I can't have you running to the bathroom when I need you."

"Don't worry."

The jet leaned sideways, leaning Jeremiah against Janice and Janice against the window. The mountains rolled, the leafless trees making it seem she was looking at the bottom of a lake instead of the bottom of a forest. The pilot said they'd be landing in Charlottesville shortly.

* * * *

On the way to the Hang 'Em Up City Motor Inn, Jeremiah confided in Dennis Manley, vice president of the Upright, Downright, Just Plain Right Americans for Social Justice, and his wife Theresa. "I don't know where this is going."

"The next step is *The New York Times*." Dennis Manley looked away from his driving at Jeremiah with an adoring look in his eyes. Janice had forgotten how tall and stark he was. She felt slightly nauseous, sitting in the back seat because she wasn't used to riding over hills.

"Do you think Thelwell will produce five busloads?" Jeremiah asked.

"He keeps his promises."

"The liberal media will have to pay attention now."

"Janice has arranged for them to cover it, haven't you Janice?" Jeremiah craned his neck around to look at her. Dennis glanced in the mirror. She felt ganged up on by two mustaches.

"*The New York Times, Publishers Weekly, Time, Newsweek, The New York Post, Newsday, US News and World Report, USA Today,* CBS, ABC, NBC, Fox and CNN all promised reporters," Janice said.

"I'm afraid we'll be the first ones shot once we put these idiots in power. The good Communists were the first to go in the Communist revolution," Jeremiah said balling his hand into a fist and hitting his thigh.

"But what are the alternatives?" Dennis asked. He drove slowly because a dense, thick fog had settled over the city.

"The alternatives are worse. We've got to do our best to stop this society's pervasive disrespect for human life. If we don't, anyone's life would be in danger should they become inconvenient." Jeremiah rolled down the window, letting in the damp air. It was too early for trick-or-treaters.

"The whole thing scares the daylights out of me," Dennis agreed.

"I wonder where love is in all this," Janice ventured. She saw a dummy hanging from a tree, and ax in his back, and three tombstones.

"I know what you mean," said Dennis's wife, Theresa. Like Dennis she was tall and big boned, and very regal. Yet she wasn't afraid to speak the truth and could make a person feel very at ease, despite her beauty. "We have several couples in church who've gone through terrible divorces, and no one lifts a finger to help them. Dennis and I were exhausted trying to help one woman. Once when we reached the end of our rope, she told me that she wouldn't be alive today were it not for us befriending her."

"The Holy Spirit sure grabbed us by the ear on that one," Dennis said.

"Seems like our society is sliding into a pervasive selfishness," Jeremiah said. "Where was the rest of the church?"

"People are stretched thin trying to survive the demands of corporate America," Janice said, thinking about how her life consisted of work and sleep.

"Are you saying something about how busy Godspeed Press is keeping you?"

"Not at all." Janice could see tatters of the fog moving across the sun. She was hoping a hot bath, as hot as she could stand, might sop up the ache in her legs.

"I need to polish my speech for tonight," Jeremiah said as he opened the car door.

The cold and damp swept under Janice's dress as she stepped out of the car, taking her breath away. She didn't want to move from the sidewalk because she didn't want to move the air and become even more chilled, so she watched Jeremiah limp into the lobby and then back out along the long row of rooms. She walked to her room thinking how it would be nice to soak in the tub, to watch HBO until she drifted off to sleep.

The next morning, Janice rubbed the sleep out of her eyes

as she called Jeremiah's room. He sounded blurry, still asleep. "You told me to wake you." The comforter was draped over her shoulders, too light. It had taken a long time to warm up, to sleep. She'd snapped awake at seven twenty nine, a minute before she'd promised to call Jeremiah.

"I'm not doing the interview." His voice sharpened with a snobbish twang.

"They're expecting to call you at eight. It's National Public Radio's Sunday Morning." Janice tried to clear the sleep out of her throat. Of the many appointments she'd made for this trip, she was proudest of this one because NPR commanded a national audience of thinking, creative people.

"Not doing it." Jeremiah had never turned her down.

"Why?"

"I have a sore throat and don't want to waste my time on liberals who will trip me up, especially since I didn't get a good night's sleep."

"What am I going to tell them?" Janice swung her feet over the bed and pulled the sheets around her. She pulled her feet up, so she sat cross-legged. Her nightgown rode up. "You'll figure it out," Jeremiah said, his voice fading.

Janice pushed down the hook switch for a couple seconds, then phoned the producer. "I'm sorry. He had a late night. It'll be a long day today." Janice closed her eyes to the crack of light coming in through her drapes. "I'm so sorry."

The phone rang again while she was in the shower, her hair soaped up. Janice shut the water off and picked up the phone. "How big an audience did you say they had?"

"National. What Congress listens to on their way to church." Janice dripped onto the carpet.

"My wife said I was a fool not to," Jeremiah sighed.

Janice told him to stay by his phone. She pulled a towel off the rack, wrapping it around her body. She pulled another one for her soapy hair. Janice called the producer back.

She turned on the radio as high as it would go, so she could hear over the shower, and stepped back in, pulling the faucet on and letting the water pour over her face and hair. When she stepped out and rubbed the damp towels along her body she heard a soothing voice introduce Jeremiah as an articulate voice coming out of the New Right.

Jeremiah sounded humble and respectful as he talked about how the general bookstores and secular media ignore work by Christians. He mentioned the titles of his books several times, and where they were available.

"We're listening." The interviewer sounded so smooth Janice thought of olive oil poured into boiling water.

"You're the exception, not the rule." Jeremiah conceded. As was *Publishers Weekly, Weekly News, The Today Show, The New York Times Book Review, The Washington Post* and all the other secular media outlets who had agreed to do stories.

Suddenly the phone rang with Janice one leg in and one leg out of her panty hose. She hopped over to pick it up. "Hello, this is Matthew."

"Yes." Janice couldn't keep the coolness out of her voice. She'd resented how he'd made her feel beholden to him because he bought a hundred and fifty grand worth of books.

"Jeremiah wants to meet with me." Matthew sounded too flat, too definite.

"He does?" Janice sat on the bed and reached the bunched up pantyhose to her toes, she slowly unfurled it along her leg.

"Today at one thirty." Matthew's voice faded like he'd put his hand over the mouth of the phone. Janice pressed her ear to the phone.

"Didn't you say you liked going through channels?" Janice stood up and pulled the control top over her belly and rear, unwinding it so it laid flat across her waist, and smoothed out her bottom. "He's booked solid." Janice pulled the dress her father bought her over her head.

"We need to talk today." Matthew emphasized the "to" in today.

"It won't work today. Tomorrow?" She closed the button, the waistband pinching.

"Tomorrow's too late."

"Do you have a number where we can reach you?"

But the phone clicked off. A thrill of fear shot through her when she heard the frightened tone in Jeremiah's voice. He sounded like he was about to go over the edge and say something outrageous. Not that it mattered, since she'd be quitting her job a few weeks after the tour, but Jeremiah could hurt Godspeed Press, and they were good people, putting out good books for the most part. One cuss word could result in thousands of returns.

"I'm at a loss for words," he said.

"If you've just tuned in, five abortion clinics were bombed this morning across the Southeast. We don't know if there are any casualties. We're interviewing Jeremiah Sackfield, whose book *An American Treatise* says not paying taxes and even the use of violence might be an option for dealing with this issue."

"Only as a last resort," Jeremiah said authoritatively. "We aren't even close to exhausting peaceful means for resolving this issue. Godly men and women picketing abortion clinics have already shut down a number of clinics."

"Do you feel responsible?"

"It's not my responsibility if people don't know how to read things in context."

She'd heard that before. Then who was responsible? Janice buttoned up the three buttons on her blouse and fumbled with the tie, because it was unseemly to listen to such terrible news partly dressed.

Maybe she should have called the FBI. Maybe if she had, this would not have happened. But Jim had said they were blowhards, nothing would come of it, and she'd believed him. She could barely breathe with the weight of it. She took out the Normans Kill water and poured it over her hands. She poured the bottle out, terrified with guilt, expecting a man in a black suit to knock on her door, wrap her hands around her back, cuffing them, all the while accusing her of not telling them there was a problem, when there was. Would they consider her an accomplice?

But it was all out there in the news. The FBI surely must read *Weekly News*. Jim had sent a warning. He'd made the call she'd been afraid to make, by writing the article.

The phone rang.

"Now is Jeremiah willing to talk to me?" Matthew Sparks' voice hit her like a fist.

Janice was silent.

"One thirty at the lobby of your hotel."

"We'll be there," Janice said, not sure if Jeremiah would agree to the meeting, since they were supposed to strategize about the New York demonstration after church. Her heart was beating so hard it felt like it was going to jump out of her chest. *Was Matthew somehow responsible for the clinic bombings? Would he be stupid enough to admit to it?*

An hour later, Janice sat in the pew with Dennis Manley listening to Jeremiah give his spiel about fighting abortion and the godless media. He said nothing about the bombings. People applauded when he was through. Then as a transition to the sermon, the congregation turned to the hymn, *I Love to Tell the Story*, the only hymn Janice remembered hearing her mother sing, a hymn she'd chosen for her funeral. The tears streamed down. Good thing Jeremiah was sitting up there on the podium because he would have leaned over and whispered in her ear, "Janice, I'm telling you, you need to knock off that Diet Coke." She smiled to herself as she looked at her mother's engagement ring on her right ring finger, where she could see her blurred reflection in a facet, the tiny prism she could flash at the pew in front of her, making a rainbow colored spot. She wanted her mother back. She wanted her integrity, where she didn't have to let people like Dennis think she was a true believer when she wondered if all their souls were in danger. Or was it just hers? And now her silence had blood on it. People had died in this morning's bombings.

If this was Christianity, she wasn't sure she wanted it. It seemed like all these men were trying to control God and everyone else. Dennis reached his arm behind her shoulder. He squeezed her close. He was trying to be kind, she knew that, but his arm felt like he'd swung rope after rope after rope around her arms and shoulders, and tied it tight, so she was like one of those women in the old movies just before the bad guy dropped her on the tracks to wait for the locomotive.

A woman sitting behind Janice tapped her with a tissue. Janice took it and wiped her eyes. Dennis leaned down and said, "Great stuff." Janice knew he thought she was crying because the preaching was so powerful. She hated it.

"I'm going to preach on the definition of true Christianity," the tall, skinny Harry Thewell said. His face was as pointy as the black Justins he wore. He looked like a man capable of whipping his daughter for not living his true definition of Christianity. He certainly was whipping up the congregation with his words. Janice didn't trust the demon look on his face. The words came out of his mouth, not his heart and he didn't speak with the authority born of words from the Lord, words that soothed and encouraged a broken spirit, but with shouts that clawed after authority like a runner clawing after a finish line tape.

"If any man among you seem to be religious, and bridleth not his tongue, but deceiveth his own heart, the man's religion is vain," he read from James in the King James.

Janice wiggled her mother's ring around to the front of her finger and closed her fist over it, so it bit into her flesh. "Religion that God our Father accepts as pure and faultless is this: to look after orphans and widows in their distress and to keep oneself from being polluted by the world," read the tall skinny Harry Thelwell with the demons on his face.

She looked up at the chandeliers in the sanctuary, sparkling like her mother's diamond. The church was so smooth with soothing light blue walls with cream trim. The seats were like theater seats and easy to sink into and listen to long sermons. Janice smelled the rotted mud smell of death and saw again the fine rib bones lying on top of the mud and leaves, the long narrow skull with pointed teeth and holes where the eyes and nose had been.

Dennis leaned over and said, "Excuse me. My wife's burritos playing havoc."

Jeremiah glared at Janice from the podium as she buried her nose in the tissue trying to make the laughter sound like coughing.

The preacher's voice shouted, "I remember when I was a boxer and was in the ring against an athlete that outclassed me. I swung at him, and he just stepped back. This went on for ten rounds. Then when my arms were too weak to defend myself, he hauled back, and I could see his swing coming, as if in slow motion."

Janice watched the man raise his arm and slowly swing it through the air.

"There was nothing I could do to stop it. Pow!" His voice echoed against the blue walls and cream trim.

"That's like some Christians who are exhausted keeping the faith against the assaults of the devil. They swing and swing until they can't swing anymore and get knocked down by sin. They're neutralized. They can't do anymore. They're no good to God."

Janice bowed her head and closed her eyes. She felt her mother's ring against the scab on her palm. "Pow! I should have called the FBI. Pow! If I had, maybe some people would be alive today. Pow! My mother died of cancer. My dad sounds so tired. My brother won't speak to me. Pow, pow, pow.

She heard Thelwell shout, "Repent of your sin. Don't be knocked down, useless to God. Get back to the winning side."

Janice didn't know being in the fight was a sin. Or that being wounded in the battle was her fault. That God judged her for her wounds, wounds hurting so much her eyes blurred with the pain. *Isn't that was Christ was for? Salvation not the judgement? Didn't he come "to seek and save that which was lost?"*

While Thewell's face fell to something more soft, beckoning people to come forward for extra prayers, or even a commitment to Christ. Janice flipped open her Bible to Matthew 18. "Children, don't keep them away from me," Christ had said. "If you cause one to stumble, it'd be better for a millstone to be wrapped around your neck." *The terrible responsibility. What happens if you're the child who is stumbling? What about the children of the people who died this morning?*

If this is Christianity, Lord forgive me, I don't want it.

She read on. "Don't look down on one of these little ones. Their angels in heaven face God." Janice bowed her head, eyes smeared with tears. *God send me an angel to lift me out of this desire to reject you, this nausea to puke what these men call 'things of the Lord' right out of my system. Send me an angel. One with marvelous wings, four pair, with hands underneath to hold me, an angel who shines because he faces God. Send me an angel to stand over and shield me from all this spiritual battle raging overhead. One with a flashing sword to slice the pinions reaching down for my shoulders.*

She read more of Jesus' words. "What do you think? If a man owns a hundred sheep and one of them wanders away, will he not leave the ninety-nine on the hills and go to look for the one that wandered off? And if he finds it, I tell you the truth, he is happier about that one sheep than about the ninety-nine that did not wander off. In the same way your Father in Heaven is not willing that any of these little ones should be lost."

Janice imagined herself still on the rock ledge. *Somewhere beyond the lip, a man was coming; she could hear the ropes and pitons clanking as he walked. He was calling her name.* "If your brother sins against you, go and tell him. If he hears you, you've got him back. If he doesn't get someone to go with you. Confront him then. What you forgive, you forgive. What you curse will be cursed."

Then a rush of rope hurled, snaking over the rock ledge. "Knot it around your waist," *the man whose voice sounded like a rifle shot across a creek, shouted. Jim? The man Jeremiah and Dennis hated?* "Keep coming up." *My God the view. Like the drive she took to Northwestern Illinois, where the land glowed from inside—luminescent greens and blues, the sky bubbling with white clouds that were about sunlight, not yet about rain. Like cultivated fields rolling up and rolling down, men's handiwork, working the land, making her yield food and beauty. Something about a garden that could put a woman's soul back into her body. She'd made the right decision. She was going home.*

"Keep coming," the voice said, quietly.

Janice imagined she stood up and grabbed the rope, the fibers burning her palm. She pulled it into herself. Of all people, it was her father, who rappelled down to her, and showed her how to wrap it and tie it to make a sling for her butt, to keep herself upright and balanced despite the pure, raw, terror she felt. Janice stepped over to the rock wall, began feeling for handholds, footholds. He said, "Here, put your foot here. Trust the tread on your boot." She lifted her foot as if she were mounting a horse, stretched out her fingertips to a tiny hold. She pulled herself up, the rope pulled along with her. "I didn't know you knew mountains," she said.

"Ski troops, 10th Mountain Division, same thing. I was well trained." Her dad as a young man, all power and force, exuding virility, a man who'd seen adventure. A hero. A warrior defending freedom and all that. And she'd never known. She'd only wanted to get away. He patted her cheek and grinned, her own frightened face reflecting in his mirrored sunglasses. "You'll find your way to the top."

Janice opened her eyes. She saw the diamond imprint on the meat of her palm from her mother's ring. The scab from Marcel's ring had begun bleeding. She gripped the tissue and pushed her mother's back to where it was supposed to be, showing the world its icy beauty, the commitment her father made to her mother, and that he made to her.

Dennis leaned over, "We've got to get out of here quickly if we're going to avoid the traffic in the parking lot. Buck will see Jeremiah back to the reception."

Janice stood up to hear Thelwell say, "Let's bow our heads and say a prayer. Every eye is closed. Lord thank you for bringing justice to those innocent babies being killed. Thank you for those lives that were saved. We ask that you rightly judge the souls of their murderers. Bless Jeremiah Sackfield's work calling us to value life at all costs."

* * * *

Janice couldn't even look at Matthew as they sat around the fake fireplace in the Hang 'Em Up Motor Lodge. Surprisingly the gas logs threw off a bit of heat. He had been waiting when they'd walked in from Jeremiah's sermon at the Hang 'Em Up Baptist Church, which irritated Janice because she had hoped for a moment to stop in her room and phone home.

Matthew's emotions darted across his face like cloud shadows across mountains. His washed out eyes were so lit up they were hard to look at. Her eyes darted off to the glowing gashes of fire in the logs. What she couldn't understand was how the Upright types were going to continue with the demonstration after the bombings. Sure they prayed for the victims during the service, but there was also a tone of glee in their voices as they remembered the babies who wouldn't die at those clinics. Jeremiah and Dennis weren't afraid of violence; they welcomed it.

"You didn't have anything to do with it did you?" Jeremiah cut to the chase.

"Why would you think that?" Matthew's face coalesced into horror.

"Because you blew portions of my book out of proportion when we last talked."

Matthew closed his eyes as though he were singing a favorite hymn. "God brought me up short when something happened in church last week. I swear revival was beginning. The Spirit was so present I could taste Him. Old enemies were saying they were sorry to each other." Matthew opened his eyes slowly and leaned back waiting for their reaction. "Reconciliation is the greatest miracle. The man who tried to put me out of business asked for my forgiveness. I asked for his."

Janice thought Matthew's eyes looked like they knew things.

"Then one of the members of my *American Treatise* book group started talking about how the only true Christians were the ones unequivocally against abortion." Matthew looked disgusted and disappointed, but also like he felt sorry he looked that way and was trying to look more pleasant, even trying to understand the person's side.

"That's right," Jeremiah said.

"Then it died. The apologies. The forgiveness. The Spirit left. I could feel the miracle fly out of there like air let out of a balloon. Do you know what it's like to see a miracle? I got to thinking we're doing this in the flesh, not in the Spirit. We're following our own way, not God's. And He can't bless it. I'm sorry I ever thought bombs might do the trick. Three people died this morning. For what? Not God's work." Tears welled up in Matthew's eyes.

"What about those groups you started?" Janice asked gently. "Did someone from there?"

"I pray not," Matthew interrupted. "When I leave here I'm going to visit each group, tell them my message, and hope to turn them around."

"Thank you for your concern," Jeremiah said, leaning back against his chair and locking his hands finger to finger. Janice saw the muscles under his shirt strain, but Matthew kept talking.

"The Lord laid it on my heart to come here." Matthew said.

Jeremiah released his hands and rubbed his palms on his khakis. "The Lord has blessed this work tremendously. Tomorrow I'll see Speaker Jim Wright. We're invited to a party at James Watts' place tomorrow night. Thanks to Janice I've appeared in major newspapers and on TV. What better proof of God's blessing do I need?"

It was Matthew who stood up, ending the conversation, leaving Jeremiah rocked back in his chair. "The Lord told me to tell you what I learned," he repeated quietly, jamming on his Atlanta Braves baseball cap.

"You know what they say when you start hearing the Lord's voice."

"Suit yourself," Matthew shrugged. He reached his hand out to Janice. It was warm, dry, firm in her grasp. "Thank you for setting this up," he said. "If you're ever in Georgia and need your clothes cleaned, look me up. Washing people's clothes is what God has called me to do." He stepped away before Janice or Jeremiah could respond.

"At least he bought some of my books," Jeremiah said.

"More than a few," Janice said, thinking as Matthew walked away with a straight back, that she'd just been sitting with a true man of God, who'd been willing to change directions, and admit he'd done so.

"That old pietism went out years ago. Christians need to be active in our culture, or we'll lose everything," Jeremiah said.

"But didn't Jesus say you can gain the world and lose your soul? Isn't the true work of God repentence," Janice paused searching for non-pietistic words, "Changing from violence to peace like Matthew?"

"Janice, Janice, Janice, if America goes down, then the Gospel will cease to exist. This country preaches God's Word all over the world, if we don't do it no one will."

Janice was about to say, "You've got to be kidding," but Jeremiah changed the subject asking what his bookings were for the next day.

"The *Today* show wants you to comment on this weekend first thing. Thelwell has offered to fly us to New York on his private jet, then on to Washington in time for your meetings on Capital Hill. I'm working on Nightline for tomorrow night."

"You see God can even turn bombings around, so something good comes from them." Jeremiah patted her hand.

"In other words, three people were killed and five buildings destroyed, so you could get some publicity."

"These are career making events. You should be pleased."

"I'm not."

"I like that I know where you stand."

"We have an hour before Dennis picks us up for the airport," Janice said as she walked up to the front desk to check her messages. The clerk handed her five pink slips saying to call Lucian, call home, call Lucian at their aunt's house. Janice swore so loudly that Jeremiah jumped. Her father had cut out on her and Lucian. That had to be what it was with all those messages.

Janice excused herself as quickly and politely as she could. Her knees felt like they'd give way if she didn't start walking to her room and the call that would pull the ground from under her feet.

* * * *

"I was just starting to feel good about life again," Janice muttered as she walked across the tarmac to the Lear Jet she would board along with Jeremiah and Dennis and Harry Thelwell, knowing she should be devastated. Instead she was furious. "Dad, why did you have to die now, just when I was starting to heal?"

She hated the interruption of death and the long work of grief that had been doubled by his death along with her mother's. The hope she'd felt at the prospect of moving out to the country and starting a new career was gone. She looked at the long nose of the jet, the wings that swept back gracefully. The arrogance of boarding one of these machines, the wheeling and dealing she'd done to arrange Jeremiah's appearances gone.

How could she even think these things? But if she didn't stay angry, she'd break apart. Not in front of these men. Please not in front of them. Tonight would be soon enough. Her body ached, like rain seeping through the leaky seams of window panes. An armed guard stepped to the side as they climbed aboard.

Dennis directed her to sit towards the front of the plane. "We want to meet privately back here," he nodded towards the back.

Janice sank into the soft leather and pushed her briefcase under the seat. Jeremiah touched her shoulder as he walked past. "You won't have me bugging you about sleeping your life away," he said with a soft smile.

"That's right." Janice looked out the window, listening to the engines whining. Then she saw her worst fear, black Suburbans driving across the tarmac, looking like vehicles from the pit of hell. *It's your fault the clinics were bombed. Tell them you want to talk to them. Tell them. You should go to prison. You put the books in the bomber's hands that day when you took the check from Matthew, that day when you did not call the FBI. You stopped short by talking to Jim, who patted you on the head and said they're just blowhards.* The engines quieted so still Janice thought everyone could hear her terror speaking.

"What's this all about?" Dennis whispered as he stood up and walked to the front of the cabin. Jeremiah followed him, sitting down next to Janice. "You let me do the talking," he said. "You're just the flak. You don't know anything. We never had lunch in Savannah."

It was like on TV. They flashed their badges, announcing "FBI" saying they had questions about the bombings. Signed copies of Jeremiah's book were found in backpacks left in front each building. They all wore suits and scared Janice. Grief and fear smashed each other like waves going in opposite directions. She felt herself rise up, but Jeremiah was right there, his strong arm around her shoulder. She reached for her bottle of Normans Kill water, but it was poured out. She'd packed it because it was empty. She'd washed her hands with it. Matthew's hands holding blasting caps. The side of a mountain shattered in smoke. Matthew saying he was going to set up cell groups centered around Jeremiah's book. At least it was Sunday.

"We have a flight plan to New York, an interview scheduled with the *Today* show. Her father died this morning. We need to get her home." Dennis nodded at Janice, who shoved herself against the window. She did not want to be used as an excuse to not talk to the Feds.

"Our condolences," the first suit said. He wore black pinstripes with a red tie. He was devastatingly handsome. He invited Jeremiah to a seat across the aisle.

A woman sat next to Janice, who wasn't dressed as rigidly as the men. She wore a khaki skirt and white blouse and reminded her of her aunt at her mother's funeral party or a very good therapist who could make a person feel at ease. "I'm sorry to hear about your loss."

"Thank you," Janice said, looking out the window at the wisps of clouds. Funny they moved opposite from how the wind was blowing. "I'm sorry about the trouble this morning," she murmured. Her eyes watered but she wasn't crying.

What can you tell me about the bombings? Did anyone you worked with say anything about this? That's what Janice would have asked, what she expected the woman to ask. But she didn't. She asked her about her father.

Janice felt grief sucking on her, drawing her into its belly like a wide, muddy current, the Normans Kill up and fat and sassy the weekend her mother had died, the loosened water shoving against the banks. Her clothes squeezed her thighs and belly. She felt like she'd leaned down against a tree and ticks crawled up her skin biting.

Janice closed her eyes against the woman's kind blue eyes, the woman who'd said her name was Becky. She waited, a presence as comforting as the ground might have been from ten thousand feet up. Janice tried not to think of Lucian coming out of the shower hot and clean, looking forward to church, only to find their father gone. She wondered what was it like for her brother to be in that house those minutes after Dad died and before Uncle Merle arrived?

Becky waited. She did not put her hand on Janice's hand. Janice rubbed the fabric of her dress—the dress her father bought her, his last gift. She'd not taken it off since she'd picked up the five messages saying call home, call your brother at Aunt Sarah's, call Lucian. She rubbed the sheer cloth like the curtains she pushed back when she watched for her father's lights top the first hill, a mile out their road, shining in the blur of snow, heading home, soon to be safe stamping his feet in their kitchen, holding boxes of cookies tied in string.

"My brother said, my dad died this morning...quietly, so quietly." Janice forced herself to breathe in, breathe out. Did her father hurt going from here to there? Had an angel taken his hand and pulled him out of his body? Or even their mother? Had she come back for her husband, taken him home to be with the

Lord? Would she feel their presence in the house?

"I just told my father I'd quit my job," Janice looked around at Jeremiah whose face was as dark as when he preached, but whose voice was very respectful, a gentle boy's voice. "My dad said he wasn't feeling well and that he was proud of me no matter what," Janice's voice trailed off. All the panic and all the sadness had emptied out of her. She felt like a husk, a carapace, utterly empty. Had her news broken his heart?

"I'm going to be an English teacher at a community college back in Northern Illinois."

"That's a far cry from this," Becky said quietly. Her face was filled out with wrinkles and a tan, like she'd worked the land, not a desk.

"I still have to promote writing." Janice made a mocking sound on the word 'promote.' "At least I believe in what I'm doing."

"You don't believe in this?" Becky looked at Jeremiah and Dennis, then around at the fancy jet, then back to Janice.

Janice knew she wasn't far from saying how all the talk of revolution had scared her, how Matthew held blasting caps in his hands, adding fire power to his threats. But Matthew had repented. He'd said he was one of Christ's own, a classic story of repentance, of turning one way, then turning another. Or had Matthew lied because of the bombs?

So Janice stayed with her grief story because it was easy to hide. "My father said I could just as easily teach at one of the colleges by him. That hadn't even crossed my mind." And here's the explanation. Right here. Here. Her father had acted like he had a crush on her. Should fathers have crushes on their daughters? Could someone love you too much? So their love weighed you down? So you chose not to come home when you could?

"You feel guilty for his death?" Becky stated kindly but flatly.

"I do," Janice said firmly, as though she were stating her marriage vows. But what about Lucian? Why hadn't he tried to revive him? He knew CPR like the back of his hand, even bragging about bringing back a drowning victim. Was Dad that far gone that Lucian couldn't try? He didn't say he tried. Wouldn't he have said he tried?

"Are you angry at Jeremiah for making it so you had to quit your job?"

"No. I'd rather teach."

"What is it about teaching you like better than this?"

"I'm not divided against myself." That popped out before Janice could say something smarmy and bland about making a difference helping kids.

"I would think this job would be perfect for a sincere young woman who loves God and who likes to travel."

"Have you read Jeremiah's book?"

"There hasn't been time."

"He urges people to care about unborn babies. I can't think of anything crazier than making a woman's womb the place of death. Anyone else can defend themselves or at least run but not a baby in the womb. He believes in peaceful protest. On the other hand, he doesn't say anything different than the founding fathers in the Declaration of Independence." Janice couldn't believe she was defending this side of the argument, but as rigid and obnoxious, as Jeremiah's followers could be, they had a point.

"And what does the Declaration say?"

"You know," Janice mumbled.

"You sound like you don't have trouble with what he says, so why do you feel the split?"

"I'm just telling you what's in his book. Is it a crime to write a book, to urge Christian people to act on what they believe? Nobody was trying to hide its contents. Everything is out in the open. You read the *Weekly News*?" Now Janice couldn't believe she was saying what Jim had told her. She was speaking for things she hadn't taken as true.

"I did catch the story. We want to see how Jeremiah is connected to these bombings. The copies were signed. When somebody tells someone to shoot someone, they're just as guilty as the shooter."

The hands. The blasting caps. Twisted pieces of wire and paper. Matthew bullying her. She could have called the FBI, but she called Jim at *Weekly News* instead. He'd said Matthew and Jeremiah were just blowhards. He'd said these guys couldn't effectively prod American indifference.

"We sell premium copies to groups around the country, including the Upright folks here. Jeremiah sometimes signs them before we send them off. It's not like he walked up to the bomber and said, you have to do this. People write about violence all the time."

"So why are you quitting your job?"

Janice sighed. She stayed with her story of grief. "I lost my parents this year. I need to be quiet."

"We're done here." The pin striped suit was standing, his face relaxed, almost jovial. "Thank you for your cooperation." He shook Jeremiah's hand. Janice could imagine the force of Jeremiah's handshake, showing even the FBI didn't frighten him, showing the force of his personality.

"I'll sign my books for you," Jeremiah said, digging for his pen. "Janice?"

Janice reached into her briefcase, past the empty bottle of Normans Kill water and pulled out the books. They were copies she'd hoped Jeremiah would sign for her brother.

Becky handed Janice her card. "If you think of anything, call. I hope you find some peace."

Nobody said anything until the jet had lifted off and was circling around the Blue Ridge Mountains, headed toward New York. There was a thin ribbon of chartreuse on the horizon and flecks of color on the cloud ceiling. Jeremiah sat next to Janice. "What did you tell them?"

"That my father died today. That I feel awful."

"Janice, I thought for sure you'd tell them all about our crab dinner and Matthew's show and tell."

She shook her head. "You didn't want me to."

"You let me take care of it. Good. Good. They'll be talking to Matthew about the blasting caps. I told them he was setting up study groups here in the south and that I signed a bunch of books for him. They won't need to talk to you now. And you won't need to lie."

Janice thanked him. "I didn't know you had it in you to betray The Cause."

"I can't lie to the Feds. It's not our fault this happened."

"But if I hadn't done my job so well, maybe the bomber wouldn't have read your book. Maybe he wouldn't have been inspired to hurt these people."

Jeremiah broke in. "You're not responsible for anything but doing a great job. From what I gathered, I would have been in more trouble if the book hadn't been publicized. It's public. If it had been a secret manifesto, then yes, maybe I'd be in trouble."

"I can't shake feeling guilty for the bombings, my father's death, the rain out there."

"Jeremiah, I'm leaving after the tour." She'd given two weeks' notice when she left for the tour, and Pete had begged her not to say anything until it was done. He'd offered her a thousand dollar bonus that she had been unable to refuse.

A smile came up around Jeremiah's eyes.

"Why didn't you say anything?"

"I was curious to see when and how you'd resign."

"Always testing people aren't you?"

"You picked as good a time as any with your dad going home to be with the Lord. I'll encourage Pete to triple that bonus if you come back for the demonstration."

"I'll think about it," Janice said hesitantly.

Janice was relieved she'd cleared the air with Jeremiah and a little put out when Dennis stood by their seats. "We're deplaning in a few minutes. I'll see that Jeremiah gets to the NBC studios. We're booked in the Plaza Hotel. The Albany airport is closed due to ice. You may be able to catch a late train or stay with us until the morning. We'll see that you get home." Dennis was peering into her eyes as if he were searching her soul, not unlike Becky.

"Thank you." Janice hoped there'd be a train out of New

York tonight because she wanted to step ahead of her grief until she made it to the safety and privacy of home. Janice leaned against the leather headrest and closed her eyes. She heard Dennis opening and closing compartments, heard, "Hmmmm." She opened her eyes to see him take out a snub nose revolver, crack the wheel to see it was fully loaded, then put it back.

"Whatever happened to trusting God for your safety?" Janice asked.

"Thelwell has a lot of enemies."

"After today, I think you need to worry about your friends more."

"Thelwell said Buck could take Jeremiah to Washington, Dallas, and L.A."

"That would help."

"Janice, it's time to deplane," Jeremiah said gently, clasping her shoulder with that grip that was stronger than he meant.

She stood up, tipped sideways between her seat and the seat in front of her. The smell of jet fuel, diesel and the grey New York skyline held no allure, no not any longer.

"I liked your father. He was a good man," Jeremiah said.

She looked at him in the eyes, how dark they were, and bright with answered desire, a desire she'd found a way to meet by doing her job. There was more to Jeremiah Sackfield than his rants and even his fixed up kitchen. Where would those deep currents of grace take him?

"I can manage without you. Go be a teacher." He clapped her hard on her arms so she felt it, the force of his intensity. "You're the best of the best my dear." Then he was off limping to pick up the bags the pilot had set beside the plane. There wasn't anything more to say as they climbed into the limo that would take them to New York and their separate ways. A fine drizzle smeared the windshield as Dennis struck up a conversation about evangelicals becoming a force to be reckoned with. "Some babies were saved today," he said.

CHAPTER SEVENTEEN

November, 1983. The Normans Kill Farm.

Back home, Janice was celebrated by King and Arthur, who curled around her, wagging their tails so fast their tails bruised her legs. She bent down and roughed their necks, looking into their bright intelligent eyes. "Someday you'll meet my boy, Joshua. He's bigger than you, dumber, but he's my friend, because you have to stay here. Janice missed Joshua, who made her apartment come alive, but she was glad he was with Betty, romping with his own family of berners. "Go play." Janice flung her hand out and the dogs jumped looking for where she'd thrown the stick, but all the sticks were buried in the snow.

Then she took a shovel and began digging into the snow from the same storm that caused the fog in Hang 'Em Up City. She hauled it away from the parking lot, so people could park when they came for the funeral party. She heard the wind high up, but not blowing any snow because rain had sealed it to the ground. It felt good to chop at the snow. She wanted to know what happened. She wanted to hear Lucian's voice.

"Odd weather," Janice said, not knowing how to talk to her brother. "It's early to start winter. Maybe we'll still get Indian summer."

"We already had it two weeks ago."

They fell silent. Janice didn't know what to say. She focused on using her shovel to cut the snow, then lifting it and carrying it away from the road.

"You know we're worth a half million," Lucian said suddenly. He added how shocked he'd been by how much The Farm was worth along with the insurance payments and bank accounts.

"I don't want to think about that," Janice said, suddenly feeling the weight of the responsibility of all that money, feeling the difference it would make in her life. It felt like greed, unseemly the day after her father had died. It meant she could walk away from Godspeed, right now, and easily afford to move, maybe even buy that farm house. She could even stay with Lucian until after Christmas.

They shoveled silently for a few minutes until Lucian looked at his sister, his eyes filled with admiration.

"What?" she asked. She was shocked because they'd not spoken since the fall.

"You're a genius."

"Me?" Janice stood up. "For what?" The small of her back felt like two fists had punched her, the muscles were so tight. She was still wearing the dress her father had bought her before she left for the tour.

"For things of the Lord." He explained how people have different intelligences and how he had always been good at putting things back together. "But you, my sister, are good at God." He leaned on the shovel, his cheeks and the tips of his ears red.

"You were always the smart one," Janice said. She looked at the crimson light along the horizon in the west, and then she swung around to look at the moon poking through the trees in the East, the same low moon her father had seen when he was alive, and the rare glitter of moonlight on iced up trees.

"Which is better, smart or wise?" He sounded desperate, which unsettled Janice.

"I don't know," Janice brushed aside his persistent compliment. "How are we going to manage?" she asked, leaning on the shovel, feeling the presence of the barns behind her, the foundation that needed shoring up in the one, the siding that needed painting on the other, the corncrib whose slats were dropping off one by one. Since Caleb lost his tractor, who would keep the fields separate from the woods? Since her parents died who would keep The Farm separate from their lives? Or would tending to it because it was theirs overtake them?

"We'll be fine." He turned to his shovel and dug at the snow.

She felt a little bored, asking Lucian the same question she'd asked when their mother was dying. He gave her the same answer, "We'll be fine." How could they be fine? Their parents were dead, laying grief on unhealed grief.

"What happened with Dad?" Janice began shoveling a path from the house to the road.

"I don't want to talk about it."

Even though his tone stung, Janice persisted. "But what happened?" Her ankles and calves and knees had stopped burning with the cold.

"Nothing really. When I got out of the shower, I heard something. Then he was gone." Lucian said each word like he was pounding a hammer. He heaved the snow and gravel to the bank, the gravel soiling the snow.

"Was it sacred?" Janice felt the cold air wheezing into her lungs and out, the sweat trickling down her back. "You know, like having a baby is sacred? Did you feel God's presence?"

"No I did not." Lucian scraped up a line of snow his shovel left and tossed it to the bank. "It was evil. He was here. Then he was gone. He turned white. He smelled bad."

Janice's calm welled up in the face of his anger and hurt. "Have you cried?"

"I had my time before Uncle Merle came."

"Awful." She wanted to hug her brother, but the way he was shoveling the snow said he wouldn't allow it.

"How about you? You cry?" Lucian's belly pushed against his snowmobile suit. His feet turned out. His cheeks were blotched and his eyes were wide. He looked like an angry, old child.

"As a matter of fact, no. Jeremiah was with me when I first heard the news. I swore a blue streak. But then the calm welled up pretty fast. Have you felt that? The calm? The odd knowledge that death is dead, you feel in your bones? That somehow time is doing funny things and that the Resurrection is happening now?"

Lucian continued to cut the snow with his shovel and then heave it out of the way.

"Lucian?"

"Sure. Sure, death is dead," he mumbled. He stabbed down in the snow. "Why don't you go on inside? Your legs look red."

Suddenly there was a wall between them. It was so wide that Janice felt that the kindest thing she could do was leave him be, even though she wasn't sure she wanted to be alone in the house where her father died. "You don't need me?"

"I'm fine," Lucian stabbed at the snow. His face looked so washed out then, like he'd just finished crying, like he was pleading with God for something. He nodded toward the house, each window glowing with light, all the way back to his bedroom. There was steam on the kitchen windows.

The warm air of the kitchen burned her legs and hands. Janice pulled off her mittens and stocking cap. Creamed chicken simmered in her mother's slow cooker. Janice saw a cookie sheet of biscuits waiting for the oven. The room smelled of pure comfort. How kind of Lucian. She noticed the dining room table was set with her mother's flow blue china, and the heavy pillar and thumbprint glasses. It must have cost him to prepare these memories.

Janice kicked off her walking shoes and shoved them against the radiator. She stood next to them, letting the heat find her toes and when it did, she opened the oven door and popped the biscuits in, the tin clattering on the wire rack. Janice wanted to pull off her nylons, and finally the dress she bought with her father, and put on her sweat suit, but she stood in the doorway, her hands on top of the radiator, her feet below. Her eyes watered as the sting returned to her fingers and toes. The rest of her body tensed in the chill of her damp clothes.

She pulled the boxes away from bags of frozen peas and corn and dropped them in boiling water. The creamed chicken was popping and bubbling. Janice stirred it, trying to calm the boil. The timer on the oven went off. Janice bundled up a dishtowel to pull out the golden biscuits.

The door scraped open and Lucian stamped his feet. "I don't like how the sky looks."

"They're calling for rain," Janice said, pouring the chicken into a flow blue tureen.

"Strange storm," Lucian said as Janice slid a spatula under the biscuits and dropped them into a wooden basket she had lined with a red checked cloth. Suddenly they heard the hard heavy drops of rain as they sat down to eat. The house felt good, like their father and mother were sitting with them, and there was delight like when they were children. It felt like a gift, this one last meal when they were together, if not in body, at least in spirit.

"Lucian do you feel our parents, with us, now?" Janice said as gently as she could because she wanted him to feel it too, the deep comfort knowing they were sitting there. "What do you mean?" He sounded irritated and sad and a little afraid.

"Like they're pleased to see us having supper together."

"No," he said slowly. "See that's what I mean about you being a genius for God. You sense the supernatural in ways the rest of us don't."

"If you say so." Janice dropped her eyes. He was telling her the best thing, but she felt weary, like anything anyone said about her and God was not true. She made too many mistakes with people. She was too self-centered. She'd left home when her parents needed her.

"Marcel and I made up," he said.

"That's good."

"She called when she heard about Dad. The horses are coming back when the roads clear."

"Good," Janice said over enthusiastically. She had made an

enemy out of Marcel; she was sure of it. And she was Lucian's love, Lucian Janice's only family. How would they ever reconcile?

"You never should have interfered," he said.

"You would have broken up without me." Janice's defensiveness flared up. "You always do."

"She was going to marry me as soon as we could have gotten blood tests."

"I know. I was there. But you did not want to hear it. You drove off."

"So it's my fault?"

"You didn't let her finish."

"All those things about not marrying into all this grief didn't change her mind?"

"If you were meant to be together, what I said wouldn't have made a difference."

"Don't you even think about interfering this time. Marcel and I have started talking again. I don't know where it will lead, but you stay out of it."

"I doubt she'll talk to me."

"She feels badly for both of us and our loss. She forgives you. I haven't."

"Now more than ever we need each other."

"You sound like Dad."

"Is that so bad?"

"I'm doing just fine."

Janice spooned more chicken onto her plate. Suddenly she was so hungry she wondered if she'd get enough to eat. "All right," Janice said. "All right." The food tasted salty and creamy and very, very good.

"Don't you have a job to go back to?"

Janice explained that she was done after this tour and that she'd start at Apple Valley Community College after Martin Luther King Day. "I was thinking about staying here from Thanksgiving until after Christmas."

Lucian picked up his plate and walked out. King and Arthur

trotted into the kitchen when they heard him set his plate on the floor. He walked past Janice mumbling how he was going to watch TV. The phone rang. Luican picked up. "Hello," he stated angrily. "Janice it's for you," then dropped the phone on the couch. Janice heard her own voice, more tired and distant than she cared to sound even after she heard it was Jeremiah and she asked how he was getting along.

"How are you doing?" Jeremiah said with that wild edge of concern for her that coated his own self-interest.

"I'm all right." Lucian had not forgiven her. He did not want her to stay through Christmas. "How did Nightline go?" Janice ran her finger through the dust on the table.

"I'm going on in an hour. I thought I'd find out if you have any suggestions from the *Today* show?"

Of course he hadn't done it yet. It had been like this when her mother died too. The timeless quality of the whole funeral routine, made her lose track of big, important details like his being on the *Today* show.

"I held my breath the whole time you were talking." Janice had caught the show at her aunt's house where everyone had gathered, saying they were proud of her, but they wondered why she'd keep working at a time like this. She honestly didn't know, except that her mother and father always told her to finish what she started. It was the last thing her father said. Shouldn't you honor your dying mother's wishes?

"That's a new one. I can read the headline now, Christian Author's Publicist Dies from Holding her Breath."

"You were about to cuss somebody out," Janice said. "You have this certain tone that slips into your voice. The next thing I know, a string of invectives flies out of your mouth, but you held off."

"You know me, don't you?"

"Yes I do."

"I'll miss having you around," Jeremiah said.

"You can always call," Janice said. "I'll tell you the same thing I always say. Then you'll be bored. You're next publicist may do an even better job."

"I doubt that. Are you all right? You don't sound good."

Janice didn't know what to say. Ice started ticking against the windows. Jeremiah sucked in a deep breath like he was smoking, even though he wasn't a smoker, and said very gently, in fact his tone was so gentle, Janice wanted to cry. "Thank you for all you've done for me and my family. By rights you shouldn't even be talking to me at a time like this. You are one courageous woman. Well, I need to get over to ABC. Any tips?"

"Stay cool and stay charming."

"Thank you Janice. I'll pray for you in the difficult days ahead. You are coming back for the demonstration aren't you?"

"I plan to."

Every so often the house creaked in the wind. She went out to the kitchen to shut off the lights and clean up their dishes. She stared at her reflection in the window. Behind it, down an icy hill were the flat and the Normans Kill. But all she saw was darkness. She wondered what the river was like on a night like this. Was the water moving or covered over with ice or a little of both? Did the trees clatter in the wind and ice? Were the night creatures out despite the weather or was everyone hunkered down? She'd never walked that way at night. She'd always followed the road or the woods nearby on the headlands. She'd never walked the flat, no not at night. Though once she'd taken Whisper down there in a moonlight bright as day. But the horse kept her safe, even at a gallop. To go alone, to go down, at night, with a river on three sides, no she wasn't that brave or spiritual to imagine they were just fields and woods and river and not a dark wood and cold river that would accept her crossing, but never let her come home. She watched Nightline instead.

CHAPTER EIGHTEEN

Janice's car skidded as she drove the short cut over to Caleb's farm. She crossed the Normans Kill with blocks of ice washed up on the banks, the river itself smaller and greener than she remembered.

Janice was relieved Caleb's truck was parked by the Butler building, not his house because they could talk without his mother listening. The corn dryer was roaring, and corn inside rattled like a powerful waterfall.

She opened the door and saw no one was there, just the breasts and smooth thighs of the topless woman dressed in a thong lying on a beach. Next to her was a calendar with an International Harvester tractor plowing a field. She opened the door to the machine shed and saw him bent over his big farm truck, the hood up. She walked past the 7700 John Deere combine towering over her, as big as a house, the nose cones like dunce's caps. She walked past a big John Deere tractor, bright bilious green. There were hardly any mud stains on the tire treads. Good for Caleb. He figured something out. All that worry for him, needless.

Caleb pulled his cap off, and wiped his brow, a big smile on his face. He was dressed in dark blue coveralls that brought out the blue in his eyes. His dark golden hair stuck out from the sides of his new John Deere cap.

"I didn't think I'd see you today." He wiped his hands on his greasy rag.

"I couldn't stay away." Janice walked toward that smile, though she'd forgotten how deep the creases on his face were around his lips and eyes.

As he wrapped his arms around her, she smelled the roasted corn smell. If there was a time for Janice to cry, now was the moment. Her idea of heaven had been to be wrapped in a man's arms, only to have him dry her tears. But now she was quiet.

"He looked so lonely at your mother's funeral," Caleb said kindly. "Losing a mate's a bad thing. My mother never got over losing my father. Love and marriage aren't worth that kind of pain."

"You may be right." Janice looked down at her shoes. Her dress felt thin under her coat.

"I didn't know he had been sick."

"Neither did we," Janice said, even though she'd heard the apathy in her father's voice just a few days ago but she'd been on top of the world, she hadn't checked further.

"He was such a kind man. You take after him." Caleb looked down at her, his eyes blue like the Helderbergs on a clear day.

"I should have taken care of him, but he wanted me to stay at my job and tell my stories."

"And so close to losing your mother." Caleb's eyes searched her for what seemed hours. Then he kissed her. She could feel the chapped strings of skin on his lips. "Somebody taught you to kiss," he said, his voice hoarse.

"I think it comes naturally," Janice murmured. His lips felt good on hers, quieting the words and questions that wanted to fly out of her mouth.

He swept his hand underneath her coat, up her back. She felt his calluses ease an itch she didn't know she had. Their coolness pressed her closer to his chest. For years she'd waited for this moment, for this floating, her knees weak, her belly warming and swelling at the touch of his lips.

Caleb drew his other hand along her chin, cupping it firmly, so she could feel his control, his barely contained passion. "Come sit on my lap," he whispered, taking her hand, which felt so warm and hard and so in control as he lead her past the 7700 and his shiny John Deere tractor.

"Your tractor?" Janice pointed at the shiny new machine.

"We sold off fifty acres. There will be houses here next spring."

"Oh Caleb. I'm sorry."

"We still have three hundred running down to the Normans Kill. And I can keep my job."

"Your hay? Did you ever get your hay in?"

"The flatbed driver took his time getting here."

"Sometimes good comes of it." Janice smiled up at him, feeling the same kind of hope she'd felt a few short days ago.

"We could go to a motel." He looked into her eyes with a kindness she'd never seen before. Then he opened the door to his office. The rain stapled the roof, one of Janice's favorite sounds, the sound of water on the move, whether in a river or shoved out of the sky.

"The roads are terrible. We'd be stuck once we got there."

"I could think of worse things," Caleb said as he plugged in the heater, the coils turning orange then deep red. He unzipped his overalls and peeled them one arm at a time, one leg at a time off his body, kicking the pants legs away from his shoes. The crease in his Levis looked so defined she thought they might cut her hands. He wore a grey SUNY Albany sweatshirt, with a maroon flannel shirt underneath. He unfolded a blanket that was on the back of the couch. "Come," he said as he sat down, taking her hand and pulling her towards him.

Janice settled down slowly, so she rested across his legs and her heels dug into the cushions. The heater had already eased the chill in the room. "Hold me." She didn't like how she pleaded because he'd run from her neediness, he'd always had, but she didn't care if he ran. She needed those arms around her, right now, right today.

She thought of a tree and leaned into his chest and lifted her face to his. He kissed her gently on the cheek. His lips felt like a gentler rain than the one outside, tapping the leaves. When they touched her lips, she touched the tip of his tongue. He touched hers. He traced the outline of her lips. She traced his. As they breathed each other's air, she thought of the rotted rich smell of woods in early spring.

"Such a woman," he groaned and sighed, a deep sigh that blew into her grief and calmed it. "Don't be nervous," he said as he settled her back on the couch and leaned down to kiss her. She watched the top of his head, hair that had been creased by his hat, and thought of the woman with the perfect breasts leaning in the sand above them. Janice felt his beard scratching and ran her hands along his shoulders and back like she'd seen actresses do in movies.

"Why haven't we done this before?" Janice whispered.

"I didn't want to hurt you." Gently he settled her on the couch.

"You didn't think standing me up would hurt?"

"Not as much as making love. Not as much as your leaving after we'd been close." He spoke hesitantly, like the words were very hard to pronounce, like he was a child just learning to speak.

"What if I fall back in love with you?"

"What if I fall in love with you?"

"You won't."

"I might." Caleb looked so open, Janice thought maybe he already had.

"Please don't."

"That doesn't sound like the Janice I know."

"I don't live here."

"You could."

"No I can't."

"Of course you can," he whispered.

"No, not now." Janice looked at the orange coils of the heater. "I've taken a new job. Out there. I've put a deposit on a new place."

Caleb sat next to her, holding her hand, "You just buried your father. It's not fair of me to take advantage."

Janice touched his lips with her finger. "Yes it is." She ran her hands under his shirt. *"Sometimes a woman needs comfort and nothing but this will do."* Sometimes a woman needs to shake her fist at God, at every understanding she ever had of Him, the rigid, we'll-make-America-right,-we'll-step-into-everyone's-bedroom,-way to God Jeremiah and the Downright types preached. The preachers used to hammer at sex: If you have sex before marriage you are committing the worst sin. *All right, that's what I'll do*, Janice thought. Besides she was flying out of her skin. She needed Caleb, a man she'd loved for years to hold her deep in her grief that was still stove up and numb.

Caleb pulled off his shirts and long underwear. His stomach rippled like the Normans Kill over its shallow bed. He closed his eyes and kissed her lips gently, his fingers playing her like he'd play a guitar. He guided her hand to the button of his jeans, the zipper. Janice's fingers trembled. She looked away, suddenly shy. Janice became aware of the heater ticking, the cold air being pushed back gently, the smell of bread rising. As Caleb took her hand, she could feel his calluses.

She felt the gritty cushions against her back, smelled the heater's burned smell as it glowed redder. She never thought she'd lose her virginity here in Caleb's machine shed, the huge machines waiting on the other side of the wall when it was the big machines that made her fall in love in the first place.

He leaned forward and kissed her. Janice's heart began racing. She did not want to become pregnant, not now, not with so much grief. But his warmth, his skin against her skin felt so kind, so gentle, it was as if he was showing her where she began and ended.

She began here along her ribs and thighs and knees. Here where his warmth felt good as warmth, as a man touching her center, her deepest sadness and being there with her, bringing quiet and calm she hadn't known in that place. Here where his lips touched hers, where his lips stilled her questions and words. Here where his eyelashes brushed her eyelashes. Here was where she was, lying on this gritty couch, being touched by a god of the earth. But he wasn't a god of the earth. He was a man, a plain man with a tiny piece of snot clinging to a nose hair.

Janice ran her finger along Caleb's cheekbone, down across his lips. Just being covered by him, the length of his warmth, his living skin against hers, toe to toe, calf to calf, his body like the beam she crawled under, the beam that held up the corner of the big barn. The comfort of him. The peace she felt had to count for something good even if he'd not even been able to come inside. Not like Jesus who'd entered her heart when she was a little girl. It was like the psalmist was right, God had put truth in her innermost parts, and they had said no even though she had said yes, let's make love, all the way, let's love. But no, her body was wiser than her. No, there's too much grief, her father in that box at the front of the church. It was too soon for the happiness of bodies meeting.

Caleb pulled her up so she was sitting next to him, and handed her the blanket that had fallen on the floor, tucking it around her.

"With all your heart I think you wanted to make love to me," he said.

"I did," Janice dropped her eyes. He'd brought her quiet, calm, not passion, but she was sorry. "Thank you for putting me back inside my skin, for comforting me."

He pulled her into his arms and nestled her under his shoulder. His eyes looked so open and sad, Janice remembered her mother saying, "Don't be using him." She'd had no clue what she meant until now. She had used Caleb, to shake her fist at God, without caring about his feelings even though all these years he'd held himself back from using her, when he knew there was no future. His standing her up, when they'd come so close had been a mercy.

"That's what friends are for. I know how hard it must be to lose both of them." He kissed the top of her head. He slipped his pants on quickly, and grabbed his shirts, sliding them over his chest. "It's a bit brisk I'd say," he said smiling.

Janice pulled on her underwear and nylons, feeling more naked than when he was touching her because dressing seemed like an intimacy reserved for people with a commitment. Suddenly he pulled her against his chest. "You're a good, good woman. Don't ever forget that," he whispered. His eyes were as blue as the Helderbergs on a steel gray day when a front has moved in and it's fall, and the clouds hang low and dry and curled back like a plowed field. His eyes were kind and full of a smile. "Maybe I'll catch that plane in a week or so," he whispered. "I'll take you to one of those fancy Chicago hotels, and we'll do this up right, the way you deserve."

"I won't be living by Chicago." Janice turned away from a vulnerability that frightened her, signaling for Caleb to zip her dress. She was used to being the one too much in love, her feelings flashing around like a garden hose with the water turned on and no one holding it. But now she felt quiet and calm and grateful to this man who'd held her all the way down to her deepest, most private place. "I found a new job teaching in a junior college." Janice felt how his fingers were clumsy on such a small, woman's thing as she listened to the zipper ride up to her neck. "I'm renting a house on a big Illinois grain farm about twenty miles from the Mississippi."

"You'll have some real farmers to chase." Caleb joked.

"You're a real farmer." Janice put her arms on Caleb's arms, feeling the round muscles of his biceps, feeling like she had to reassure him when she felt pity. But he was right, she would be chasing the real deal. And what had she been thinking, jumping into his arms, when there was Fred, who'd shown her an owl in his barn, which was no big deal, but it was something intimate and private and just between them. Caleb was right about her chasing them.

The phone rang. "Yes Mother. It's Janice. I will tell her. I will be right up." He threw the phone on the cradle.

"My mother sends her condolences. She wants me up to the

house for dinner. And you should go before the salt stops work-ing on the roads."

Janice wrapped her coat around her and let Caleb take her by the elbow and lead her to her car. She stepped between the ice patches, feeling her foot slide when she stepped on water, but Caleb held onto her.

* * * *

Janice drove down the low spot in front of his sheds, speed-ing up a little, so the speed would carry her up the hill, past her tires skidding on the ice, water spraying out. The wind had shifted, roaring up from the south. She signaled to turn onto the main road, and looked over her shoulder at Caleb standing.

Back home, barns and the house were too quiet. The floor-boards cracked under her feet and then cracked where she wasn't walking. The house smelled old and damp, and it felt like the life had gone out of it. Where her father used to sit, Janice saw how the fabric was worn on the arms of the loveseat and the back where his shoulders rubbed. King and Arthur curled around her legs, wagging their tails, asking to be let out.

Janice changed her clothes and walked back outside, the dogs skidding over the thick crust on the snow until they cir-cled behind her. She punched through the crust into the soft snow underneath, breaking a trail for all of them. The air had changed, she couldn't see her breath, and she began to sweat. She cut across the field to the backside of the pond where the drainpipe stuck out of the side of the embankment. She grabbed onto a Scotch pine branch to slide down into the gully that began there and widened to a full, flat swampy valley that crossed the neighbor's barbed wire fence into their cow pasture.

When she was a girl she used to hide under these pines and think she was safe from enemy eyes, if one should fly overhead. The pine needles felt smooth and thick and solid under her mit-ten. Arthur's nose butted up against her calf. She stomped down to the edge of the tiny gully carved by the drain. The ribs on the pipe reminded Janice of a peppermint because of how they alternated with the low parts that looked like twirling valleys. A hollow icicle connected the pipe to the ditch. She could hear water trickling through the ice.

Janice pulled the bottom of her parka underneath her and sat. She felt her mother's ring pulling on her brother's fat ski glove and way underneath she felt the soreness from Caleb's trying. But she also felt a calm pushing away the nothingness like clear skies pushing away the back line of a squall. The preachers never said anything about the power of skin on skin, how two people could touch each other and feel deeply healed. A loneliness Janice had felt since she was a baby, that drove her to cry in the woods for someone to hold her, to wrap her up in their arms and hold her tight, like Jesus wiping away her tears, was healed. That loneliness was gone, kaput, done with, filled in. Oh it was more filled in than the pond, on the other side of the goldenrod and burdocks and hay sticking into the sky, that was filled in with silt and water and ice.

And the preachers said once a man's passion wound up, it couldn't stop. But Caleb, as full of desire as anyone, had rolled off her when it didn't work, when she couldn't, when her innermost parts, with their own wisdom, said, "No not today, our Janice is too full of grief to open and let you in." He'd been nothing but kind and gentle and tender with her inexperience.

The preachers had lied about the guilt she would feel from having sex; they lied about how this was the worst sin. *"You've done it. You've used Caleb to comfort you. You can come back now. I've called you to be Janice, not Lucian. Not Jeremiah. Janice. Even so, come,"* a quiet voice, not quite her own, said.

When she thought this way Janice never knew whose voice it was. It sounded like God, but who was she to hear God speaking in her mind? At the very least the voice came from her wiser self, her kinder self, the self schooled in the Bible stories that talked about how God was a friend, and schooled by her father because he was the one who bandaged her knees and said if you stumble, just get right up and keep walking.

Her vision of glory was shattered. She no longer saw how the light fell on him, the kind of golden light that slants across the fields as the sun drops to the horizon. Caleb had become a man with a sweet bread smell, and snot on his nose hairs. Janice had used that light to find her way, but it had gone out. Making love to him, flesh to flesh, as powerful as it was to deeply comfort her and put her back in her skin, had blown out the light, but she wasn't in darkness, no it wasn't a day dying, but rather a day rising. The gold and amber faded to green and brown.

The voice repeated, *You can come back now. Even. So. Come.* Melted snow had seeped through her parka and into her jeans. Her bottom was cold, which felt good to the soreness she felt there. King and Arthur trotted down to the gulley to lap up water between the ice column and ice covering the stream. Janice brushed herself off and slid all the way down and stomped on the ice. How good it felt to make it break, her feet dry in her boots, but still feeling the pull of the water. She filled up the bottle with water from the heart of The Farm, the pond. She heard the wash of a truck and trailer passing the pond. Lucian and Marcel were back home with the horses. It was time to walk to the house, help them unload them, just to be around horses again.

CHAPTER NINETEEN

Lucian and Marcel had become a couple again, the gravel-sized diamond appearing on Marcel's finger. The sweetness and the intimacy between them was hard for Janice to watch. Marcel had thanked Janice for her help finding a place for herself and her horses and seemed grateful for these months to grow up and be on her own. Janice had been dumbfounded that Marcel had truly forgiven her and that her brother was, again, engaged.

The next day, Janice stood in Lucian's doorway while he was dressing. She could leave this evening or early tomorrow morning to meet Jeremiah in time for the demonstration. He'd called nearly every day saying how well the interviews went, telling her how brilliant she was, and how books were flying off the shelves.

Lucian grabbed his jeans and stepped into them. With Marcel marrying him a little more than a month away, Janice wanted to know, "What will we do with The Farm?"

"We'll *both* have to keep it. I can't afford to buy you out." Lucian's eyes were wide and angry, his furious cat look.

"You live here rent free," Janice exclaimed. "You make more money than I will in my new job."

"I've spent thousands fixing this place, supporting our parents. Dad would have left the whole thing to me, if there'd been time." Lucian zipped and snapped shut his jeans.

"But he didn't," Janice whispered. "I own half. You own half. When are we going to settle up?" Almost, her mother's last words to her were: *Watch Lucian. He thinks he has certain rights. He's lived here all this time.* The drawn look on her face when she said it.

"There's nothing to settle."

"Yes there is. I want my half of the furniture, the land, the house."

"You got your half of the furniture after Mother died."

"No. That was different, separate from this, and not half by a long shot." Janice pronounced each word, so he would understand what she was saying.

"My sister the saint has turned greedy."

"I'm not interested in what's rightfully yours," she said calmly, his language not fazing her.

"Why now, so soon after his funeral?"

"You brought up how much we were worth the moment I arrived. You sounded ready to talk. We should do this before Marcel becomes your wife."

"Dad died in front of my eyes, Janice. No matter how peacefully he died, it was a terrible thing to behold." He squeezed his eyes shut, shaking his head. "I don't want to think about it."

"Why didn't you do CPR?" Janice blurted. She hadn't meant to say this. No, she had not.

"I couldn't," Lucian whispered.

"So you let him die." Janice's voice sounded harsher than she meant.

"He didn't die alone."

"But you could have tried to save him." How desolate her father must have felt seeing his son standing by and not even calling an ambulance until he was gone.

"For what, Janice? What would I have saved him for? Being alone without the woman he loved over half his life? Rattling around this house with no one to talk to?"

"And that gives you more right to The Farm than me?"

"Where were you when my mother was diagnosed? Or when

she went for radiation treatments, or came home puking her guts out? Playing publicity girl in Chicago. That's where you were."

"I would have come home in a flash, but Mother and Father told me to stay put."

"Where were you when my mother died? You were in New York playing at the *Today* show. And when my dad died, you were jet-setting around the country."

"They said they were proud of me."

"If it was up to you, they would have died alone."

"But you didn't help Dad," Janice whispered.

"You called saying you quit your job. The one thing Dad cared about was how you were doing in that job. No you couldn't move back home. You had to move further west. You broke his heart."

"He said he was proud of me," Janice repeated, the ground dropping out from under her feet.

"You weren't here when he was sobbing his eyes out. Then he was dead."

"Lucian, you were here with him. You could have tried to save him, but you didn't. The Bible says, 'Thou shalt not kill' and you killed him by not helping, not even calling an ambulance."

"How can you say I let our father die, when your self-centeredness did him in?" Lucian shouted.

"How? I wasn't even here." Janice's terror was pounding in her ears.

"You broke his heart Janice, by not coming home. That's how."

"Mother said to watch out for you." Let him feel what she was feeling, betrayed by her parents because they didn't tell her the truth.

"What do you mean?"

"She said you'd say I'd have no right. I do have a right. Just as much as you," Janice hissed.

Lucian jammed his hands in his pockets and clawed his own thighs.

"We need to decide," she said quietly. "Why not now?"

"Not now," Lucian shouted, his hands wildly snapping out of his pockets, about to reach for Janice. Instead he ran through the house, the creaks and groans of the wood underfoot, like the house crying out in pain. He slammed the living room door so hard, it sounded like a banjo with a string popped, a crack splitting one of the windows.

Janice followed as Lucian ran to the barn and grabbed his father's ax. Outside the moon was setting over the Helderbergs, a pale furnace door, glowing with a steady white glow, like she'd seen when her father opened the oil burner's door and showed her the fire.

He slammed the ax against the flesh of the mountain ash, the tree planted in her honor when she was born. The tree she had leaned on right after her mother died. Her tree. The gray bark chipped away. A glancing blow. He slammed it against the tree again, the grey bark chipped off.

"Lucian what are you doing?" Janice screamed. The dogs were barking, diving at him, then backing away.

"Cutting down this tree."

He slammed the ax again, the sound of the steel thocking and echoing against the wood. He pulled it out, the ax head behind his head, behind his shoulders, pulling him back and down to the ground. He pulled it forward out of the air, his muscles straining and slammed it against the pale meat of the tree, the mouth opening wider and wider into a scream only a tree could make.

"Lucian don't," Janice screamed, grabbing his arm to stop him. Only he turned at her, yanking his arm out of her grip and hauling the ax over his shoulder, threatening her. The dogs tugged at his pants cuff. Lucian swung at them, but Janice grabbed their tails, yanking them away, so Lucian hurled the ax back at the tree like that had been his intent all along.

"Come. Come," she screamed with all kinds of terror in her voice.

And the border collies turned on her, their teeth bared.

"King. Arthur. No." She dropped their tails and ran towards the house, the dogs nipping her heels. Out of the corner of her eyes, she saw him yank the ax out of the tree and step to the other side to open another mouth, so the tree fell.

The house echoed as she ran through it to gather her things, so she could leave—for good. She glanced at the couch where her father died, saw the grease spot where his head rested. And wondered at the pain he must have felt when his son stood by while he was dying. The loneliness cut a hole in her. She stuffed her clothes in her garment bag and threw her Bible in her briefcase. She looked at the desk and shelves her parents lovingly made for her when she was ten. The dogs were chasing each other, their mouths open, playing, vying for dominance. She could not leave them here. They had been their mother's dogs. They were not safe with him. She crammed their dog food bag under her arm and stuffed their bowls in her briefcase. She would buy water on the road.

Janice stopped when she saw Lucian twisting the knob on the propane lighter. Blue and orange flame, blue by the nozzle whooshed out. He set it to the dried leaves, the fire exploding back toward the stump, her mountain ash, now lying on its side. He couldn't just chop down her tree, he had to burn it, an effigy of her.

* * * *

It was almost beautiful how the fire and smoke rolled through the crown, catching leaves and branches, making them more themselves than when they were just plain leaves and branches. Burning leaves and sparks flooded the sky. Smoke filled her nose, stinging her lungs. Her ears ached with the crackle. Moses was lucky God spoke from the burning bush, saying this is my name; I want you to lead my children from bondage into freedom. She strained to hear His voice but heard no words.

Then she felt the fire burning along her legs and arms, curling along her fingers. It swept up her mouth and face and eyes.

"He is like a refiner's fire, and like fuller's soap," the Bible had said. Janice felt it scrubbing her legs and arms and head, scraping through the flesh into the muscle, down to her bones. The sun poured along her skin, corded through her muscles, sparked along her bones.

She was burning, and blessing that, the blessed thought when her darkness would be turned to light, her selfishness—wood, hay, stubble—turned into heat and light, leaving her clean as a newborn who'd never been left by her family. The ropes tying her to The Farm glowed with red hot filaments like the tobacco in her mother's cigarettes and then charred, falling away.

She took one last look at Lucian's face so blotched and furious. "I wish you'd never been born," he screamed.

"No, Lucian. I am glad I was born," she shouted. "God willed that I be your sister. We had no choice in the matter." But she could not stand. Lucian started towards her, the ax hauled back over his shoulder. The dogs dove to her ankles nipping, their teeth more flames along her Achilles tendon. They whirled around, barking and snapping at Lucian.

"King. Arthur. Come." She threw open the back door of the car. Threw the bags in. King jumped up front. Arthur jumped in back. Arthur barked and snapped at Lucian out the back window.

The car sprayed gravel as it spun out of the driveway, leaving Lucian shouting. Janice did not look back. Her throat tightened, battened down like there were two thumbs pressing her windpipe. It was just like in the Bible. Jacob hated Esau, stealing his birthright and inheritance. Somehow that theft was God's will. How could a person fight God? But after eighty years and wrestling with an angel—Jacob crossed the river and saw God in his brother's face. Was she seeing God in Lucian's face? When Jacob's hip was thrown out of joint, was it fire touching his thigh?

In the rearview mirror she saw the gas can pop like a depth charge and land in the woodshed... "Lucian, you are on your own," she said as she kept driving. The black smoke billowed between the house and the barns.

Oh my God! Marcel's horses were still in the barn, Janice thought, immediately making a U-turn and heading back toward the house.

By the time she reached the house the fire from the burning mountain ash had leapt onto the little barn, which was now smoldering. Janice dashed into the house to call 911.

"The Farm," she panted, "is burning."

"What's your address?" The dispatcher sounded bored, like this happened all the time.

"The Westfahl place. Off Font Grove."

Janice heard roaring. "Please don't burn," she said to the house.

Why don't you come home to stay? She heard the house's voice running along the beams holding up the floor. *You and Lucian could make a life. You could be family to each other, without me dividing you.* The voice eased into her feet, curled along her ankles, slithered towards her heart. It was an evil feeling, the need to pour every resource into owning and keeping up The Farm, especially when it was too much.

She heard Lucian's steps on the roof, and saw the water pouring down the windows. Each branch of the mountain ash glowed. The pump house kicked on. Roaring filled her ears.

As she ran outside, she saw flames licking around the roof of the Little Barn. Marcel's horses screamed and banged.

"Janice don't!" Lucian screamed, but she could not stand the thought of Marcel's beautiful horses burned up, or Marcel's inconsolable grief. She felt the cool shade of the front part of the barn, as she ran past his motorcycle, and Old Town canoe, and the tractor with the brush hog. She shoved open the big sliding door, the wide pine planks that would soon light up. Arthur and King pushed past her knees, buckling them. She slammed open Martha's stall door and then Johnny's. The fire overhead sounded like children running back and forth upstairs. Smoke poured out of the door leading up to the loft. Janice grabbed a rag and held it to her mouth, smelling camphor and Vaseline.

Martha and Johnny's legs were locked. Both were vibrating

against the back of their stalls, their heads facing the corner, their tails pressed against their buttocks. The roar was almost deafening, but thank God, the wind was sucking the smoke upward and away from the barn. Sparks cascaded down on the Big Barn.

"Shhhhh. Get em. Get em. Get em. Shhhhh," she hissed at the dogs. And King and Arthur barreled into the stall, savaging Martha's fetlocks and hocks, until they were more terrifying than the fire. The ceiling began smoldering. The dogs drove them hard into the pasture. Janice grabbed Martha's halter and lead, brushing a burning straw off her shoulder and ran after them. She closed the gate, so they would not run back. The dogs barking, the pounding of the hooves as the horses galloped was all she could hear. They sounded like her breathing.

She felt the heat of the barn fully engulfed, and ducked as a belly of flame hurled into the sky. She ran hard after the horses, her footsteps melded into the sound of their hooves. The cuffs of her jeans chapped her ankles, and her legs felt heavy as she ran into the pasture. She felt the terrible heat pouring off the barn, smelled the wood, hay and Lucian's toys burning up. The horses were circling the old apple tree, foam sliding between the inside of their legs. "That'll do," she panted when she ran up, her feet soaked by the snow. The dogs trotted to her, their eyes bright and tails wagging. They danced on their front feet, asking to work again. "That'll do," Janice repeated. They shook their heads and backed up, lying down, watching her. The horses stood, their nostrils red, their sides heaving. Then they dropped their heads to nuzzle the snow and graze.

Janice could barely hear. The sirens of the fire engines. Hurtling in the road, a whole parade. Along with state troopers, county sheriffs, neighbors. Janice leaned down her hands against her thighs, her legs shaking.

How would Lucian explain the burning tree? Small flames scampered along the ridge of the Big Barn as fire outlined each timber of the Little Barn. "Get back, it's going to go." It was a familiar voice sounding the warning. It was Caleb, one of the first volunteer fire fighters to arrive at the scene.

And she watched, the roof of the Little Barn caved in, the timbers breaking and cracking, not unlike the sound of trees groaning in the wind, or logs settling. A rooster tail of water shot over the house, drenching it. Lucian had saved it, wetting down the roof until the firemen arrived.

Flickering red lights of the emergency vehicles now filled the yard. A hook-and-ladder truck pulled up to the Big Barn and began raising the ladder so the firemen could pour water down on the roof. How graceful that ladder looked, and the water pouring out of the hose, turning the red wood, black, blessed black, the wetness that might save the barn that Janice thought of more as a cathedral, a place that opened the air, so she could feel God.

A fireman flung open the barn doors that circulated air. As a girl she'd plunged her hand between bales and felt the heat smoldering in the new mown hay. Who would have thought hay would make heat? Smoke poured out of the barn, and flames lapped along the door. Suddenly a gust hit the barn. Marcel's three hundred bales had caught.

She touched her throat and felt the unicorn necklace Lucian had given her. She'd not been happy for him or Marcel because she'd wanted him to be her brother, to stay her family—just Lucian—with no one else between them. She had been the one who'd given Marcel the easy way out by telling her about Judy's farm as a place to board horses.

And yet after all that, he'd said she was a genius for God, a person pure in heart. The pure in heart shall see God. But no, she had been unspeakably selfish, wheeling and dealing because she was good at it, even though it wrenched her soul. She'd not visited the sick—her own mother. She'd not comforted the grieving—her own father. She'd pressured Lucian about the estate and judged him for not saving their father at the end. She'd interfered with Marcel. She'd been cruel to both of them, in the guise of being helpful when all she wanted was to keep things the same.

But the mystics said the way to God was down through your

own self. And the psalmist said, "He was near to the broken-hearted." And she had plunged down into herself to find a God who was wholly other, as fire is, burning her up. "Where your treasure is, there will your heart be." Where your treasure is. It wasn't The Farm. No, she had a new life waiting for her. Her parents had succeeded in pushing her away from The Farm. And Lucian had stayed. He'd die if he couldn't keep it. That she knew for certain. And she couldn't bear to have him dead and gone—even if he hated her. She didn't have to own The Farm to walk here, to revisit old places and old memories.

* * * *

The timbers of the Big Barn appeared as the siding burned up. The shiny aluminum roof glowed red in the heat. The barn glowed orange and red in defiance of the water the New Scotland volunteer firemen were pouring. Janice figured the pond would be sucked dry. Her beautiful barn whose timbers soared over her like flying buttresses, when she sat to pray, all those years ago, was being judged as she had been judged. Had her prayers in both places, pulled her wild, fire of a God, down on these buildings?

How could it?

It was Lucian who'd burned up her tree when the wind was roaring up from the south. Suddenly the roof buckled like a horse folding her legs to lie down and roll. Smoke billowed up. The smell burned Janice's nostrils. It would be hours of pushing over the hay, pouring water on it, before that fire died.

As Lucian walked toward her, his head down, Janice stood up to meet him. She called the dogs, but they sat back a few feet away, panting. The Farm was his now. He could explain himself to the firemen, the police, and the neighbors. It was time for her to finish what she started with Jeremiah, and then drive home to Illinois.

"I'm sorry," he said, his face tear streaked, his eyes full of pain.

Janice didn't know what to say. Her anger had blown out of her, but his act remained, and the meaning of that act remained.

"You saved the house," she said.

"You saved Marcel's horses."

"I'm giving you my half of The Farm." Suddenly she was so light, she swore her feet lifted off the ground, and she was giddy with that lightness.

Lucian looked hurt when she said this, more hurt than when he'd walked up. "But that's not fair," he said.

"Who said fair is good?" She saw that she was the one with the power because she was freely giving him her half of The Farm. She had been set free, utterly and completely free, as someone who had nothing more to lose was free, and utterly light, no longer tied down, because the ropes had been burned, so free she had set his fate by giving him what he wanted.

"Our parents." He swiped the grass with his foot, not looking her in the eyes.

"They didn't know everything."

"But they wanted me to share everything equally," he paused, the words hard to say, "with you. I can do that now. They tried to teach me this since I was a little boy. And I could not, for the life of me, change, no matter how much I confessed, repented, ignored my hatred for you. Until today. With my whole heart I want you to be my sister." He said this while looking down at the ground. He couldn't meet her eyes.

"The Farm is more than my soul can bear." Janice heard the wind playing the white pines marking The Farm's border with the Genovese's. She could not look at Lucian either. "You'd do me a favor by taking it."

"You're a better soul than I am." He lifted his face, his eyes as earnest, as full of prayer, as she'd ever seen them.

"You're the one who stayed, who did the hard work of tending the sick, comforting the grieving—the only work God says marks a righteous man." She put her hand on his shoulder and with all her might, wished blessing on her brother.

"You're a good sister, but you need to let me buy you out.

This is the only way to make it right. You have as much right as I do. You are my parents' daughter."

"You said you couldn't afford it." A horse might as well have kicked her in the belly. All this, she looked at the burning barns, could have been stopped, if he'd said this before.

"I think I can if you hold the mortgage without a down payment. The bank won't finance it with the well the way it is. The water doesn't pump fast enough."

"I can do that," Janice sighed. "You're my brother. You always will be, but I need to leave now. I'm taking King and Arthur and Mother's car."

"Your half of Dad's life insurance money should help you get settled. When this is settled," he nodded back towards the smoldering buildings, "I'll fly out there to help you pack and move."

Janice didn't have the heart to say he didn't need to help her, or that she didn't think he'd make it, or that he was on his own for his wedding and Christmas because she needed time to heal, as a charred field needed time to find the new grass. No, she didn't have the heart.

"What are you going to tell them?" she asked.

"The truth."

"That you hated me my whole life and took it out on my tree?" What a waste this was.

"I'll figure something out." Lucian dropped his eyes and scuffed the snow.

"Burning the barns was an accident, but I don't know if the fire marshal would believe you." Janice had to admit she was glad Lucian was going to be held accountable for what he'd done. Or at least he'd have to stand before some men and answer for himself. And it would happen in this life, not the next.

"Why would I want to burn up The Farm?"

"Lucian I can't answer that."Janice pointed at the slender figure walking up the field. "Marcel's coming."

The look of love and relief on Lucian's face said where he held his heart.

Janice slapped her thigh. "King. Arthur. Come." They rose

to their feet and trotted after her. Her feet were barely able to step down through the snow, they were so cold. She lifted her mother's diamond to her lips, feeling the four prongs, feeling the smooth surface like a tiny frozen pond. Lucian might have the land to remember their parents by, but now with their parents gone, the land was just a shell, a carapace of the real love that Janice felt growing up from her finger, a love that was a barb, that held pain in those silences when her parents sat across from each other drinking coffee, the stillness of wire between barbs in a fence, a wire that set a boundary saying this place is ours and not that one, the one on the other side. And on the other side of that wire grazed a happiness that was pure and simple as the two horses tearing at the dried grass.

Janice kissed the diamond. It must have been blessed with her mother's and father's love, a gritty unselfish love, that had set her free to drive out that road to the little house on the hill, surrounded by land so well tended it was more like an ornamental garden than a farm. She tucked her hand in her pocket, pushed the diamond to her palm and squeezed, something from her parents she held in her hand.

She walked behind the ash heaps of the barns, the glorious rafters and beams, now charred stumps sticking into the air. She could see all the way across the fields to the woods now. The smoke stung her nose. The dogs trotted by her side, their heads down sniffing. A man dressed in fireman's garb handed someone else his fire hose. He walked towards her. Janice did not want to answer questions about what happened because she wasn't sure she had the story straight even though she'd been there. She kept walking toward her mother's car. She would be able to drive through a gap between cars parked on the road and head down to New York City. She'd promised Jeremiah she would do this—meet him for the demonstration.

The man took off his hat and grabbed Janice and pulled her into his arms. Caleb smelled like the smoke of her beloved barns. His canvas coat scratched her. The dogs tried to nudge their way in between them. "Honey, " he said, his voice filled with sadness and weariness. "I need to breathe," she said, pushing him back gently. He had fallen in love. She had used him for comfort and to shake a fist at God. She had used him. Used. Like a man uses a woman, only she'd used a man. And the sex hadn't even worked, but still the tenderness in his face betrayed that love, but still it wasn't enough for her to call her back here to live.

"You're not coming back."

Janice looked down at the dancing paws of the dogs, sniffing and swirling and nearly chasing their tails with impatience. She could not look at that love. "No, I am not."

"What happened here?"

"You have to ask Lucian. I have to be in the City by this evening." Janice opened the door to her mother's Chrysler and called the dogs to jump in, wet paws and all. They sniffed the bag of dog food. And sat on the velour seats.

Caleb put his helmet back on. "I guess that's it."

Janice thought of the line in the old hymn about Jesus on the cross: "Sorrow and love flow mingled down." She shut the door on the dogs and opened her own door. "I loved you so much. Once. But I can't give you my heart and my life. You'd find yourself too busy if I did."

She sat down and put her key in the ignition. The dogs sat behind her panting.

"You can think that." Caleb said. "But this isn't the end."

Janice smiled and pulled the car door shut. She heard him tap the top of her roof and then she backed around. He waved her to stop. She rolled down the window. "Check the quarry as you go by on the Thruway. They break the rock today."

"Goodbye Caleb." She'd seen enough for one day. The field rocked under the car and the tires skidded as she pulled onto the muddy road, driving slowly past the cars lined up on either side. She did not want to see the glint in her neighbor's eyes from her family's misfortune and was glad to finally turn left onto Font Grove Road and head toward her final obligation.

CHAPTER TWENTY

November, 1983. New York City

When Janice parked at the Broadway Parking Garage, she let King and Arthur out to relieve themselves. She shivered in the gray light, the dogs' red, white and black coats seemingly the only living color in the whole place. Janice felt like ashes. Her brother had cut down her tree. He'd cut her down. And then he burned her because he could not set Janice on fire. She poured a dish of water and offered the dogs a drink. She thought of the word *provide* while she listened to their lapping. She was providing them with water, some kibble, and safety. And they were providing her with company and humor as she drove away from The Farm. Both had jumped on the bed at the hotel, curling their backs against hers until she fell asleep, warm bodies holding her. Then she loaded the dogs back in the car and walked over to *The New York Times*, trying not to look at the street people begging.

Jim stood at the back of the crowd, his collar turned up against the wind, his shoulders hunched forward. Janice's heart skipped a beat and then she was angry. She clapped him on the back. "Now do you think evangelicals are apathetic?"

His face brightened and his eyes crinkled in warmth. She saw how glad he was to see her. He reached into her and kissed her lightly on the cheek. Instead of bursting into tears, she'd thought she'd burst into tears at such kindness, she drew strength and calm. "How are you?"

"My dad died."

"God must like you," he said, his face darkening.

"Or hate me."

"All of God's friends have it hard. Just look at Jesus."

"Doesn't give us much hope does it?"

"Or all the hope in the world." He said it in her ear, like it was secret to be guarded. Janice thought about telling him about her brother's fury, about the fire, about the dogs sitting in the car but she didn't. Instead she told him about the job and the house she'd rented and her hopes for community.

"Good. Good for you." Jim gave her one last squeeze. "Keep in touch."

"I will," Janice said looking into all that ferocity, that had softened on account of her. "Who knows what stories I'll find that you might find interesting?"

He touched her cheek with his lips again and Janice was off walking to the stage where Jeremiah was talking intensely to a microphone. He literally glowed when she walked up to him. He clapped her on the shoulder, "God I admire your courage."

"Now, don't be taking God's name in vain on my account."

"Your father just died. And you're here."

"I said I'd come didn't I?" It felt good to be with someone who had no idea how awful that was.

"You're as good as your word."

"I need to finish this and talk to those guys." Janice pointed at the reporters setting up their microphones and talking to their cameramen. She walked over to check in with ABC, CBS, NBC, FOX, CNN. Buck, the flak for the Upright folks, was making a name with producers, who were already settled and lined up with interviews to talk to Jeremiah and Dennis. She was surprised smarmy worked so well. Maybe it was easy because the Upright folks offered a good story on a slow news day.

* * * *

Janice looked up at the buildings, not terribly tall, but large enough to make the street a dirty canyon. The wind cut through her, clouds raced overhead and the street was wet, and grimy.

Janice rubbed her arms with her hands. Her body ached with loss and she did not look forward to the long work of grief. She rocked back and forth to the "Battle Hymn of the Republic" sung by the Upright Choir. There were a few police officers on horseback keeping the door to the *Times* clear, guiding their horses like she'd seen cutting horses work cattle. The people going back to the *Times* pulled up their collars and looked down as if they were being pelted by heavy rain.

Finally, Dennis Manley, vice president of the Upright, Down Right, Just Plain Right Americans for Moral Justice walked across the stage. The crowd clapped and broke into a chorus of "Amen" that had been urged on by the Upright's music director. Even though Manley was walking, he looked like he was loping, he was so tall.

He introduced Jeremiah, by saying, "We're all involved in a revolution. We perceive the dangerous things going on in our society for those who believe as we do. We must win the battle by being serious. We must take over the press, the culture, and infiltrate it on every level. If we don't we're lost; our country is lost. Without further ado, let me introduce Jeremiah Sackfield."

Jeremiah looked around and put his hands between his legs and clasped them like he was shaking his own hands. He wore a black wool coat. His blonde hair and dark eyebrows added to his ferocity.

Then he stood. We need to stop thinking that what we do at our jobs, in the voting booth, doesn't count for God's Kingdom. We are either with God or against Him. How we behave is either for good or evil in all areas of our lives. It is up to us to make the Kingdom come.

"And when our work meets high standards, we should demand it be recognized. My book has sold as many copies as the number three book on *The New Times Bestseller List,* but where is it? We are making the secular publishing elite recognize we are a force to be reckoned with." He shouted the word "force" so loud it hurt Janice's ears.

"We are exposing the media's censorship of what is good, and right, and pure, and holy. The pornographer has more First Amendment rights than we do. He can write his slime and sell it. But God forbid if we want to put up a manger in a city park at Christmas. God forbid if our children pray in school. Or a teacher places her Bible on her desk. We are sent to jail, not the man who degrades women and children for his pornographic slime. Thank the Supreme Court for this."

Janice's knees felt like they'd climbed seven hills and stuck her hands in her pocket and wished she could slam a Diet Coke to wash away the headache blooming from behind her ear, and running down the side of her face. The crowd tensed. People shifted from one foot to the other like they were bored, but they weren't. They were like the police horses tossing their heads, tired of standing in one place. The police looked across the people to each other. One spoke into his radio. The crowd pushed toward the door to the *Times*. People stopped going inside. The buildings slid closer, the sky narrower.

"We're not under the Constitution anymore. We're under the Supreme Court. Most people don't know our system of government has changed, giving the Supreme Court the highest authority." Jeremiah leaned into the podium, whispering.

"I attack this premise in *An American Treatise* and am forming an organization to defend our people. Two people who called an abortionist a murderer were sued for half a million. Others were arrested for picketing an abortion clinic. A teacher was fired for posting the Ten Commandments. Lawyers for Moral Justice will defend them. This is the Second American Revolution." Jeremiah smoothed the pulpit and then slammed his palm down, the microphone echoing the crack. People jumped.

"The Second American Revolution is taking over every American institution, restoring what's good, right, holy, pure, what's been lost, to each one. The Second American Revolution is restoring this country to a Christian America." Whisper to screaming, Jeremiah was sawing the crowd's emotions back and forth.

Janice could smell the diesel exhaust of the city, but there was no combine, no Caleb or Fred. Farmers plant their fields in patterns. Where are the patterns? Weren't Christians about making order? Her mother always said things should be done nicely and in order. But what was this but a challenge to upend things in the name of Christ, when Christians were no different than the people they resisted?

She pushed through the crowd his voice in her ears like the roar of the barns burning. "My job is to prod the sleeping giant. The secular elite is made up of a small group of people—Did you know only two hundred and forty people control the media? Once you take them out we can gain control. A tiny number elite control academia. Get rid of them and we can restore standards to our education. You reach a point where the emperor has no clothes. The academic elite, the media elite. They don't have the numbers we have." Jeremiah was talking reasonably again. He shrugged off his coat, letting it drop. He was down to white shirtsleeves plastered against his body despite the cold.

"*An American Treatise* is galvanizing a minority within a minority within the great majority of Christian people in this land to grab the sleeping giant by the nose and yank." Jeremiah twisted his hand like he was twisting someone's nose.

"If one hundred thousand of the ten million of us become activated we could run the country. If what we're doing becomes fashionable the apathetic majority will join us.

"Messianic madmen have taken what I'm saying as a Christian call to arms. Five clinics were bombed this weekend, three abortionists died. This scares me, but what is even more frightening is the apathy of American evangelicals who allow one million babies to be slaughtered every year." His voice raised to a shout. The cords of his neck stood out. "Unfortunately life isn't divided into convenient choices. Every choice left is crazy." The "zee" sound of crazy pocked off the buildings.

"If we lived in the Twenties in Germany someone would have to warn the Jews and perhaps be so inflammatory that the result would be to gun down the SS guards and their wives. What's the lesser evil?"

Janice couldn't take it any more. People had died who didn't need to die. They left grieving daughters and sons, fathers and mothers, sisters and brothers. Jeremiah was still riling his audience. *Lift up your heart, lift it up unto the Lord.* That's how she felt, her heart lifting up with righteous fury. She squirmed through the gaps between people, inching towards the podium. "Excuse me. Excuse me," she said. But people wouldn't let her slip past.

She heard Jeremiah's rant and pushed between coats, people giving her dirty looks. "The people who are against abortion are the best people I know." Jeremiah railed. "Hard core, good people. I think it's the absolute acid test for righteousness. It identifies who is on our side, who true Christians are. Politicians don't understand what religious conviction means."

You don't either, Janice thought. She slipped between a gap of two women and found herself staring at the podium.

"My books *A Christian Bestseller* and *An American Treatise* are available for sale at the tables set up in Times Square. Twenty dollars will buy you the definitive plan of our movement. To give people a chance to make their way to the tables let us sing."

Janice could feel the power in her breastbone as the crowd poured their nervous tension into songs. She heard Jeremiah leading them, singing the old hymn, "Stand Up, Stand Up for Jesus." She heard arrogance and defiance. She hated that in some Christians, their cockiness in the face of an aching world when there was so much ache, so much mystery. Christ might be the answer as they said, but Janice felt he was more a man, a God, who drove people to the question.

When they were done, Jeremiah shouted, "Who is on the Lord's side?"

The crowd shouted back, stronger, louder, more in unison

than in any evangelistic rally, "We are."

"Who is?"

"We are." The crowd shouted louder. Their words became one voice. They sounded like Niagara Falls or the ocean whipped up by distant wind. One woman standing next to Janice shrieked, "The Spirit is here. Praise you, Jesus." Soon others had picked up her words. Their voices, "Praise you, Jesus. Praise you, Jesus," were revved up, nervous as if they were working themselves into an ecstasy or a headache.

Janice could smell expensive perfume mixed in with the diesel exhaust and fumes of the city as she pushed towards Jeremiah. People's coats ballooned against hers. Her coat seemed thin, not only against the cold, but against their touch.

* * * *

Janice stepped on the wooden steps. One, two, three, four. She stood on the platform and walked up to the microphones. Stood in front of them. She held up her hands and leaned into the mike. People fell silent, waiting to listen. All those eyes and ears turned to her.

"Are we following Jesus here? Are we?" She paused, a little startled at how canned and loud her voice sounded.

"Are we called to be bullies? Are we?"

The crowd looked at her silently. She could hear a pigeon cooing on the ledge behind her.

"Didn't Jesus tell us to take up our cross and follow him? Didn't he say we need to die before we die? That nothing on this earth compares to following him?"

"He didn't say take over the government. No, he said, 'the Kingdom of heaven is like a mustard seed,' a little tiny seed." She held up her hands like she was pinching off a dash of salt. They felt cold and chapped in the wind. "That will spread its branches so that it becomes the biggest tree in the forest. Hasn't that already happened? Hasn't God's kingdom spread throughout the world?

"He says, 'We'll stand someday, all the tribes and nations, before his throne. And you know who will lead us? A lamb that was slain. He will take us to springs of living water. He will wipe away our tears.'"

"But Jeremiah has just told you how to be afraid, how to be bullies, how to throw your weight around, when this poor, sad woman standing before you needs your humility. If this is Christianity, I don't want it." Janice turned away to leave. Then she turned back, leaning her mouth into the bulbous microphone like she was going to kiss it, like she was going to kiss Caleb or Fred. Tears sprang to her eyes. She blinked them away. She did not care if her voice wavered.

"But you know what? It's not. It's found on our knees asking the Lord and our neighbor to forgive us the things we've done wrong. How many of you have ever gone up to someone you've gossiped about and said you were sorry? Or said to the author they were promoting, 'I betrayed you.' Just like Judas, I sold you, but not for silver, no, not silver, just a story."

She turned to Jeremiah who looked shocked as a neighbor whose dog broke her grip and leaped for Janice's throat. Her dress felt damp underneath her coat. Her feet burned.

"Jeremiah, I'm so sorry. I betrayed you. For a story or two. I didn't believe in your cause. I never, ever did believe in it. I publicized you because I wanted to expose you. I wanted to kill your power. I'm asking you to forgive me for being double tongued— one way to your face, one way to the journalists."

Jeremiah looked startled, like she'd slapped him in the face, his eyes not fierce, his mouth not tyrannical. No, in that moment he looked like a little boy just before he said I didn't mean to.

"But the bombs that went off in Georgia, they're the fruit. Murder. Death. By their fruit you will know them."

Janice turned away from Jeremiah and looked out at the milling crowd. She heard a horse's hooves strike the pavement, one, two, three, four.

"People. Consider this. Do you want to follow Jesus? Whose fruit was loving us so much he died for us. Whose fruit was springing out of the grave?

"Or do you want to follow Jeremiah?" She threw her arm behind her and pointed at him, "Whose fruit is bombed buildings and dead people?

"Choose this day whom you will serve. As for me I'm serving the Lord."

By now Jeremiah was standing beside her. He was reaching for the mike. Janice took his hand. She squeezed it with all her might. "The peace of the Lord be with you," she said. For the first time since she'd promoted him, she felt peace, the kind of peace when her two faces slid into focus and became one. Finally she had spoken the truth as she had seen it.

"And also with you," he replied. He leaned into her and hugged her, so close she could smell the woody smell of his cologne. "I forgive you," he said. "I've known all along that you didn't believe in The Cause. But you got me the stories. That's all that counted." He pressed her even closer and hugged with all his might, so she couldn't catch her breath. There was all the intensity of love and respect. "But too many babies are dying for me to step down." He said another thing and released her.

Before Janice stepped down from the stage, she set the bottle of water from The Farm on the podium. She would not need it where she was going. She sighed at the mob she had to walk through like snow up to her knees. People clapped her on the back. "You blessed my soul. You are so blessed," they said, their smiles like too much candy. *What are they thinking?* She'd just challenged their idol, and they were saying she blessed them? Was the microphone that powerful, they liked anything anyone said just because it was amplified? All Janice could say was, "Thank you" because she'd found the blessing in Connor County, twenty miles from the Mississippi River, in a farm family who said she could be one of them.

ACKNOWLEDGEMENTS

Since this novel took thirty years to set down straight, many, many people helped. I'd like to thank Anne Brashler for taking me on as a student and teaching me how to write and question my work, so I could find the joy and magic of revising. John Bradley listened so well I heard myself, and slowly changed into the writer who could write this. Carolyn Dickey gave me hope when I didn't have much, tending to a smoking wick. She turned me back to revise this story, and revise it again so that I found a peace that is beyond price. My voice told her as much as anything, what advice she should give concerning which I should go. Darlene Elsbury and Christine DeSmet supported that decision with some good hints on what direction to head.

Betsy Amster was the tree I plowed to as I worked and reworked this book. She gave me a big gift by introducing me to my editor, Helga Schier, who held the ropes while I walked down the cliffs of my character's lives and listened to their voices. Helga helped me find my voice and said it's all right to be the writer you are. Nichole Argyres at St. Martins was the other tree I aimed for as I turned to go up the field the other way.

Bev Jednyak, Joe Jackson, Rita Mae Brown, Vicki Davis, and Frank Schaeffer read this book in late stages and offered wise encouragement. Sharon Oard Warner kicked me into the final, publishable draft. Jim McNiece read this early on, saying you've got stories but not a novel, setting me on the journey into my imagination. Julie Murphy was my very first reader, gentle with my first run at the story.

John Dufresne, Larry Woiwode, and Jack Butler offered encouragement when I needed it. Maureen Barron and Deb Doran were booksellers who listened and repeated, "Steady. Steady." Jonis Agee taught me a few things saying, "Publication will happen for you like it did for me." Rachel Simon consoled and counseled me on how to keep working.

Dana Tautz showed me the farm twenty miles from the Mississipppi. Paul R. Huey helped my research on the Normans Kill and Ken Dovenmuehle filled me in on how to blow up rock. Ginny Aulik, Deb Rogers and Laura Bird listened.

Robert Self, John Schaeffer, Michael Day and Ellen Frankin of Northern Illinois University offered the practical support of a job and a decent schedule. Without them I wouldn't have had the time or energy to write. Thank you to Myron Siegel for easing my colleagues' and my working conditions and for cheering on this project. Thank you to David Giannasi for helping fund the actual publication of this book. I would also like to thank the Abercrombie Foundation for a scholarship to the Writers for Racing Project, which broke the ice for my attending much needed summer workshops.

Thanks for the prayers of the congregations of Christ the Rock and Christ Lutheran Churches. Troy and Janice Hedrick were the inspiration for Madeleine and Pastor Ted.

John L. Moore made the connection between myself and Koehler books. Without his generosity, this book would not have been published.

I can't thank John Koehler and Joe Coccaro enough for taking a risk on publishing this book.

Cane, Bundy, Laager, Nate, Booker and Night sat at my feet and watched over me for the long hours of work. Sometimes they brought me a toy to throw. Onyx the cat has been supervising. Beau Ty, Tessie and Morgen have taught me to enter my body, from which the best writing comes.

Most of all thank you to my husband, Bruce whose love made this book possible.